To Hear The Ocean Sigh

ALSO BY BRYANT A. LONEY

Exodus in Confluence
....
A NOVELLA

Take Me to the Cat
....
A NOVEL

Sea Breeze Academy
....
A NOVEL

BRYANT A. LONEY

TO HEAR THE
OCEAN SIGH

VERONA BOOKSELLERS
TULSA

Published by VERONA BOOKSELLERS

Contact info@VeronaBooksellers.com for information about special discounts for bulk purchases.

The author does not in any way endorse, condone, or encourage engaging in any conduct depicted in this story.

December: "The Canterville Ghost" by Oscar Wilde; "Ode 3.30" by Horace / February: "Will the Circle Be Unbroken?" by Ada R. Habershon, Charles H. Gabriel / March: *Metamorphoses* by Ovid; *Elegies* by Sextus Propertius / May: *The Prince* by Niccolò Machiavelli.

Publisher's Cataloging-in-Publication Data

Loney, Bryant A.
    To hear the ocean sigh / Bryant A. Loney.
    p. cm.
    ISBN 978-0-692-38111-3 (paperback)
    ISBN 978-0-692-41552-8 (ebook)
    Summary: Jay Murchison believes he is a nobody at his high school in Oklahoma. After a mysterious girl named Saphnie in North Carolina mistakenly texts him, an unlikely relationship develops that affects Jay's self-perception and influences the rest of his sophomore year.

[1. Friendship—Fiction. 2. Self-esteem—Fiction. 3. Interpersonal relationships—Fiction. 4. Coming of age—Fiction. 5. High school—Fiction. 6. Oklahoma—Fiction. I. Title]

PZ7.L8443 To 2015
[Fic]—dc23   2015901939

Published in Tulsa, Oklahoma, U.S.A. by Verona Booksellers
"Where Books Are Still Sold!" www.VeronaBooksellers.com

Cover design by Deranged Doctor Design
First Edition: April 2015
10 9 8 7 6

To my loving mother. Thank you for everything.

I had always assumed Mercer was jangling spare change in his weathered palms before that red sky morning. Upon closer inspection, however, it turned out to be a total of four seashells. I approached the poet, startling him in the process, causing him to drop a single shell into the fading water below us. After begging his pardon, I asked him of their significance. He replied simply there was none, nor should there be.

—AMOS METRES II, *Rudderless at Sea*

Oftentimes it seems to me the night is much more richly coloured than the day... When you pay attention, you will see that certain stars are more lemony, others have strong pinks, greens, blues, forget-me-not. And without insisting further it is evident that to paint a starry sky, it does not at all suffice to just put white dots on some blue-black.

—Vincent van Gogh

TO HEAR THE OCEAN SIGH

PROLOGUE

"Life begins with a single push," Aunt Nancy shared with the family one Thanksgiving dinner. My parents blamed her outburst on the red wine, but the older I got, the more often I came back to ponder that infamous saying. While I doubted there was any metaphorical reason-ing behind it, *Life Begins with a Single Push* sort of became my motto, at least in the way my father attempted to explain it: "A fresh start yields a greater potential at glory." And because I couldn't engrave it into Aunt Nancy's headstone when she died of liver failure, I took the liberty of sewing it onto a little pillow in middle school home econom-ics and hung it next to the bathroom door across the hall from my room when I was finished.

It was that phrased pillow I noticed again the day I got my first text message, three years later.

The bell rang at 3:50. High school students rushed out of the building, and I was the first of them on the bus. To some, it might have looked like I was in a hurry, but unlike most people, I had no place to be. No extracurricular activities, no group to hang out and chat with, nothing. As far as I was concerned, *school's over and home is where I'm going.*

I sat down on the right side and looked out the fogged window at the road cluttered with the remnants of fall—leaves of almost-but-not-quite-yet-dead brown. I watched as Nick Behr walked onto the bus and sat one row ahead and to the left of me. He wore a blazer over a red t-shirt promoting a "PS" band I did not yet know on that particular day. His arms were covered in wristbands, and his blue denim high tops seemed to complement the paisley socks on his feet. He put my sense of fashion to shame.

We had never met, although I'd had two classes with Nick my ninth grade year. He was a charismatic and outgoing guy, which occasionally made him the target of hateful jokes. The worst were about his curly hair, which had earned him nicknames such as "Permetheus" and "Permafrost." Word had also gotten around that his flamboyance was because he was gay, but as Nick had dated two girls in ninth grade and another the following summer, his rumored sexual orientation seemed unlikely.

But who was I to judge? "Introvert, extrovert," I would hear in the hallways from the mouths of those quick to criticize. "Type A, Type B"—always one or the other, it seemed. The remarkable thing about Nick was that none of this appeared to faze him, and from what I saw, he was a genuinely nice guy. He wasn't much into clubs besides Student Council and Speech & Debate ("It's not what you know, but who you know," he would say with a smile that suggested he knew quite a few people), and he made up for this with the fact that everyone seemed to know of him, from the current ninth graders to the seniors the year before. He got around, and I had to acknowledge him for it.

Nick was listening to his music, earbuds in place, when we both noticed a small girl step aimlessly onto the bus. She walked farther toward the back—toward me—holding her belongings in front of her, and it was evident from her watery, red eyes she had been crying. The girl managed to get past all the knees and backpacks in the aisle, sit in the row across from me, and lean against her window. She clutched her book bag to her chest and watched the students congregating outside.

Sure, I wondered why this girl was so upset, but it never occurred to me to *do* something about it. I had learned to keep to myself, maybe establishing me as a loner by some definitions, and was therefore generously minding my own business. If this girl wanted to talk to someone, I figured, she wouldn't have sat by herself.

It was at that moment when I noticed Nick was looking at her, too. He frowned, paused whatever song was playing, and slipped his phone into his pocket as he shuffled back one row. He sat down next to her.

"Hey," he said, pulling out a sheet of paper. "Can you help me for a second? It's this zoology question that keeps getting at me. Do you happen to know how much a polar bear weighs?"

She said nothing.

"Enough to break the ice!" He smiled and extended his left hand. "I'm Nick."

"I don't want to talk," she said in a quiet voice. Nick sighed.

"I know life can be rough sometimes," he allowed, "and there's bound to be a day of suck for every good one. But each can be overcome, right?"

She shook her head slowly, then spoke.

"Have you ever thought about killing yourself?"

His frown returned. "Who hasn't?"

She was crying, and her body still faced the window. So Nick tried again.

"The day we all learn to stop pushing each other to our breaking points is when we'll all be saved." He was looking at her brown hair, where her eyes would have been on the opposite side. "Until then, we're all we've got."

She turned to him. Nick put the blank sheet of paper down, opened his arms, and she came in for him to hold.

"It's OK," he said, stroking her hair as she wept. I see it now as a sort of cliché, but it worked for him. "Everything's going to be OK."

The bus pulled away from the school and onto the long road ahead. I glanced over at the girl, still weeping in his embrace, and Nick turned to me and nodded with an expression devoid of emotion. I wasn't sure what he meant by it, but I nodded back before facing the front of the bus and closing my eyes.

There I was, keeping to myself. And then there was Nick, who was bold enough to do what I would not. Why was that? Because I was embarrassed, too, like her? Was it because I didn't want to get involved (which had admittedly gotten me into some trouble in the past)? No. Instead of facing the tough decision, I had ignored it once again.

I needed that single push Aunt Nancy had drunkenly described— something to push me in the right direction. In retrospect, I suppose I got it, as that was the first night Saphnie texted me.

I only wish it hadn't come at her expense.

DECEMBER

one hundred and seventy-eight days ago

I came to the realization I wasn't popular on December 18th of my tenth grade year, a.k.a. my birthday. I had always secretly suspected it, of course, but I reached this conclusion because (1.) no one had mentioned my birthday, (2.) when I had told people, the recognition was at most an overly-animated thumbs-up, and (3.) no one had commented on my status update about it, which was ridiculous, since most teenagers rarely logged off their computers, let alone moved their fingers away from their phones. Granted, most of my updates were weird facts I came across on QuickSearch or quotes from Ronald Reagan, but whenever I did post something witty, I expected my virtual friends to take notice, and yet they never did.

Some people were simply created with the right genes and the proper social skills, I figured. They ended up at a lunch table with a group of good-looking individuals, like them, who did what all good-looking individuals managed: making the rest of us feel both envious of them and sad for ourselves, intentional or not. They had activities outside of school and followers online—people of social necessity who sat at home on Friday nights and "liked" popular posts in hopes that they, too, might one day be as attractive and personable.

And I was OK with that. Not happy, just OK. I knew there were far worse things for me in life than being unpopular: I could have been a nicotine addict, or a high school dropout, or been born into poverty or to a janitor with a bad mullet who wears the same t-shirt every day. But nope—I was too tall and too skinny, lived in one of those suburban McMansions, and was unpopular.

And I was OK with that.

When I got home from school that day, my parents told me there was a birthday-related surprise waiting for me on the dining room table. Naturally, I dropped everything I was carrying and dashed there to find my very own cell phone, still in the box.

Although my parents could have easily afforded to give me a phone when I was much younger, let alone sixteen, my mother was lovingly overprotective of me. So when I saw my brand new TSC Serenade 7-Plus Ultra Pro (whatever that all meant), I hugged my parents, "thank you, thank you," went to my room, and posted on my CoffeeFolder profile page.

Jake Murchison

I've finally decided to join the rest of the world and get a cell phone! Text me your numbers. 918-555-0121.

Like · Unfollow · about a minute ago near Arminster, OK

I closed my laptop and only briefly opened it every so often to check my post. As expected, no one had left a comment. So I waited.

Four hours had passed, and there were still no new texts. I was frustrated, as I had seen cheerleaders and potential underwear models doing this all the time before, and they would get twenty some-odd comments and forty-something "likes" before I even scrolled down.

While anticipating the moment when the masses would message me, I played with some of my Serenade's gadgets. But after browsing a bit through the camera's filters and effects, I got bored of waiting for my imaginary friends. I ended up watching a rerun I had already seen of *$tore Wars: Florida*, a reality show about teams of professional bidders looking to buy abandoned shopping centers in hopes of selling their contents for profit.

"It's not the mermaid-themed antique place I met the wife at," recurring buyer Laine told the camera about the decrepit building onscreen, "but if Meredith wants it, then you bet I'm all in to stop her."

"I have enough properties I'm trying to keep afloat," rival Meredith said separately, "but this used to be a Julian Morrissey store—the fancy watchmaker. If any of his brand-name merchandise was left here, this one could be worth some *real money*."

It was about as interesting as it sounded. I dozed off five minutes into the episode, a plate of birthday cake in my lap and my new phone on the empty couch seat beside me.

My mother woke me up.

"Honey, you've got to get ready for bed," she said, a hand on my shoulder. "It's almost ten, and tomorrow's the last day of finals week."

"Mom, most kids my age turn off the lights at midnight or later. It's my birthday. You should be paying me to go to sleep this early."

"Your good grades are payment enough," she said, knowing she had won the argument. "So go to bed."

"Bleeearghh…"

I got up, turned off the TV, and took my new phone with me. "You'll thank me one of these days!" she called out after I had already left the room. Some say a boy's best friend is his mom, but while I lacked any real friends, let alone a best friend, my mother did not fill that position.

Climbing the stairs out of the den—and then climbing some more stairs after that—I went into my room and collapsed on my bed. The door was still open, and I spotted across the hall the needlepoint pillow I had hand-sewn in the seventh grade. *Life Begins with a Single Push*, it promised.

It was then that my phone did this little chime and vibrated, scaring me so much I dropped it onto the bed. It read: ONE NEW TEXT.

I slid my finger across the screen and read the message.

Jason, it's been nearly six months and I'm getting tired of waiting. I need to know if you've moved on so that I can, too. We had some wonderful times together. I hope all is well with you. Saphnie

I didn't recognize the area code, I didn't know a Saphnie, and I certainly wasn't a Jason. I responded accordingly.

Me: My name's Jake, not Jason. I think you have the wrong number. Sorry about that.

And then she confused me even further with her next text.

Her: Like Jake Palaver?

Me: Who?

Her: He was the bachelor who cried on every single episode during his season of House of Love. He even chose the wrong girl! He's kind of a mini-celebrity where I live.

Me: Well, my name's Jake Murchison. Some people call me Jay, but yeah, no Jason or Jake Palaver here. Again, sorry.

She responded back a few minutes later.

Her: I guess I saw this coming. Thanks anyway, Jay.

She called me Jay. Was she flirting with me? Was this what flirting looked like? We weren't friends, but she still called me Jay. And was she implying she was ending the conversation? My plea of desperation:

Me: Wait! I just got this phone for my birthday today, and no one's really texted me yet, and I'm kind of alone… Wanna talk?

When she didn't initially respond, I knew I had made a mistake—the first person to text me got creeped out because I was overeager. But then she replied.

Her: Okay. Happy birthday. How old are you?

Me: I turned sixteen. I'm doing Chemistry homework, but not to celebrate!

Her: Nice. I turn 16 in May. Are you sure you're not some perverted old man trying to get some nudes from a teenage girl?

Me: WHAT?? No, I'm not! Besides, you texted me!

Her: I guess sarcasm is hard to detect over text, huh? So where are you from?

Me: Arminster, Oklahoma, where we ride horses to our one-room schoolhouse and partake in unfair trades with the Native Americans. Oh, and we get tornados about every other week! Haha. Not really. That was my own attempt at sarcasm.

Her: I'm from Arminster! \(^o^)/ The tornados are usually during the spring, though I get what you're saying. Now I live in Windhaven, NC. It's by Monkey Junction if you've heard of it.

Me: That's cool! My sister lives in North Carolina, but what's "Monkey Junction?"

Her: Supposedly the zoo was transporting monkeys to their awaiting exhibit when their van crashed and the monkeys escaped from their cages. That's the most plausible explanation I've heard, but I can't corroborate.

Me: You said you were from Arminster?

Her: Arminster County. My family and I left in early June after middle school was over. That was two summers ago. It wasn't fun. Jason was my boyfriend back in Oklahoma. I guess long-distance relationships really don't work out. Moving takes its toll on life.

Me: And you said you were fifteen, right?

Her: Not exactly phrased like that, but yes. Why?

Me: Well, you come across as very... articulate, y'know?

Her: People say I act differently when I text, like I'm so serious or something. Maybe I feel I can be more honest (or vaguely honest).

Me: So how do you really act? If you don't mind me asking.

Her: Like it all matters. Like I'm happy, like I actually care about who's dating who, OMG-did-you-hear-what-happened-well-let-me-tell-you, etc., etc.

Me: So you're popular?

Her: I'm included in a lot of things. I'm a popular choice of company, but it really depends on who you ask. Again, why?

I could have suggested I was popular to try and impress this girl—Saphnie—but that would have been nonsensical. She lived in North Carolina. I'd never be able to meet, let alone date, whoever she was.

Me: Because I'm not exactly popular. No one cared about my birthday today, no one comments on my posts, and you're the only person I've texted all night. *That* isn't fun.

I felt bad after sending that, as I was making this all about me when I should have been helping her get over her ex. Yet she didn't seem to mind. Maybe she was used to people telling her their problems.

Her: Being popular isn't everything, Jay. Sometimes I don't even know which side of the fishbowl I'm on. I can't tell you how important it is to find your REAL friends. Each person perceives different actions as admirable and celebrates accordingly. "Popularity" is merely someone else's opinion.

Me: Wow. You are articulate, aren't you? :-)

Her: Just don't let your new phone get to your head, okay? You'll go crazy trying to change things beyond your control. Leave popularity to those who think it matters. (Hint hint: it doesn't.)

Me: I'll remember that! But it's past 10:30 here, and my mom's getting mad at me on the other side of the door, so I should probably go. G'night!

Her: Go iron the ol' ear, as they say in Oklahoma!

Me: What? Ironing your ear sounds painful! :-P

Her: It's an idiom. An iron makes things flat. Your ear gets flat when you sleep on your side.

Me: Oh, OK. Sorry about you and Jason, by the way.

Her: Me too. Text you later.

I shifted from my position on the bed and noticed both the clock and her text's timestamp read 10:39 PM. I had spent more than half an hour texting. Texting a girl. It didn't matter that she lived three states away. Had we been flirting? Maybe. Did I like it, whatever it was? Absolutely. Talking in person would have been much better, but just texting Saphnie was good enough for me. Good practice, that is. With years of experience to catch up on, Lord knew I needed it.

And maybe she did, too.

one hundred and seventy-seven days ago

Concerning the great nation of Canada, Aunt Nancy once noted that it's a "*ghetto-ass, frozen nation!* They've got a fuggin' marijuana leaf as their flag, the GPS doesn't work because it's a third world country, and there's no swimming 'cause all the damn lakes are solid!" She then went on about how all Canadians live in igloos, ride their polar bears to their log cabins—where they learn about the lumberjack trade—and the whole community goes ice fishing on the weekends, eh?

I can't admit to having traveled to Canada, although I'm sure there were people who thought similarly to my aunt when it came to Oklahoma, with teepees, saloons, cowboys, and Native Americans alike. Then there were those who thought of themselves as a little less ignorant—people who imagined Okies living off farmland and driving pickup trucks everywhere. But the cultural city of Arminster may as well be the same as any other American metropolitan of 400,000 individuals, with supermarkets, movie theaters, performing arts, and many kinds of sports, restaurants, and outdoor recreation. Natural beaches were the only missing feature, the state being distinctly landlocked.

Finbarr Hennigan High School, like the rest of Oklahoma, was built on a hill, or in the case of the school, many, many smaller hills. Formerly Arminster High and renamed after the city's first mayor, the building consists of four floors, with entrances to all but the fourth. Using this setup, if one were to stand at the base of the third floor's entrance, it would appear as if the fourth floor was actually the second.

I was wandering those halls the first day of high school when I met Ethan, a fellow ninth grader with an unfortunate case of major acne, which made his red hair even more prominent. At the time, neither of us knew our way to Spanish II, but we'd helped each other since.

A year later, and Ethan and I weren't best buds or anything, but we were friendly enough. I guess that's how I was with most people: They acknowledged me, but only to an extent, as only a few knew my name. I didn't force myself to talk to people, which was probably the reason why I was always alone—I didn't try hard enough.

I once thought I'd had friends in my home state of Florida, where my circle of childhood playmates and I went to school together, prayed at church together, and ate together at each other's houses. The move to Oklahoma happened before CoffeeFolder and the "like" had been invented, so I lost contact with those kids. It was only months later when I realized we had formed our associations based not on mutual interests, but the convenience of it all within our little cul-de-sac—an awareness that seemed to permanently hinder my social capabilities in the years to follow.

Throughout most of middle school, my friends consisted primarily of the sons of my mother's co-workers (before her job was outsourced and she switched to a career in real estate). These boys tended to be two or three years younger than me, and consequently, we never had much in common. So we played videogames, and I was OK with that up until they discovered friends their own age and my sister Elena left for college, leaving me to play those two-person games by myself. In eighth grade, I hopelessly searched for anyone who would allow me into his or her company, and I eventually came across a girl who had moved to Oklahoma from another state and was also searching. In fact, we ended up dating for a couple of months until she abandoned me for another group right before I left for Hennigan High and she went elsewhere. Ever since, I had found myself consistently regressing to the point of being an active observer rather than an eager participant. Ethan was short and loud with a slight country accent—and even he had a girlfriend. What was my excuse? Where was my friend group?

In most situations, I messed up entirely.

"Hey, can I borrow that pencil you're using?" a girl asked one day.

"Um, yeah," I answered. "Here you go."

"Thanks. You're Johnny, right?"

"Jake. Or Jay, actually. I—"

"Right. Duh. I'm Reagan."

"Oh, like the president?"

"NO! I FUCKING HATE IT WHEN PEOPLE SAY THAT."

I clearly did not receive her friendship that day, as she stomped off with both my pencil and hopes of finding a companion.

The day after my sixteenth birthday was not only a Friday, but also the last day of testing for semester finals, which meant I would have two full weeks of Winter Break. After my Chemistry final and a two-hour study period, all that was left was the dreaded Spanish III exam.

Once everyone had either finished or given up, Mrs. Beckham put on a movie for us to watch as we talked among ourselves. I was playing blackjack with Ethan, whose acne seemed to have gotten worse with age, when he put his cards down and faced the film enlarged on the TSC GALAXIAN Interactive Whiteboard.

"Ethan, what are you—?"

"Shush!" he said, his attention focused on one character laughably hitting another, who then fell backward and wailed in pain (dubbed in Spanish). "These guys are great!"

I shook my head and—when Ethan wasn't looking—reached into the deck, took out a King of Hearts, and replaced it with my seven, equaling twenty-one with my Ace and ten card. But since he was still watching the movie, I pulled my phone out of my pocket and browsed the contacts list: Bradford, Ethan; Murchison, Dad; Murchison, Mom; and Saphnie. I then put it away, hoping Mrs. Beckham hadn't seen, as she had a strict *dos semestres sin celulares* policy. We weren't watching a movie in her class because she was a fun teacher, but because she honestly expected us to have failed her test and thought we were another "lost cause of today's generation." This apparently meant we had nothing to lose by watching a low-grade classic in the public domain.

"This hand is enough to make even an onion cry," Ethan said, looking at his cards. I shrugged and watched as the wall clock ticked from 3:48 to 3:49.

"Now remember, class," Mrs. Beckham started as she noticed us packing up our belongings. She paused the movie. "Your chapter six vocabulary packet and verb sheets over the future tense are due when?"

"*En dos semanas*," we answered, all eyes staring not at her, but the clock.

"What day is your test?"

"*El próximo viernes*," we replied.

The bell then rang, and Mrs. Beckham wished us all a safe Winter Break and a "Happy Christmas" before we left. (She had moved to the States from England, which meant she spoke Spanish in a British accent. So while Mrs. Beckham could be a hard teacher, at least her voice was pleasant enough.)

I headed upstairs for my locker, put my textbooks and loose sheets of paper inside, went out the science wing exit door, and then felt my Serenade vibrate in my pocket. I was surprised for a second, thinking it was from Saphnie, which was absurd all on its own—that I would get excited to receive a text from a girl I had never met. But of course, it was my mother.

Mom: Don't forget I'm picking you up today. Love you!

I was one of the only sophomores who still rode the school bus, as my mom wouldn't even let me consider getting my learner's permit for another year. It was embarrassing, but also meant I was never bothered for a window seat by a tiny middle schooler, which was nice.

Me: OK. The Spanish final wasn't as bad as I'd thought it would be. I think I did pretty well!

Mom: What a SEXT! See you soon!

I stared at my phone, confused, and made my way outside and into the passenger seat of our fairly-new, luxury sedan. I then turned up the heater, put my backpack on the floor, and reclined.

"You know it makes me nervous when you sit up front," Mom reminded me, as this was one of the reasons Dad had purchased the car.

"Right, sorry," I said, but she had already pulled out and away from the school. "So, um, what do you think 'sext' means?"

"A surprise text message?" she guessed. I laughed. For a smart real estate agent, my mother sure had a lot to learn. Then again, so did I.

Dad was on the phone when Mom and I got home—probably negotiating a business deal with the higher-ups in Chicago. She went upstairs to her home office while I made myself a turkey sandwich with mayonnaise and ate it in three large bites, followed by a glass of water to wash it down.

In my room, I sat on the edge of my bed and took out my phone. If it was 4:30 in Oklahoma, then it was 5:30 in North Carolina. Hoping she wasn't having an early dinner, I decided to text Saphnie.

Me: Salutations from Arminster! How are you?

I realized it was silly of me to be waiting for her when she hadn't responded for ten or so minutes. I took out my verbs sheet from my backpack and started on *comprender*—"to understand"—and got to *comprenderemos*—"we will understand"—before I received her reply. This excited me more than it might the average teenager, but they had all sorts of people to text, and I had been trying not to appear too eager (or lonely, as it would turn out).

Saphnie: I'm fine. I think I did all right on my finals. Are you a sophomore, too? Have you taken yours yet?

Me: I am, and I have! I finished my last one today, so now I'm working on Spanish verb sheets (homework over the break). Which was the hardest for you?

Saphnie: Probably Latin or math. Imaginary numbers are too abstract for even me.

Me: I've always thought Latin was interesting!

Saphnie: It's okay. De gustibus non est disputandum.

Me: Yeah... What?

Saphnie: It's a Latin maxim meaning, "In matters of preference there is no argument."

Me: Wow. There's definitely truth to that!

Saphnie: Do you believe in God?

Our conversation had gotten serious fast, and I re-read the previous texts to make sure I hadn't missed one. I thought about my answer, as this seemed important to her.

Me: I grew up with the concept of God, so I would like to think so. I believe there's Someone or Something out there making sure not as many houses burn or people drown as there could be. My parents think differently, though, so I do as they do.

Saphnie: Not to jump languages, but there are two great Japanese words to describe what you're talking about: "tatemae," what you pretend to believe, and "honne," what you actually believe. Counter-attitudinal behavior. It's similar to when the toddler next door gets baby-muck all over his face and you tell Mrs Neighbor it's cute when really you're thinking, "I swear if that kid gets anywhere near me oh gosh oh gosh get it AWAY!!!"

Tatemae and *honne* described my relationship with church beautifully. While my parents had gone for the social connections—as they were just as infatuated with public perception—I had actually enjoyed

17

learning about the Word of God in the evangelical Christian church of my childhood. I knew all the worship songs by heart, memorized Bible verses in a big room with stained-glass windows, and even went to Vacation Bible School for a few summers. But when we moved states, and I got older, it became less about, "Let's read how Jesus fed thousands of people with merely five loaves of bread and two fish," to "Let's play some air hockey, watch an inspirational movie, and pray at the end." My faith had suffered because of this.

> **Me: Regarding tatemae, smoking's gross. But if we're talking honne, I still think it's cool, even if I would never do it and know it's bad for your health.**

> **Saphnie: In terms of tatemae, I'm going to follow in my mom's footsteps and become the hardworking, CEO-type businessperson she wants me to be. Honne-wise? I'll die before I ever let that happen.**

> **Me: Tatemae, I know popularity doesn't matter. But it does! Sort of. I feel like a background character in a TV show watching the main characters go about their adventures. For once, I'd like to be recognized and not have to sit around on the weekends doing nothing. I don't want to be just another name in the obituaries when I die, y'know?**

> **Saphnie: "Death must be so beautiful. To lie in the soft brown earth with the grasses waving above one's head and listen to silence. To have no yesterday and no tomorrow. To forget time, to forgive life, to be at peace." That's what I hope death is like. No heaven, no limbo, no hell. Dad's religious, but mom's not. They let my sister and I choose, but we're opposites. I want to rest in peace, "y'know?"**

> **Me: Are you making fun of me? :-P**

> **Saphnie: Me mocking Jay? Not as much as you think I am.**

Me: That's... a confusing statement.

Saphnie: Ha. (^_~) Oscar Wilde wrote that by the way, but it's often misattributed to Sylvia Plath. She died of carbon monoxide poisoning, head in gas oven, suicide. She was 30. Her children were sleeping in the other room.

Me: I'm not sure what to say. That's awful! D-:

Saphnie: New topic: What kind of music do you like to listen to? What type of books do you enjoy?

Me: I'll read and listen to just about anything. I'm easy! What genres do you prefer?

Saphnie: It's never that simple with me, ha ha. I read a mix of young adult, horror, suspense, and psychological thrillers. One of my favorite authors has a new book coming out in January! There's also this indie band I like called Pulsar Skies. Have you heard of them? Their best song is Demon Drink, but Sedona at 12:14 AM, Lights and Limousines, Ghoughpteighbteau, and Miles in the Snow from The Nuclear Cold album are just as phenomenal. They're so good. You should totes listen to them!

Sure enough, "Demon Drink" was the first item to show up on QuickSearch. So I clicked, I listened, and I liked what I heard. The song was only three minutes long, but the combination of the music's quality, the powerful lyrics, and the deceptive simplicity in the lead singer's voice was absolutely masterful—the same being true for the other songs she had listed.

Me: These guys are awesome! I think "Demon Drink" is my favorite. Is there another voice in the "Sedona at 12:14 AM" song?

Saphnie: PS originally had two lead singers until one died in a DUI car accident. Demon Drink was from their second album and wasn't recorded with his voice. It's sort of haunting hearing the dead sing, whether it be Elvis Presley or Michael Jackson.

Me: Huh. I guess you're right.

Saphnie: "Non omnis moriar," wrote the poet Horace. "I shall not wholly die." On that happy note, do you have plans this holiday break?

Me: My parents are leaving for a short trip in the morning, but other than that, doubtful. Yourself?

Saphnie: I might head south to Myrtle Beach and rent a cabin with some people from school, but no swimming or anything. It's too cold for that. We would just sit around a fire, eat crappy junk food, and retell stories. Sometimes I feel so disconnected from it all. I don't know. I better get going. Bye, Jay.

Me: OK. See you later!

Pulsar Skies had many songs I found incredible, but I kept coming back to "Demon Drink"—it forced its listeners to ask, "What happens after death?" Are we ghosts in limbo? Do we meet our Creator in a better place and suffer for our actions here on Earth? Or do we get to finally rest in peace, as perhaps Sylvia Plath had dreamed of doing?

I'd always thought of Heaven as being a castle in the air, like I was taught. I had never before imagined it being an individualized experience—something personal.

Christmas Eve

The snow fell gradually, at first, with one of the weather forecasters predicting three inches, at most. That alone would be enough to close down the surrounding towns, but Arminster had a couple of plows, so not too many people were concerned. But as highways started to pile up with the snow banks while supermarkets began to run out of milk and bread, the governor declared a state of emergency. Three people ended up dying from those thirteen accumulated inches of snowfall and wind-chill factors as low as -30 degrees Fahrenheit, and evening meteorologist Russ Carpenter was fired subsequently.

I'd been at home for almost four days by Christmas Eve. This was unusually long for my business parents—who had left for France on Saturday morning to celebrate their 25th wedding anniversary—but not their fault, given that Arminster International had since been closed due to the weather. Pros: I had electricity (for the time being), TV, Internet, 121 recorded episodes of *$tore Wars: Florida*, and my phone. Cons: I was running low on food, out of milk, and was getting bored. Still, what was called the "storm of the century" on Coffee-Folder didn't stop my mother from calling every hour to check on me.

It was on that fourth day when I realized the freezer was out of microwaveable chicken pot pies, BBQ Buffalo wings, and sausage pancakes. There was only a big, frozen, spinach pizza Mom had so kindly left for me. And since my stomach felt close to empty, I picked up my phone and sent Ethan a message.

Me: Hey, how do I cook a frozen pizza?

No response.

I remembered he had gone south to visit his cousins in Texas, so I tried Saphnie, instead.

Me: Hey, how do I cook a frozen pizza?

No response.

Saphnie tended to reply promptly, so I was worried, and combined with my hunger and anguish:

Me: I'M STARVING, I'M ALL BY MYSELF, I'M LOW ON FOOD, AND HOW DO YOU COOK A FROZEN PIZZA??

Saphnie: You're 16 and you don't know how to bake a pizza?

Me: Please. Tell. Me. How.

Saphnie: Do you know how to preheat the oven?

Me: Nope.

Saphnie: Find the Bake button and set it to 400 degrees.

Me: I did that 15 minutes ago. Do I put the pizza in now?

Saphnie: Yeah. Use oven mitts! Don't burn yourself!

Me: And bake for 15 more minutes?

Saphnie: 12-13 should do it.

Me: My oven goes in five minute intervals.

Saphnie: Set yourself a timer (there's a timer button, but use your phone if you need it) and take out the pizza in 13 minutes.

Me: Do I press Bake now?

Saphnie: It's already baking.

———————————

Me: Oh, my God. This stuff is good.

Saphnie: Welcome to Common Knowledge! We're glad you could join us. (^_~)

Me: My mom is overprotective and doesn't like me handling the oven. She even has to know my CoffeeFolder password!

Saphnie: I've never understood why people find CoffeeFolder so appealing.

Me: You don't have one?

Saphnie: CoffeeFolder's motto is literally, "Your Business is Our Business." No thank you.

Me: Think about it this way: Oklahoma's in the middle of a blizzard. I can't get out of the house, but with CoffeeFolder, at least I can read about the lives of other people in the same situation as me!

Saphnie: That doesn't help your case. Besides, it only leads to drama. CoffeeFolder is one giant soap opera. THAT should be its slogan!

Me: Ronald Reagan once said, "Information is the oxygen of the modern age." It's good for that!

Saphnie: When I was little I lost a tooth during school and a kid said that if you write letters to the tooth fairy she would write back. I wrote one that night and stuck it under my pillow with my tooth and got a note from her the next day. I ended up doing this for every tooth I lost until my last tooth in seventh grade when my mom told me it was she who was writing those responses. If someone is happy, why point out reality at their expense? It doesn't seem fair. Ignorance is bliss. End of rant. When do your parents get back?

Me: Um, sometime after this storm passes. When do you leave for Myrtle Beach?

Saphnie: I have to stay and help my mom with my sister. The universe has a strange sense of humor in regard to putting us in our place.

Me: How old is she?

Saphnie: 18. She had a heart attack due to a heart abnormality. The lack of oxygen flow caused her to be mentally disabled. This happened during a summer party with her friends a while back. Everyone was too drunk to see she was unconscious on the floor and they got her help a little too late. She can't really talk anymore. Some say she's lucky to be alive, but I'm not so sure.

Me: Oh, gosh. I'm sorry. :-(

Saphnie: Don't be. Everyone's always so sorry. But it's fine, really. Besides, I told anyone who's asked I'm flying to Chicago with my dad instead. It's too personal.

Me: But are you all right?

Saphnie: I don't like people being sorry all the time, okay? "Oh goodness, I didn't know," and "We are so sorry for your family, dear." I want to say, "Yes, wonderful, but we don't NEED you to feel sorry." It gets annoying sometimes. I want the best for Valerie, but I think we've all come to accept the tragedy as a part of her now. People don't know what it's like because it's never happened to them, similar to how only you can feel the hunger in your stomach or the pain of a bad breakup. No one can understand your suffering as greatly as you can.

Me: I see what you mean. I'm only a text away if you need me, OK? And you don't have to pay me! ;-P

Saphnie: Good, since we're close to broke. Anyway, I should go. Have a good evening and a Happy New Year!

Me: Same to you! Merry Christmas!

Although I had started and ended the year without any true friends, I had met Saphnie in mid-December. She was smart, funny, put up with my lame sense of humor, and I appreciated her. So even though my social situation wasn't any better than it had been a year before, I was still determined to make the most of the next one. I figured that if it had taken me almost a full year to make that one friend, then those twelve months weren't wasted at all.

Yet I did not know of Lily and the role I would play in her schemes, and the same could be said of Ethan, Sandy, and Nick. I knew only Saphnie, and even that was an overstatement. But those four had history—past events which had linked them together and would eventually reveal their secret, self-centered ambitions to me. At the time, I was ecstatic just to be involved. It was never about me, though, nor was it really about them. It was Saphnie and her undying passion for true, deserved greatness in a world corrupted by the company with whom I would surround myself. That is the reason for her suffering. That is the reason why the next five months can only be described in a pensive, almost mournful expression of thought.

January

one hundred and sixty days ago

My parents and I had our own Christmas morning when the weather began to clear and they returned from France. I got some money from far-away aunts and miss-you-much uncles, a Verona Booksellers gift card, the fifth book adaptation of the *Annihilation!* videogame from Elena (who could not make it to Arminster due to the storms in her state), hygiene stuff, and a couple of small things like socks and underwear.

Scattered snow slowly melted and remained as sleet periodically fell from the pale blue sky to the brown grass, with the only signs of life coming from the evergreens. The temperature would stick to thirty-three for a while, then drop to thirty-two, then thirty-one, but would make its way back up to thirty-four within the hour. For kids who wanted a snow day the first day back to school, it was frustrating, as the new year brought many familiar things: the return of school, the hugging of friends who acted like they hadn't kept in touch with each other, the loud laughter from holiday inside jokes, and people like me unable to participate.

I wandered into first-hour Chemistry right before class started at 8:45. I sat at my table and took notes as Mr. Kukowski tried to explain chemical reactions in water. Eventually, Kukowski bored even himself, so he threw up his hands and played some "hip hop hippity hop" music on his GALAXIAN board. So my classmates talked among themselves, ignoring the fact that Kukowski was on one of those dating websites he frequented. Considering his profile picture was a close-up of himself—displaying his full beard and mustache, bald patch, and tufts of hair on the side of his head—it was deemed unlikely he would receive many responses, if any, despite him insistently referring to himself as "ruggedly handsome."

By the time seventh-hour Spanish arrived, I was too tired for Mrs. Beckham and her British accent. So I opened my textbook on my desk and put *Annihilation! Book Five: Moonlight Requisition* (featuring the return of Commander Ace Thunderbolt) between its large pages.

"Mr. Bradford, please wake Jakob."

I felt a tug on my shoulder and looked up to Mrs. Beckham standing beside me. The whole class was watching us.

"Mr. Murchison, I asked how you say 'rubbish' in Spanish."

"*Basura*," I answered without much thought. On the floor between my feet was the *Annihilation!* book. I bent down to grab it, but Mrs. Beckham slid it into the aisle with her foot and picked it up herself.

"This, children, *es basura*," she said, holding up *Moonlight Requisition*. "If the author—a Mr. Ted Errikson—had changed the characters and spiced up the plot a little bit, he would not have to write fanfiction."

When Elena was a teenager, she got a gaming system from her boyfriend-at-the-time as a Valentine's Day gift. (She kept it after the breakup, of course, as any reasonable young woman should.) Inside was *Annihilation!*, a first-person shooter set in the year 2114. The game consists of a cooperative single-player mode where the player assumes the role of teen-cyborg and playboy Damien Strong under the persona of Commander Ace Thunderbolt. He and his friends would then attempt to rid the galaxy of Interplanetary Industries, a corrupt and Rockefeller-esque transportation business controlled by Damien's father, William Strong (who is holding Damien's girlfriend Victoria hostage).

27

The game received almost universal critical acclaim, yet that wasn't enough to garner any sequels. In fact, it sold so poorly that the game's studio went bankrupt. So lead designer Ted Errikson took it upon himself to write a novelization of the game and a bunch of backstory afterward. Elena would preorder these books and let me read them when she was finished, so even though there was a seven-year age gap between us, we still had *Annihilation!* to talk about, which is why she had gotten me the fifth book for Christmas. With me in high school and Elena working as a photographer for a newspaper in her seaside city, it was nice to have something we found mutually enjoyable—Sci-Fi shooters and cheesy one-liners alike. ("Looks like you just got… *annihilated!*" to quote Commander Thunderbolt.)

I didn't tell all of this to Mrs. Beckham, though.

"But he got *paid* to write a *novelization*," I noted. "And money's money, especially in these poor economic times." That got me a couple of laughs.

"Nonetheless, you should neither be reading—nor sleeping—in my class."

She put the book on my desk and went back to teaching. She managed a few sentences before the bell rang, ending her lecture and our school day.

I finished *Moonlight Requisition* on the bus ride home. Mr. Errikson always did such a great job with the banter between Sergeant Mysti Moreno and "Binary Jack" Dixon (Damien's best friends, and in the case of Binary Jack, Victoria's brother) that I was laughing to myself the whole way to the bus stop. Despite Damien, Mysti, and Binary Jack being only videogame characters, I'd always enjoyed reading about their adventures, like with those who had added me as their friend on CoffeeFolder—it was almost as if I, too, was a part of their fun.

The bus dropped me and a few others off at my neighborhood. While walking home, I got a text from Saphnie.

Saphnie: JAY! RUDDERLESS AT SEA COMES OUT IN 15 DAYS! BESTILL MY HEART; I'M BARELY BREATHING.

Me: What?

Saphnie: The book by my favorite author that I preordered? It comes January 20. I'm skipping school and picking it up at the bookstore. It's going to be great!!! \(*^o^*)/

Me: Skipping school? Is it that good?

Saphnie: Oh yes, you deprived child! It's that good and better!

Me: I'm older than you. :-P

Saphnie: That you are. Have you ever heard of Amos Metres? QuickSearch him if you haven't. He's written a bunch of other novels. You need to read those too so I can discuss them with someone.

I was already on my laptop by the time she had sent her last text. As most students do when attempting to research, I indeed started with QuickSearch. Under "Amos Metres," it listed information on his childhood, career, writings, personal life, bibliography, and various awards he had received. The picture on the right showed a lean man with a pale, narrow face, blue eyes, and thick, brown hair above his wrinkled forehead. He looked much older than the age it listed him as—maybe it was in his genes, or maybe he didn't get enough sleep, enough sun, or both.

According to his bibliography, he finished his first book when he was seventeen, titled *The Vanishing Act*, and his bestselling novel was his twelfth and latest, *Die in Peace, Sinner*. His first adventure book, *Rudderless at Sea*, was to come out on January 20th. I clicked the link.

RUDDERLESS AT SEA from QuickSearch, your fishing expedition: an upcoming <u>epistolary</u> novel written by author <u>Amos Metres</u>. The novel is estimated to be around 400 pages.[citation optional]

Metres described the plot on his website: "Edward Merry leaves the small village of Keydale as the Captain's First Mate aboard the *Apricity* after tragedy strikes his family. An unexpected maelstrom knocks the vessel off course, and Edward becomes shipwrecked on a seemingly-deserted, South Pacific isle. With Captain O'Rourke missing, can Edward lead the small band of survivors while uncovering the dark secrets of the Island and the mysterious disappearance of its inhabitants who have long since fled? Free from society's constraints, Edward's journey will lead him to the brink of madness, as he has found himself Rudderless at Sea."[1]

Me: Seems like an interesting guy! How do you pronounce his last name? "Meters?"

Saphnie: MEH-tress, like mattress with a short "e" for the "a." Also, I went to the Arminster City-County Library's website and searched for Rudderless while you were looking him up. People have already placed 42 holds on the book and it hasn't come out yet! I suggest you go out and buy it yourself. Please? (;_;)

Me: I got a Verona Booksellers gift card for Christmas, so yeah, I'll buy it. Speaking of which, how was yours?

Saphnie: Great! I got a Latin-English dictionary, a Frank Sinatra album, Beatles memorabilia, pajamas, and a necklace with a charm shaped like my cat Minerva. She has three legs and only half her right ear. I also got a boatload of Ivy's Innuendo stuff! (I know they completely sexualize women, but my mom used to work there, so she gets credit from her former boss. My future boyfriend will appreciate it.) A guy I know even gave me a free 8th of weed! \($_$)/

Me: Awesome! And that last bit is… cool?

Saphnie: I didn't smoke it, Jay! I thought it was a nice gesture. That's all. De gustibus non est disputandum! Speaking of Latin, I need to go and start my homework. Bye!

Me: See you later!

I connected the phone to its charger, turned on my laptop, and then went ahead to VeronaBooksellers.com, "Where Books Are Still Sold!" I preordered a hardcover copy of *Rudderless at Sea* for twenty-one dollars—plus four for shipping fees—and received another text while closing the browser.

Ethan: With hot colds

Me: What?

Ethan: It's a pun. You know. Hot colds like hot coals. I dunno you asked me how to bake a pizza. Thought there was punch line or something

Me: Oh, OK. Sorry about that!

Ethan: You seriously didn't know how? Read the goddamn instructions, Murchison! Anyway that sucks what Beckham put you through today. You play Anal Nation?

Me: I think you mean, "Annihilation!" And not recently, since I haven't had anyone to be the second player. Do you have the game?

Ethan: Damn autocorrect. That's sick. I never typed that before. Anyway I sometimes play with my little sis. She gets us killed tho and there's usually friendly fire. You should come over and get us passed the last few levels

31

Me: Definitely! That'd be fun!

Ethan: K. Is the Spanish test this week?

Me: I don't know. I was sleeping, remember?

Ethan: You better study your balls off!!! Later bro

I had never been invited to someone's house—let alone told to learn so much my sexual organs detach—so this was new to me. I was excited for making another friend, which was worth getting belittled for in another language.

one hundred and forty-five days ago
Saphnie's text woke me up on the morning of January 20th.

Saphnie: Got my copy of Rudderless at Sea! I'm already 50 pages in. I adore Mercer. He's so sensitive and emotional! I swear to God if anything happens to him I'll cut a bitch. Anyway I'm turning my phone off for the day so people don't disturb me. <3

Me: I was sleeping. This book better be worth it.

Saphnie: I CAN'T HEAR YOU, LA-LA-LA.

I found a package in the mail when I got home after school. I brought it inside, waved at my busy parents (who nodded in recognition), and went to my room. With no homework that night, I focused solely on the words of Amos Metres.

The opening sentence: "This jeweled coast does not shine, for its gems are coated with grit."

one hundred and forty-three days ago

During the late hours of January 22nd, I finished *Rudderless at Sea*.

Me: That book was amazing! :-D

Saphnie: You finished it too?!

Me: Yes! I'm not gonna lie, I cried at the end of day twenty-one!

Saphnie: Omg all the emotions. So much sobbing. Asdfghjkl

Me: What did you think of the Island and all its mystery?

Saphnie: I believe the Island itself is not supposed to be a tangible, physical place, but a metaphor for the circumstances Edward and the crew find themselves in.

Me: What? You're over-thinking it. I think he's on an actual island. Wasn't it hinted at somewhere early on he had been there before?

Saphnie: You can't take the text at face value! That's not what Amos Metres books are about. You didn't think they actually lost a rudder, did you?

Me: … Maybe.

Saphnie: (>_<) I'll try and forget you said that. You're such a left-brain AND a kleptomaniac. Quit taking things literally and there's hope for you yet!

Me: Well, does the Internet say anything?

Saphnie: Just a lot of fan speculation. The only thing Mr Metres has said is that it's meant to be left open for interpretation.

Me: But now we'll never know!

Saphnie: I think it's important there isn't a direct explanation. It lets people analyze it more while allowing for seemingly endless possibilities. Kind of like what we're doing now. (^_^)

We continued our plot analysis for the next hour or so, discussing everything from Edward's love interest Paluure to the poet Mercer's true identity. But it was after we had said our good-byes and finished texting when it occurred to me that Saphnie hadn't shared this with anyone else—only me. And then, for one crazy moment, I doubted her sincerity, like O'Rourke with Mercer when the latter's name didn't show up on the ship's manifest. While I'm sure not every person in the United States had a CoffeeFolder profile, it did have close to a billion active users. Was it even logical to think Saphnie might be fictional?

one hundred and forty-two days ago
During the three weeks after Mrs. Beckham scolded me in class, Ethan and I bonded over our shared liking of *Annihilation!* and our mutual dislike of the Spanish language. (Nothing against Spanish speakers—it was just harder than what the juniors at my Freshman Orientation had made it out to be.) He had yet to invite me over, as his family was refinishing their floors, but we still talked about the game frequently. It gave us something in common, similar to how it was with Elena and me, and it was nice getting to experience new emotions from Ethan while he talked about a subject he was passionate about (unlike Spanish). It was those moments that were special to me—when a person could be real without fear of judgment.

I was aware of this sensation again the next morning while re-reading *Rudderless* in Chemistry before class started. In fact, I was actually startled when I heard the mixture of shrieking and squealing behind me, which could be interpreted as, "Dude! You read Amos Metres books, too?!"

I turned around to see a girl with sleek, shoulder-length blonde hair. She was wearing tight jeans and one of those Ivy's Innuendo V-necks that was see-through enough to show just a little of her red bra. In her hands, she held her own copy of *Rudderless*. Its cover was the same as mine: a nighttime view of an island with crimson smoke from a fire mixing with the golden storm above it, which caused quite the scene as the falling ash intermingled with violet lightning, striking the mountainous landscape, which was so blue, it was almost black. The top of the cover, among the dark clouds, read AMOS METRES, and the bottom's reflecting ocean, in a smaller font: RUDDERLESS AT SEA.

"I'm reading it for the second time," I said, then quickly added: "It's really good!" I wasn't used to talking to girls I found this attractive—womanly curves and the like.

Her eyes widened. "I just finished it during the car ride to school. It was amazing! I was crying by the time I got to—"

"Day twenty-one?" I asked, and she laughed.

"Yes! Oh, God, that was bad. Good, but bad, you know?"

I was trying to remember where I had seen her before. Obviously, she'd been in my Chemistry class the whole year, but I felt as if I knew who she was somehow.

"You look familiar," I said, gazing into her pleasant and pale blue eyes. "Where do I know you from?"

She thought about it for a moment and then snapped her fingers as she smiled, pointing at me.

"Oh! Do you subscribe to the Tits'n'More Pussy Palace?" she asked, her face devoid of any signs she was joking. I didn't know what site she was talking about, but she laughed before I could answer. "Just kidding. My name's Lily. I'm dating Ethan. You might've seen me in the halls with him."

That's where I knew her from, as Ethan wouldn't shut up about a Lily Carswell when they had first started going out in September.

I introduced myself as Jay while she took the seat facing me. She opened her copy of the book and flipped to a page in the latter half.

"So what do you think the Island is?" she asked, still flipping pages.

35

"Do you think it's real?"

"I'm not sure. I think it's real—maybe based on someplace Edward's been to before with his daughter. But a lot of stuff about it doesn't make much sense. It's all too convenient."

"Yeah!" she said, excited. "Like the rusty car parts! It's a deserted island, so why would that stuff be scattered along a beach with no roads? It's crazy!"

"What do you think happened to Edward?" I asked.

"I think he committed sui—" She stopped herself, looking around. "I mean, after his daughter's death, maybe he tried to, um, kill himself, and now he's in a coma or something at the hospital, and it's all a dream world he constructed."

"Whoa. *Suicide?* Sure, the novel ends with him reminiscing over the past on the top of a cliff, but I don't think he jumped. Besides, it never says his daughter died. I just thought he lost custody of her."

"Maybe Paluure is a manifestation of the wife who divorced him?" she suggested, then laughed. "Or maybe Metres isn't having enough sex with *his* wife."

Kukowski was staring at us from his desk, obviously confused as to what we were talking about.

"I don't know where that conversation started or was going to end up, but sweet mother of God's holy haberdashery!" he said, starting another one of his ravings. "What on earth did any of that have to do with the price of tea in China? I don't care about your personal lives, kiddos, no matter my purest and utmost curiosity or whatever you think I have as a teacher. *¡Santa vaca!* Seriously, though, it's like no thought in this room goes un-verbalized. Keep it in your head, folks, not in the back of your sinus passages. There's no flying by the seat of your pants involved—this isn't rocket surgery, people."

"You mean rocket science?" one kid asked.

"Or brain surgery?" suggested another.

"Whatever," Kukowski finished. He took a closer look at our books, then shrugged. "At least you're taking the initiative to read. There's hope for your generation yet!"

We told him we'd be quieter, all the while laughing some more. When Kukowski decided he was actually going to teach us something, Lily got up to go to her regular seat and slid me a piece of torn notebook paper on her way there.

Call me so we can discuss Edward x Paluure some more! —Lily

She included her number at the bottom, and I quickly entered it into my phone as Kukowski showed us a video on the attractive force between atoms. He also talked about jetpacks, bunnies, pineapples, and garden gnomes—"but that's not relevant."

In Spanish class, Ethan mentioned to me Lily had said we'd been discussing *Rudderless*.

"My mom reads books by that Amos guy," he told me.

"Really?" I asked. "That's neat."

"Yeah, I guess," he added, unaware of Mrs. Beckham behind him.

"'It was like a giant maze, only to find that your destination was a dead end all along,'" she said to us. We turned to face her. She was smiling, which was uncomfortable for everyone involved.

There was an awkward silence, followed by Ethan asking, "Uh... what?"

"It's from the Metres novel *Die in Peace, Sinner*," she explained.

"I've only read *Rudderless at Sea*," I said.

"I don't read," Ethan deadpanned.

"Ah," Mrs. Beckham said, either disappointed that I hadn't read the book she was referring to or that Ethan didn't read, period. "Well, I'm going to borrow *Rudderless at Sea* when my son is finished with it, as it was his birthday present. He is a slow reader, much like Mr. Bradford here, so it may take some time before I get to it, unfortunately."

"Yeah, I'm *right here*," Ethan pointed out, but she paid him no attention and walked away from us.

"That was weird," I said.

"I find it gross that both you and Lily have something in common with Mrs. Beckham," Ethan whispered so she wouldn't hear him. "But anyway, I just feel sorry for her kid!" We then laughed for the remainder of the hour at the thought of our teacher chastising her son in a British accent.

———————————

Mom made Dad and me toasted sandwiches with her panini press for dinner that night—"nothing fancy," as she said she wanted to "keep it simple." While we ate, Mom asked me how school was.

"It was a normal day, I guess."

"What does that mean? Did you make new friends?" She asked this not because she was honestly curious, but to be sure that I wasn't hanging out with potentially-bad influences.

"Actually, I met Ethan's girlfriend Lily. She—"

"Girlfriend? Lily? What's her last name?"

"For the love, Karen, let the boy live," Dad told her.

"Maybe I know her parents!" she said defensively, then turned back to me. "Her last name?"

"Carswell. But as I was saying, she's Ethan's girlfriend, and she—"

"Oh, OK. I know her mother." She turned to Dad. "We met her at the company banquet, honey, don't you remember? The woman who missed her husband?"

"Mhmm," Dad said, his mouth full.

"Anyway," I continued, "we were discussing *Rudderless at Sea* in my first-hour—"

"By that Amos Memphis, right?"

"Metres," I corrected her. "And it turns out Mrs. Beckham—my Spanish teacher—has read his books, too."

"*Tulip Beckham?*" Dad asked, spitting out his food onto his shirt in surprise. Mom raised an eyebrow, causing him to laugh at her. "You really think I'd cheat on you for that witch of a woman? I only asked 'cause she was Nancy's teacher back when I went to Arminster High—thirty years and just as many pounds ago. *Before Florida.*"

Mom rolled her eyes at him, then turned to me. "It's good you're making friends, Jakob."

"Yep," Dad said in between bites, still chewing. "We're very proud of you."

The rest of my dinner was spent listening to my parents remind themselves how great their trip to Paris was, how much healthier the people were ("They ride their bikes everywhere! Can you believe it?!"), how small the houses were, how amazing the onion soup was, how it's just a common misconception that French people are rude, et cetera. Then my phone started to vibrate repeatedly, and since I had finished my sandwich, I excused myself, went upstairs, shut my door, and then answered Lily's call.

Me: "Hello?"

Lily: "Hey there! What's up?"

Me: "Nothing much. Finished dinner. Yourself?"

Lily: "Not much. Working on our Chem homework. So! What did you think of Edward and Paluure?"

Me: "I think she missed the Captain too much to fall in love with Edward. Like, if someone ends their relationship with you, and then somebody else comforts you, you might think you're interested in that person, when really it was all in the situation."

Lily: "Maybe you've been watching too much reality TV! But seriously, that moment between them in the jungle was *completely* unnecessary! Does Amos's wife not proofread his books? Hold on, I have it right here—"

Me: "No! No! Not again!" (Laughing.) "They were about to die. It wasn't the time to be thinking clearly! But sex-scenes aside, I was grateful the characters didn't cuss without purpose."

Lily: "Yeah, only when it's needed. For *emphasis*, unlike—" (Buzzing.) "That's Ethan calling me. Crap."

Me: "You should probably answer."

Lily: "Wait! Don't hang—"

Me: "Yeah?"

Lily: "I know we just met and all, but... Would you like to go to church with me and Ethan this Sunday?" (Pause.) "I know this is kind of random, but it'll be fun! Pleeeeaase?"

Me: "Well, I'm not so much a fan of most churches. At least, my parents aren't."

Lily: "It's the one on 12th and Redbud Avenue. You know it?"

Me: "Maybe?" (Pause.) "I'll think about it. What time—?"

Lily: "The 11:30 service, after worship. Sound like a plan, Stan?"

Me: "Um, my name's Jay."

Lily: "It's a joke, silly! See you then?"

Me: "Sure. See you then."

I plugged my phone into its charger after she hung up. I wasn't so keen on the idea of going to church, but I needed to get out more, so what the hell?

I opened my Chemistry textbook and started reading about ionic bonds, in which electrons from an atom are detached and added to another atom, leading to negative and positive bonds attracting each other. Then CoffeeFolder notified me that Lily had added me as her friend and was requesting my approval.

I accepted and browsed her many pictures, status updates, videos, and tags by her hundreds of friends. There was a video of her eating Italian food before Winter Formal with a large group of people at Ricchezza's downtown. A filtered picture showed her and a girl I knew as Darian dressed as retro nurses in a Taco Kick restroom mirror on Halloween night, and another of Lily and Ethan kissing at a Hennigan home football game. A screenshot of her phone's camera roll consisted primarily of images of shirtless actors. Its caption read, "So many men to have crushes on <3," and her latest post: "Thank God for lattes and novels and all the lush vibes."

one hundred and forty days ago

Dad dropped me off in front of the Redbud Avenue church on Sunday morning with fatherly advice: "Support whatever they think as long as it doesn't offend or discriminate, and don't ever say their beliefs are false." I took my Bible and went inside the brick building with the cross on top, eventually making my way up past the sanctuary and the nursery to the small room where Lily and Ethan's youth group met for the 11:30 lesson. It had plain walls, shag carpeting, a TV and a couch in one corner, a plastic table against the wall, and a massive Bible on a podium with three rows of chairs in front of it.

"Look who finally made it to church!" Ethan exclaimed as I walked in, a goofy grin on his pimple-ridden face.

"'I sought the Lord, and He heard me,'" I replied, quoting scripture. "Psalms 34:4."

"Sounds good," he said, then focused his attention back on the TV, a marathon of *$tore Wars: Florida* playing. Lily was in his arms, and she smiled in my direction from the couch they were occupying. A girl with dark hair sat beside them.

The door opened from behind me, and in came a bald man in his mid-thirties with seemingly nothing better to do on Sundays than to preach to teenagers. Ethan would later explain to me it was mostly due to a combination of his love for the Lord and the fact that his wife had forced him out of their apartment for the eighth time—and each was never his fault.

"Whew! Sorry I'm late, kiddos," he said, dropping a pile of papers onto the table. He took a drink of his coffee, straightened his yellow tie, and opened the Bible on the podium. "Good morning, fellow disciples of Christ!"

And then, in monotone unison, the three of them: "Good morning, YMC. We're ready to learn about God's grace and demonstrate His abundance of love toward our fellow man."

"Amen!" he shouted. If this was routine, he never got tired of it. "I'm going to get right to taking attendance now. Let's see… Megan and Tyler? Megan, you're here. I saw Tyler earlier… Phillip? Anyone seen Phillip? No? Guess not. Sandra's home sick… How about Trisha? Hmm. All right then… Ethan?"

"Present and ready to learn about God's grace, sir!" he replied without looking away from the TV.

"Your sarcasm is not appreciated," the man said. "Where was I? Oh, right. Lily—dag nabbit, Lily! Turn off that scripted garbage!"

Fake or not, she was into the show, all the same. "Come on, Meredith," she said to the woman on the screen. "Don't let Laine outbid you! He's a total butthead! Wait a minute… wait… OHHH, YES!" She jumped off the couch, spinning around and waving her hands in the air. "BLESS THE LORD, MY SOUL, AND DON'T FORGET ALL HIS BENEFITS!'"

"'Who forgives all your sins, heals all your diseases, and crowns you with loving kindness and tender mercies,'" the bald man finished for her. "He does *not* determine the outcome of bogus television programs. Psalms one-oh-three, verses two through four."

"All right, all right," Lily said, turning off the TV.

"So we got four here, one might be here, and three absent," he continued. "Huh. Our all-time low." He then turned to me and held out a hand to shake. "I'm Carl, the youth minister here at Redbud Avenue. The kids like to call me YMC—Youth Minister Carl—but just Carl will do."

He smiled as I took it and shook it with my free hand, as the other held my childhood Bible—which he pointed out with a smile on his face, showing his teeth. I told him my name was Jay, and he introduced me to everyone, even though I knew over half the people present, considering there was a total of five of us.

"Is this your first time at church, Jay?" he asked when we were away from them.

"To this one," I answered. "My family went while we lived in Florida, but we sort of stopped once we moved here a few years back. My dad wanted us to live where he grew up, so… yeah."

"I see," he replied in a serious tone. "And do you feel disconnected from God?"

While that was an extremely personal question, I couldn't help interpreting it literally, causing me to imagine a doctor taking a large pair of scissors to cut the umbilical cord that attached me to a mysterious entity way up in the sky and past the clouds.

"I'm here because Lily invited me," I told him.

"That's fine," Carl said, smiling again. "I'm here for you, Jay, and I'll do my best to help with whatever I can. So if you need me, just ask, OK?"

"OK," I said. He seemed supportive, which was perfect for a minister overseeing insecure teenagers.

Carl then told us to take the tiny plastic chairs and form them into a circle in front of the podium. As we began to do so, his phone started ringing. He then gestured that he just *had* to take this call—and left the room as he answered it.

"Where's Ty?" Lily asked, looking around.

"Probably smoking some shit behind the church," Ethan said. Lily shrugged.

"He only said that once to sound cool," said the girl, Megan, who had a noticeable diagonal scar across her left cheek. "It was from a bake sale accident," she told me, seeing the shameful fascination on my face.

"Hey, why'd you bring your Bible?" Ethan asked me.

"This is the church sermon, right?" I pointed out. "I thought—"

"If YMC makes us look up a verse, we just pull out our phones and go to QuickSearch," he explained. "It's that easy. Plus there's nothing to lug around."

"But anyway," Megan interjected, "does anyone know what's in two weeks from today?"

"Your... wait for it," Lily said, adding a pause for dramatic effect. "YOUR BIRTHDAY! Is your family having the party at the lake again this year?"

"Yes!" Megan said, excited. "And I believe this one will, dare I say, *take the cake.*"

Lily groaned, while Ethan looked confused.

"But isn't it also—"

43

"Yeah, yeah, shut up," Megan replied, though she was smiling.

"I guess both our birthdays are lousy," I said. "They're too close to Christmas!"

"Oh, definitely. It's nice until it's over, 'cause then you have to wait another whole year. It's terrible!"

"Wait a second," Lily said, turning her chair toward me. "You had a birthday and didn't tell me?" She looked to Megan. "How do boys expect us to give them stuff if they won't tell us when their birthday is?!"

"I'm sure it was on CoffeeFolder," Ethan noted, and it was. "There's no reason why you forgot, since you're on there 24/7!"

"Not anymore, I'm not!" Lily argued, then smiled and playfully punched Ethan's left arm. He dramatically fell to the ground, faking his death. So I kicked him, and we laughed.

"We just met," I reminded her. "It's fine that you—"

"Didn't your mom give you the keys to the SUV last year?" Lily asked Megan. "That big, blue, ugly Privateer? Because she got the years mixed up or something?"

"That sucks almost as much as the band Student Council hired for Winter Formal," Ethan said, then looked toward Lily and me. "What was their name? The Orpheus?" I hadn't gone, so I couldn't contribute to their distaste.

The door opened again, and Carl returned, picking his papers off the table and taking one last drink of his coffee.

"Michelle called back from the airport," he explained as he rushed out the door. "Make sure to pray!" he shouted from the hallway.

"Well," Ethan said as he got up from the floor. "I guess it's off to the next room over to play air hockey." There was no opposition, so I followed them. I would prove to be good at that.

The following week was more memorable than others. I sensed this was because for once in a long time, I was more than OK with how things were, as I happily hung out with Lily and Ethan (and Megan that Sunday, as she went to Dunmire Preparatory). It was also nice switching lunch spots, away from the technological engineering and robotics team who merely tolerated my presence. (I was only good for providing them *Annihilation!* strategy tips, and even that knowledge was limited. And yet, after all the time I had spent sitting with them, I still didn't know a thing of computer programming.) But Lily and Ethan actually enjoyed having me around, and that was as fair of a trade-off as it gets, as I don't think the robotics team even realized I had moved on.

February

one hundred and thirty-three days ago

Both my parents were busy the next Sunday morning, so I didn't ask them to drive me to church. Instead, I logged onto CoffeeFolder and found on my homepage:

Rudderless at Sea (Official)

How many of you would like a signed copy of RUDDERLESS AT SEA? Enter for a chance to win by leaving a comment below saying what you enjoyed most about the book. This contest will run to March 3rd at midnight (EST). The winner will not only get a free book signed by Amos Metres, but an answer to any one question he or she has! Stay subscribed for more info.

Any one question? I was going to text Saphnie, though I hesitated. It had been a little over a week since we had last texted, and during the time I'd spent with Lily and Ethan, I had been contemplating Saphnie and her honesty. One thought that came to mind was that she might actually be my mother trying to eavesdrop into my social life, which *was* something she would do, but probably didn't, as I didn't think she had the ability of sounding so teenager-like, for lack of a better way of phrasing it.

Still, I wanted to test my theory. I shut my laptop, walked down the hall, and waited outside my mother's office. The door to the study was made of wood and glass, so I was able to see her typing away at her computer. Her phone was on her desk, so I sent Saphnie a text.

Me: Hello!

I received a reply about a minute later. My mom hadn't moved her fingers away from her keyboard.

Saphnie: Hi there! What's up?

Since it was a North Carolina area code, it occurred to me my mom could have asked my sister to pretend to be Saphnie. I couldn't imagine Elena agreeing to it, but I had to be certain.

"Hey, Mom," I said, knocking on the door.

She turned around. "Yes, what is it?"

"Could you please ask Elena if she's read her copy of that *Annihilation!* book series we read?"

"That reminds me I need to ask her how her work with the newspaper is going. Give me just one second."

She picked up her phone and dialed the number. When she started talking, I texted Saphnie.

Me: Amos Metres is holding a contest on his CoffeeFolder page!

Saphnie: I know! That's pretty neat of him.

Mom was still on the phone with Elena.

Me: Wait, you know? How?

Saphnie: I sort of gave in and created an account to check out the contest. v(^_^)v Now approve my friend request so I can stalk your pics.

Me: Yeah, of course!

I quickly went back to my computer and found, lo and behold, a friend request from *Saphnie Kane-Tachibana*.

With only our texts and my suspicions to go by, I did not imagine Saphnie as her profile picture displayed her: a young Asian girl with a gorgeous smile, perfect teeth, and pink lips. She had shiny, dark brown hair, and her bangs were long and side-swept—almost covering her right eye. Her nose was adorable. She wasn't wearing much makeup, although the eyeliner and mascara she had on were all that she needed to look absolutely stunning.

This made me wonder what she thought I looked like.

I went through all my profile pictures, seeing if any were embarrassing, or maybe I didn't look too good in this one or that one. A pic from a few months ago brought out the inner nerdiness in me, so I deleted it. One post about the 1919 Boston Molasses Disaster, a disaster that had killed twenty-one people, had no comments, so I got rid of that as well. I went on like this for a while, tweaking things here and there before accepting her request.

Saphnie had made her account five hours before, but she had already gained 121 friends. And she wasn't kidding when she said she was popular. Messages kept popping up on her profile page, saying, "welcome to coffeefolder!!" and "it's about time you joined <3" It listed her place of education as Tallarico Bay High School and her birthday as May 17th, which I then entered in my phone's calendar and set as high-priority.

One picture that stood out to me had been tagged by her mother. It was a family photo of four: a short, bespectacled man; a tall, pretty, Asian woman in a pink suit with her hands on his left shoulder; and two teenage girls sitting in front of them—Saphnie, in a black and white floral dress, and then a much larger version of her with glasses, who I guessed was Valerie. The man showed a strained smile, the woman wasn't even trying, and Saphnie had her arm around her sister, who was in the middle of clapping. Twenty-one people had already "liked" it, leaving comments such as, "lovely family," "cute outfit!" and "beautiful."

People were tagging her in pictures by the minute, some seemingly more recent than others: ones of her laughing at a bonfire on the beach, a picture of her lying down in the middle of the TBHS football field, one with her wearing a red bandana at some sort of concert, a few taken in restroom mirrors, and one with the contestants and host parents of *America's Next Top Foster Child.*

Me: When did you meet the ANTFC people??

Saphnie: This season was filmed in Windhaven, so I went with some other people to watch the auditions. I got so mad when the family chose Richard and not Brian. (The 17-year-old? Are you kidding me???) It's my favorite show next to Rehab Runway and House of Love. They're all a nice distraction. You know that new romantic drama movie Together Forever? Xavier's flower shop is a mile or two from my house. They don't call this place the Hollywood of the East for nothing!

Me: You're so lucky! But anyway, where did the name "Saphnie" come from? Just wondering. I mean, it's unique. I've never heard it before!

Saphnie: You'll laugh.

Me: No, I won't! I promise!

Saphnie: Most people who ask think it has some special Japanese meaning. It doesn't. When Valerie was born she liked to watch reruns of that dog detective show on TV. My mom misheard Daphne's name as "Saphnie" and thought it sounded pretty. So I got it. Yay!

Me: Well, I think it's cool! Is your last name Japanese?

Saphnie: Half of it. Kane (like sugarcane) is Welsh.

Me: Have you ever been to Japan? Curious, that's all!

Saphnie: I went last summer. It was a breathtaking experience, but after a week I just wanted to go home and eat a burrito. What's the story behind your name?

Me: Murchison? I think it's Irish.

Saphnie: No, your first name. Some people call you Jay, while others refer to you as Jake. Your mom has called you Jakob with a k several times when she talks about you in her posts. Why so many different names for the same person? Do you not know who you are? (^_~)

Mom then knocked on the door and handed me her phone. She said that yes, Elena had gotten her copy and also wanted me to read "an island book by that Amory Murdock author." I told her I would.

one hundred and twenty-three days ago

A week later, after a light dinner of fish and asparagus, I logged onto CoffeeFolder and found on the homepage:

<u>**Lily Carswell**</u> went from being "in a relationship" to "single."
<u>**Ethan Bradford**</u> went from being "in a relationship" to "single."

Lily's was posted after our lunch period—when I noticed the two of them being awfully silent toward each other—and Ethan's after school. I decided to call Lily.

Lily: "Hey."
Me: "Hey. Is everything OK?"
Lily: "Yeah, everything's fine."
Me: "I saw that you and Ethan broke up, and I—"
Lily: "We need a break from each other. God, he's such an idiot."

Me: "Well, I just wanted to check and make sure you're—"

Lily: "Was that stupid of me? To break up with him, I mean."

Me: "Why did you break up with him?"

Lily: "I don't know... He's always so paranoid, and sometimes, I wish he would stop groping me long enough to listen... UGH WHY IS THIS HAPPENING TO ME I'M A GOOD PERSON I GO TO CHURCH AND RECYCLE AND STUFF AAARGHH."

Me: "..."

Lily: "..."

Me: "Lily?"

Lily: "Sorry. I... I just wanted to get it over with, you know?"

Me: "I wouldn't know, actually. The only girl I've dated broke up with me over a phone call while I was on vacation."

Lily: "Oh. Wow. That, like, really sucks."

Me: "I'm OK now."

Lily: "Yeah."

Me: "..."

Lily: "The church has this little get-together for us teens every second Wednesday of the month where we can sing songs, recite poetry, or maybe even put on a performance... Kind of like a mini-talent show. I was going to go with Ethan—Megan with Ty—but since we... since I broke up with Ethan... Do you maybe want to go tonight with me, instead?"

Me: "Um... sure! Like, what time?"

Lily: "Great! It starts at 7:30, so in about an hour. See you then?"

Me: "See you then!"

Whereas some people might find it boring to go to church, I had spent too many weeknights alone, so any opportunity to go someplace with my new-found friends, I'd gladly take. Plus my mom was happy to know I was going to a religious institution rather than a nightclub or a party or who-knows-where.

Mom dropped me off at the front entrance, and I pulled my jacket tighter with each step from the car to the double doors. It was freezing this time of year in Oklahoma, especially as the stars came out to glisten. When my family and I had moved to the state, the grass was an ugly yellow, like Carl's tie, and the trees were cold and lifeless. I soon learned that spring would bring a landscape of lush green, but back then, it made me hate our move even more than I had originally, as leaving the peninsula of Florida for middle-of-nowhere Oklahoma did not seem appealing to a twelve-year-old who had just finished the sixth grade. As Kukowski had once so eloquently put it, "How many of you were born in Oklahoma? Yeah, never raise your hand to a question like that again. We're the mecca of beer-drinkin' rednecks."

The inside of the church was about as dark as the outside, only illuminated by a single, flickering fluorescent light closer to the front. It was downright spooky, and I fully expected someone in a mask to jump out with a chainsaw to scare me while another person recorded my reaction to upload to CoffeeFolder.

I turned the corner (all the while likening the situation to *Annihilation!* and wondering which button I needed to press to pull out my melee weapon), went to the first door with light from underneath, and opened it.

"—and there *was* a banana in my pocket!"

I had entered a room of about eight adults, all sitting in tiny plastic chairs like in Lily and Ethan's youth group two Sundays before, the difference being that these grown-ups smelled distinctly of booze.

"This is an Alcoholics Anonymous meeting," a bearded man with an eye patch said, noticing my confused look. "The kid place is upstairs."

"Oh, uh, thanks," I said in a voice much quieter than I had wanted. I turned to leave and noticed none other than Kukowski standing at the podium. He put a finger to his lips and winked at me as I shut the door.

I went up one flight of stairs and found a dim room at the end of the hallway with Lily, Megan, and presumably Tyler. They were sitting together at a table for four, surrounded by similar tables in front of a raised stage with a microphone, a piano, and a few mounted guitars. I guessed this to be the room where they sang worship music. At the back were a couple of couches already occupied by teenagers either on their phones or talking with one another.

"You came!" Lily said, standing up and hugging me. I had not been touched that way by a girl who wasn't my mom for quite some time, and instantly felt an obvious bulge in my jeans. I quickly took the available seat.

"Accidently walked in on Alcoholics Anonymous," I explained, laughing awkwardly. "Did you know Kukowski's in there?"

"I'm not surprised," Lily said, then to Megan and Tyler: "Kukowski is our Chemistry teacher. Oh! Ty, this is Jay. Jay, Ty."

"'Sup?" Ty asked, holding out his fist. We fist bumped.

"I didn't think there would be this many people here," I told them. "I mean, there were so few at your youth group."

"That's 'cause they're all too hungover on Sundays," Ty said. Megan gave him an annoyed look, to which Ty told me: "She's the pure one."

"What's that supposed to mean?" Megan asked, then turned to Lily. "And speaking of things we weren't expecting, Ty and I noticed before we sat down that the *flowers* are *pretty* in the *spring*."

I didn't know what she was referring to or why she had enunciated each syllable, but whatever it was seemed to startle Lily, who stood up to look around the dark room. Megan pointed a finger toward the stage. I followed it to Carl in the spotlight, wearing a stained, blue tie over a pale pink button-down. I didn't see the relevance to springtime flowers, especially since it was still winter.

"This on?" Carl asked, tapping the mic. "Good evening, fellow disciples of Christ!"

And then, in monotone unison: "Good evening, YMC. We're ready to learn about God's grace and demonstrate His abundance of love toward our fellow man."

"Excellent!" he said, flipping notecards in his hands.

"I keep telling him that he needs to make it gender-neutral," Megan whispered to me. "Just you wait."

"Today marks the tenth meeting of our monthly LEO group," Carl continued, "which stands for Loving Each Other. Sponsored by Redbud Avenue's worship center, our mission is to provide a safe, casual environment for our youth to share faith, poetry, music, art, talent, and life together every second Wednesday of the month. 'Come to me,' said Jesus in the book of Matthew, 'all you who labor and are heavily burdened, and I will give you rest.' This we promise.

"Our first act this evening is fourteen-year-old Barrett Carpenter. He tells me he has a few jokes to start off our night. Let's hear them, Barrett!"

Everyone clapped as a short kid with sunglasses was led to the stage by former-meteorologist Russ Carpenter. He walked Barrett up, adjusted the mic for him, and Barrett said, "I don't know who designed those stairs, but I know for certain it wasn't a blind guy. Sure, some people say you can achieve anything you put your mind to, but have *you* ever tried to stop a revolving door?"

I didn't know how to react to this, but everyone else laughed with him. I guessed that was appropriate.

"So the other day, YMC here took my dad and me out to eat at Ricchezza's. As we sat down to order, I heard someone whisper into my right ear, 'Nice shirt, handsome.' Mind you, I'd be happy with such flattery if it weren't for the fact that to my right was a *wall*, not a person.

"Anyway, while we're waiting for our drinks, I hear in my other ear, 'You're *so* adorable,' except it's not in my dad's voice, who's sitting next to me. Confused, I mention this to the waitress, who then replies, 'It sure wasn't me, but it could've been the breadsticks. They're complimentary!'"

His voice trailed off as we laughed over him. It made me happy to see this kid—who had all the more reason to be depressed—doing his best to make people smile, even if he couldn't physically see it. He just knew.

Barrett continued with his jokes, such as, "Seriously, who would actually want to go out and *see* a silent film? Yeah, neither would I! And making all our phones and tablets touchscreens? *Puh-lease!*" Carl tried to high-five him as he walked off stage when he was finished, but that didn't work too well. An older girl came up next to recite some original poems, followed by a local band performance, a long but endearing puppet show, and Ty's juggling act, which was one ball at a time.

At about ten 'til ten, Carl announced, "Our last act for the night is Miss Lily Carswell singing 'Will the Circle Be Unbroken,' one of my all-time favorite Christian hymns. The mic is yours, Lily!"

She smiled at me, brushed her skirt as she got up, and started toward the stage. I was wondering how Lily's legs weren't cold while Megan gave her a thumbs-up and a couple of guys cheered her on.

"This is for all us teenagers out there rushing through life," she told the crowd. "Don't burn yourself out just yet. Growing up isn't about the person you're going to marry or what job you're going to get. It's not about the happy ending, either. It *is* about the story and savoring every step of it—who in your life you let walk with you and who you leave behind. So let's all calm down for a change, let things go, and allow life to happen as we live it."

Carl sat at the piano, and at Lily's nod, he started playing. Other than his soft accompaniment, it was just her up there singing. It was very traditional—what I remembered growing up hearing in church. She sang slow and proud, knowing this night was hers and not mine or Ethan's or anybody else's.

There are loved ones in the glory
Whose dear forms you often miss.
When you close your earthly story,
Will you join them in their bliss?

Megan was no longer sitting at the table, as she had quietly joined Lily up on stage. Lily blew everyone a kiss while Megan took the second microphone and proceeded to sing backup for the chorus.

Will the circle be unbroken
By and by, by and by?
Is a better home awaiting
In the sky, in the sky?

As Lily sang the next verse, I looked around to see at least a dozen or so faces my age watching her intently. I was an outsider to this small community, and although I didn't know all of them, they still accepted me, and I felt honored to be included.

The spotlights dimmed, and Carl stopped playing as Lily reached the last verse. Megan rejoined us and sat down next to me. It was only Lily now.

One by one, their seats were emptied,
And one by one, they went away.
Now the family is parted.
Will it be complete one day?

Will the circle be unbroken
By and by, oh, by and by?
Is a better home awaiting
In the sky, in the sky?

In the sky, in the sky…

To have said it was beautiful would've been an understatement. I could tell the audience agreed with me, as she got a standing ovation at the end—everyone was cheering, hollering, clapping, and screaming. I was awestruck.

"Hallelujah," Carl said, congratulating her.

"More like, hot damn!" Ty said when she returned to our table. She laughed and shoved his arm as her response.

"Thank you all for coming!" Carl said as people started getting up from their seats. "I hope to see each and every one of you at our youth group on Sunday, starting with live worship at 9:30, followed by a 10:30 scripture study and an 11:30 sermon. DO NOT PARTY WITH SATAN SATURDAY NIGHT! PARTY WITH JESUS SUNDAY MORNING! Can I hear an amen!"

"Amen!" shouted the audience.

"Have a blessed evening, everybody! Drive home safe!"

As the crowd dispersed, I said my good-byes to Megan and Ty, who were leaving together. When they were gone, Lily took me aside.

"I wanted to thank you for showing up tonight," she said to me. "It really means a lot."

"No problem," I said. "I had fun! Thank *you* for inviting me."

We laughed. We hugged. As she pulled away, she kissed my cheek and left with the crowd. The bulge returned. Lily's eyes were a definite blue, but in the moment, I mistook them for gray.

Mom drove up to the curb as I left the church. Aside from Kukowski, the rest of Alcoholics Anonymous, and Carl, I was the last to leave. As I opened the car door, she asked how it went.

"It was really good," I told her, and we left it at that.

one hundred and twenty-two days ago

My opinion of Valentine's Day had always been a negative one. In my mind, it should've been called Make-Every-Single-Guy-And-Girl-Feel-Excluded Day, as that was basically the gist of it. This Valentine's Day was different, however, because two days before it, I realized I was available rather than single. And so was Lily Carswell.

I couldn't talk to her in Chemistry on Thursday, as Kukowski spent the entire hour ranting about the dog that had kept him up the night before while he was going through his alcohol withdrawal.

"That dog, I swear, is the dumbest thing in the world," he told us, leaning back with his hands on the edge of his desk. "It just kept barking! Sometimes, at nothing! Air, maybe! It might be something as important as a squirrel crossing the fence—*oh, my God, it's a home invasion!* And when it looks at you, it's not even threatening or with malicious intentions. Just barks! You know what I'm gonna do? When the dog is sleeping, I'm going to bark at *it!*"

"What if it barks back?" someone asked.

"It probably will for a day or so, then it'll get so annoyed it slits its own wrists. I might put razor-blades in its food—nah, that's only for Halloween. But that's why, in the back of the room, I'm working on poisons that won't kill a dog, but make it so sick you'll have to put the vermin down yourself. Might even test it out on you all!"

"Try it on Jay," Lily joked, then smiled at me. "He's the thinnest."

"Murchison?" Kukowski asked. "I like Murchison. Barks the least out of all y'all!"

I didn't think that was the proper time to ask her out, to say the least. I did, however, see her again after school as she walked past my locker. So I threw everything inside, shut it, and ran to catch up to her. When I did, I took her aside into a somewhat-empty hallway.

"Hey," she began. "What's—?"

"There's no reason for two people such as us to be single with Valentine's Day this weekend… right?"

"I suppose so. Why?"

"Well, I was just wondering if—" I had to force myself not to talk too fast. "—if you'd wanna go out with me… maybe?" I was ready for rejection, but she smiled instantly.

"Sure! I mean, yeah, of course!" She put her arms around me, and I held onto her tight, not wanting to let go.

"Well, that was easier than I expected," I admitted.

"Life doesn't always have to be complicated," she said with a laugh. And so it seemed.

I hadn't even open the door before my mother started asking questions, as she was already on the front porch with her laptop when I got to the house.

"You're 'in a relationship?!'" she cried out at once. "With *Lily Carswell?* YOU HAVE A GIRLFRIEND?!"

"You make it sound like it's a bad thing," I said, reaching for the doorknob, but she stopped me. "I don't see what the problem is! You didn't react this way when Courtney and I—"

"I knew I shouldn't have let you go out last night. I thought church was supposed to be a sacred place! You just met this girl!"

"Mom, Mom, calm down." She was standing, yet I was still about a head taller than her. "How did you even—?"

"I saw it on CoffeeMolder," she told me, hands on her hips.

"Coffee*Folder*," I said. "But I haven't accepted—"

"I did it for you."

I couldn't believe what I was hearing. "You said it yourself that you've met Lily's mother!" I pointed out. "I think I know what I'm doing, OK? So please, please, *please* for once in my life let me do my own thing. Is that too much to ask?"

We were silent for a moment. Then she opened her mouth, but was quiet. Finally, she spoke.

"I—I don't know anymore. You've always been my little boy…"

"Mom, look at me. I'm sixteen. I'm growing up."

"I know you are. And your father wasn't lying when he said how proud we are of you. But don't let this girl get in the way of your grades. Not like the other one."

"All right. I promise." She then hugged me, and unlike with Lily, I avoided making physical contact with her breasts.

I went up to my room after that, stripped down to my t-shirt and boxers, and fell on my bed. I wasn't just OK with how things were. I was happy with them.

Valentine's Day

Lily told me she wanted to go and see *Together Forever* for a Valentine's Day afternoon date. When Mom anxiously dropped me off, it looked as if everyone and their grandmother had had the same idea, as the movie theater we chose was full of women and the tissue boxes they all kept beside them.

A basic rundown of the plot: A woman named Marine meets a tall and large gentleman named Xavier at a local coffee house. He owns a flower shop. They fall in love. While they're on a date, Marine gets hit by a freakin' bus. She wakes up wheelchair-bound in the hospital. In a sudden twist of events, it's revealed that Xavier leapt in front of the bus to save Marine, and he died in the process. She then eats a poisonous flower from his shop so they can be *Together Forever*. Fin.

There was no kissing between Lily and me during the movie, as I had cried even during the previews I'd seen on TV weeks before. When it was finished, we walked outside, where Lily's mom was waiting for her. We hugged, said good-bye, and my mother showed up soon after.

I took out my phone as our conversation idled. Saphnie and I hadn't texted in a while, so I decided to check up on her.

Me: Happy Valentine's Day!

Saphnie: Same to you!

Me: What have you been up to?

Saphnie: Nothing special. Enjoying the reds and pinks. How about you?

Me: I asked a girl out on Thursday, and she said yes! We went to see that Together Forever movie today. It was OK.

Saphnie: How original. Way to glow! Give yourself a pat on the back and whatnot. What's her name?

Me: Lily Carswell. We actually met because she saw me reading Rudderless and wanted to discuss it.

Saphnie: YOU'RE WELCOME! Don't ever say I haven't done anything for you!

Me: How are *you* still single today? I mean, you're beautiful!

Saphnie: That's mighty creepy of you, but whatever. You probably say that to every girl who accidentally texts you. (;_;)

Me: No, I'm serious!

Saphnie: Flattery won't get you nudes, but thanks for trying. My love life is nonexistent. I'm essentially a love atheist. Besides, you have a GIRLFRIEND! Why are you texting me??? Go get some!

Me: Some what?

Saphnie: Sex, Jay. It's apparently what all the cool kids are doing.

Me: Haha... no. My mom would freak. Anyway, I need to go eat dinner. Have a good evening!

Saphnie: Guess what? Pulsar Skies is coming to Raleigh, NC, on April 21! I had HIGH hopes for it being on the 20th, ha ha. Vale (bye)!

Me: Fun! Buenas noches!

I was going to check the Pulsar Skies page on CoffeeFolder to see if they were coming to Oklahoma—and they weren't—when I saw my own.

In a Relationship with <u>Lily Carswell</u>

What did that even mean, to be "in a relationship?" The only one I'd been in had ended on a beach the summer after eighth grade, so I certainly didn't know. Whatever it meant, I hoped I was ready. Dating Lily had seemed like a good idea, but with it actually, physically happening, I wasn't so sure.

one hundred and nineteen days ago

Sunday brought the over-the-top drama that would typically be found in romantic comedies, only there was nothing funny about it—mostly false accusations, unresolved feelings, and a black eye.

I had promised Lily I would try my best to go to Redbud Avenue's 11:30 youth lesson, as I was actually curious to hear Carl's sermon and see how he preached the Bible, so long as he didn't leave again. I walked in late with Lily, as she had waited for me in the lobby, and I saw only familiar faces: Ethan, who hadn't made much of an effort to talk to me since Lily and he had broken up, sat alone on the couch in front of the TV; Megan was watching Ty play a game on his phone; and Carl was on his laptop—its screen reflecting off his freshly-shaven head. Then, noticing the time, Carl removed the computer from the podium and placed it on the table.

"Good morning, fellow disciples of Christ!"

Followed by everyone but Ethan: "Good morning, YMC. We're ready to learn about God's grace and demonstrate His abundance of love—"

"TOWARD OUR FELLOW PEOPLE!" Megan shouted. "We're a progressive society!"

"Amen," Carl said, laughing. "If it means that much to you, we can change it. Attendance time! Now, Megan and Tyler are here… Phillip? Nope? OK… Sandra's not here, either, but Ethan's here… Trisha's absent… Lily is—" He spotted me. "Ah, Jay! Good to see you again."

"Good to see you, too," I said, which was the truth.

"Now then, if everyone will please form a circle in front of the podium…"

We took the small chairs and arranged them in a lopsided oval, with Megan grabbing an extra to rest her feet. Carl put on his reading glasses and shuffled his notes and the massive, heavily-bookmarked Bible before finally getting settled.

And without warning, the Bible fell off the podium. Not even Megan's "Look out!" was enough to move his foot out of the way.

"GOD BLESS AMERICA!" Carl wailed, collapsing on the floor as he held his foot in pain. "Holy, *holy* tabernacle of Jerusalem!"

"Well, you know what they say," Ty joked. "The older they are, the harder they fall!"

"Very funny," Carl said, managing his way up by using the podium for support. "I'll just… leave it on the floor… for the custodian to… to deal with."

Bibles aren't supposed to touch the ground, but I didn't say anything. He cleared his throat and straightened his tie.

"Last Sunday we, uh, discussed how to be a loyal friend," he began, "but today's lesson is on handling your enemies. You're all, what, sixteen, right? Your, quote, unquote, enemies can be anyone from a kid at school to an unfair teacher or even a person in your group of friends.

"Who here has seen a superhero movie?" We all raised our hands. *"Live to Rise* comes out in May! And who *hasn't* cheered whenever the villain or bad guy got what they deserved?"

Megan raised her hand. "They're usually complicated individuals with their own hopes and motivations different from that of the protagonist, who—by their point of view—is the true 'bad guy.'"

"That's deep," Ty noted. I smiled.

"Even so," Carl went on, "it was a rhetorical question, Megan." He sighed. "Also rhetorical: What do you all do whenever somebody says something rude about you behind your back? Do you feel like giving them what *they* deserve, or do you turn the other cheek like Jesus did?

"Not everyone will be your fan, and even those closest will hurt us, as you may have figured out. Most of us have thought at one time or another, 'Oh, how I want to get back at that person for what they did to me!' But this is not the way Jesus taught us to behave. God has a different idea of 'evenness,' or rather, He tells us that He will handle our revenge personally. Instead of retaliating, we must seek to walk in peace and have pure hearts before God, which is impossible while we are at the same time devising mischief for those who have wronged us. That doesn't mean you're a doormat and let people walk all over you, but it does mean you should be quick to forgive even when you don't want to, as He will bless your obedience for you doing so…"

Whenever someone would talk about Jesus or the Lord, I tended not to listen as much, despite my belief that there was a God out there, somewhere. I attributed this bias toward my father's negative attitude when it came to organized religion. But for the sake of being at church, I tried to remain focused—which was more than Lily and Ethan, who kept pulling out their phones to respond to texts.

"… and when you do mess up, which we all do, you know you can go to Him with a *contrite* heart, as the psalmist King David did when he messed up with Bathsheba. Do you all know what happened then?"

All of us but Ethan shook our heads.

"Long story short, David saw a beautiful woman, had her brought to his palace, gave in to adultery, got her pregnant, and had her husband killed in the front lines of battle so David could marry her. After all of this, David knew he had sinned against God, and you can refer to Psalm 51 to read his heart-felt apology. God forgave David, and he and Bathsheba did get married… but the baby died. There were consequences even for the King.

"Kids, the sooner you know how critically important it is to be in right standing with God, the sooner life will get much easier to deal with. So when you're home tonight, talk to Him, and ask for His forgiveness. And next time, rather than permitting yourself to imagine how you can get even with the person who has deceived you, you can get alone with the Lord. Once He is ruling your heart, you'll see the situation from an entirely different perspective. Meanwhile, you'll be able to walk in peace with a pure heart before God, free from all bitterness, anger, and strife. If you take one thing from today's lesson, remember that we don't have the right to get even, no matter what anyone says. Ask yourself, 'What would Jesus do?'"

"Well," Ethan began, on the edge of his seat, "I think Jesus would be pretty pissed if one of His disciples stole His girlfriend."

"Jay didn't *steal me*, Ethan," Lily stated, furious. "Women aren't property. And I broke up with you!"

"For no good reason!" he shouted back unnecessarily loud.

"Dude, cool off your hotness," Ty said. "You've totally been staring at Meg's ass all morning."

"Tyler!" Carl exclaimed as Megan shifted uncomfortably in her seat.

"You've known Jay for a month now," Ethan said to Lily, ignoring Ty. "You and I have been dating since—"

"I broke up with you!" she repeated. "And leave Jay out of this!"

"—and you bring him in here to, what, *spite me?!*" He turned to me, his face as red as his hair.

"Hey, I didn't mean to—"

"SHUT UP!" he shouted, leaping from his chair and swinging to punch me. "JUST SHUT UP, DAMMIT!"

I blocked him, but he tripped and fell on top of me, pushing the chair away from underneath us. We rolled over, and when he tried again, I put out my stiff arms in an attempt to defend myself, which only caused me to hit the bridge of his nose and brow with the side of my hand—the terrible *whack* of fist meeting face.

"ENOUGH!" Carl shouted, and we instantly stopped. "IN THE HALL. RIGHT NOW."

Ethan got off the ground, rubbed his sore eye, and started toward the hallway. Carl went next to keep us separated, and I followed.

"What the flying fladoodle were you both thinking?!" Carl glared at us both. "In a Church of Christ, too!" He turned to Ethan. "I know for a fact I've taught you better than that. Did you even listen to the sermon?!"

We were silent. Ethan was staring at his shoes, and since I didn't want to look at Carl, I admired a stained glass window.

"While I prefer it when a person dates someone of the same religion," he said, "I don't like it when their relationship gets in the way of them and God." I turned and saw him staring at me. "Now, Jay, I know what you did was in self-defense—"

"It's fine," I said quickly. "I appreciate what you do here, and I didn't mean any harm, but maybe this isn't the church for me." And before he could argue, I walked down the hall and stairs, past the nursery and the offices, and sat on a bench outside the sanctuary.

I took out my phone and asked my dad to pick me up early. I texted Saphnie as I waited.

Me: Hey.

Saphnie: Hey. I haven't been texting as much lately because things are sort of hectic over here. I thought you should know.

Me: I understand. What's going on?

Saphnie: Family stuff. My dad's job with Adveston requires him to fly in and out of the state to meet with the execs in Chicago every three weeks or so. My mom doesn't like it, especially how they don't talk anymore. He also likes to gamble, though I know he only wants what's best for us. I miss him sometimes, but I've gotten used to it. She says she doubts they'll divorce and isn't asking me to pick sides, but I'm not so sure. Now I'm rambling. How's your family? What do they do?

Me: We're fine. My mom works from home selling real estate, and my dad works for some marketing company or another. He's been to Chicago a few times, too. I honestly have no idea what he does, but he talks on the phone a lot.

Saphnie: Ha ha. So what's up?

Me: I got in a fight with my friend Ethan at his church. He went out with Lily before I did.

Saphnie: That's not good. What happened?

Me: He got mad during the sermon, and then Lily and he were yelling at each other. I somehow got involved, he tried to punch me, and in the end, I gave him some swelling.

Saphnie: Whoa! Jay is actually a total badass!!! Maybe Ethan still has feelings for her? "Jealousy is a monster born from hypnotizing flames," to quote Rudderless. Who dumped whom?

Me: Haha. Lily broke up with Ethan on Wednesday.

Saphnie: You asked her out the next day, right? Why did you do that again?

Me: She's cool, funny, and I can be myself around her. It was also close to Valentine's Day, and for once, I knew someone who was single who possibly liked me back.

Saphnie: Possibly?

Me: She had kissed me the night before.

Saphnie: Where?

Me: On the cheek... Why?

Saphnie: Did you ask her out simply because you didn't want to be single anymore? Guys do that sometimes once they figure out someone is into them. They're excited in the moment because "OMG! OMG! Somebody actually LIKES me!" After a while it

becomes less of a relationship and more of a courtesy running off fumes. Do you think that might apply to you both? Are you merely Ethan's replacement?

Me: Hmmm. I think you might be right.

Saphnie: You should do something about it. I need to go. Bye!

Me: Thanks, by the way.

Saphnie: You're welcome. Best of luck, Mr Murchison.

It was around that time when Dad showed up. I walked to the car, got in, and we drove away. I knew the main reason he had agreed to drive me back and forth was because he felt a little guilty we'd stopped going to church as a family. With me leaving by my own decision, maybe we would all get a little more sleep on Sunday mornings.

one hundred and seventeen days ago

President's Day followed Sunday, and American students got the day off from school. Lily seemed a bit despondent, though, and said she didn't want to do anything together. So it was back to me being alone for a while, which consequently meant watching more recorded episodes of *$tore Wars*.

Lily wasn't in Chemistry the next day, and neither was Mrs. Beckham in Spanish. The substitute directed us to the GALAXIAN board for our homework: 7.1 outline, pages 221-242 (two page minimum), and 7.1 workbook, pages 91-94. The daily assignment was to "translate the following sentences from English to Spanish." Mrs. Beckham had typed the first three and had hand written the rest, and since none of us could read cursive—a fault of our generation—we took turns trying to decipher it.

"Number 4: 'She *blank* pictures of her sister,'" someone attempted.

"So what's the blank?" another asked.

"She *takes* pictures of her sister?"

"She *has* pictures of her sister?"

"She *sold* pictures of her sister?"

Ethan arrived fifteen minutes later. He explained himself to the sub and hesitantly took his assigned seat next to me.

"Hey," he said, embarrassed.

"Hey," I said back, not knowing any other way to reply.

"I'm sorry about what happened Sunday," he started. "I don't know what came over me. I just... I really love and care about Lily, and there are sometimes when I can get a little... worried. It's a long story. I thought..." He saw my doubting expression. "Well, I guess it doesn't matter what I thought. Point is, I know she can do so much better than me, but she's all I could ever want in a soul mate. And I need another chance."

"It's OK," I said. While I couldn't truly believe they were soul mates or that he was in love with her, then again, neither was I. "I'll see what I can do."

"Aww, thanks, man!" He hugged me awkwardly, and I tried to wiggle out. "It means more than a lot."

"I'm just sorry about your eye," I told him, unable to look directly at his left side without wincing.

"Meh. I sort of asked for it." He let go of me and shrugged. "But it's funny how we—as in guys—can beat the crap outta each other one day, but be total buds again the next, when girls can take weeks to get over their period-drama."

"If you say so," I said. He laughed again.

I called Lily later that evening. She told me she was absent from school because she was getting her passport renewed for a mission trip to Costa Rica in the summer. I apologized for what happened on Sunday and told her what Ethan had told me, aside from the menstruation comment. She understood and apologized for getting me dragged into this and if it ever seemed like she had led me on. I told her it was fine, as I would rather everyone be happy than let one unlucky sermon ruin the friendships I'd so recently made.

We broke up over the phone that night (which I was all too familiar with), ending our six-day relationship. Everybody's CoffeeFolder status was back to normal by the next morning, and I was OK with that.

MARCH

one hundred and five days ago

"When are we ever going to meet that girlfriend of yours?"

"Mom, we broke up almost a week ago."

"WHAT?!" She slammed her book shut and put it on the table beside her. "I leave ColderCoffee for a week to sell some houses, and look what happens! When was this?! *Was it over a phone call?*"

"Like I said, it was five days ago, it just wasn't going to work, and yes, it was through the phone again—but this time mine and not yours. She and I are still friends, though."

She was about to say something, but then decided against it and went back to reading her copy of *Rudderless*. I returned my attention toward the TV and got only a couple of seconds into this show about an arrogant chef when I felt a vibration in my pocket. Not wanting to stress Mom out some more, I clicked the remote and went to my room to check the text.

Saphnie: How are things between you, Lily, and Ethan?

Me: We're good. You were right, obviously. Ethan apologized, Lily and I mutually broke up, and now they're back together.

Saphnie: "Mutually broke up," he says. That's nice. You're all still buddies and whatnot?

Me: Yes, haha. They're back to being the best of friends I have.

Saphnie: Again, best of luck. Speaking of which, did you ever enter the Rudderless at Sea contest?

Me: I totally forgot! When does it end??

Saphnie: Tonight at midnight EST. You have two hours if you want to submit. I didn't.

Me: Huh? How come? Wasn't that the reason you signed up for CoffeeFolder in the first place?

Saphnie: Originally, but frankly the whole concept of getting answers to an intentionally open-ended book pisses me off. It defeats the purpose! Our generation is so privileged in that we have all the answers at the tips of our fingers so long as we can access QuickSearch. Sometimes I think we're nothing more than self-centered, spoiled brats who honestly believe we're entitled to this world that solely revolves around us. Seeing an author fold for that is disappointing.

Me: I'm still confused. Is everything all right?

Saphnie: Yes, I'm all right! Why can't I have a disagreeing opinion without people assuming I'm upset?! It's fine if you enter the contest. I just think it's dumb. That's all.

Me: Well, thanks for the reminder. Have a good night, OK?

Saphnie: I'll try. Sleep well.

While I understood her point, I appreciated the prompt too much to not participate—it was exactly like my discussions with Saphnie over the book, and I wanted to share my thoughts with its fellow readers. So I sent in my response with twenty-one minutes to spare and hoped

I had made a good impression.

one hundred and three days ago

"Hydrochloric acid is a strong acid, no matter what concentration you have of it," Kukowski told us in preparation for our lab the next day. "You could hold it in your hands for probably five or six seconds before you really start to feel it, but anything past about fifteen seconds, and you're gonna have some damage, 'kay? If a student dies in my classroom, homicide or not, I'm no longer eligible for a bonus next year. Plus it's a helluva lot of paperwork, and I don't have that kind of patience. That's why I have to guide you a little more on this lab. I don't want you all grabbing stuff and going, 'Uhhh, what do I do with this?' 'cause that would *obviously* be the teenager thing to do—to either drink it or pour it on yourselves. It's kind of like when you all were little babies, and you were trying to go from tipsy cups to real ones."

"*Tipsy* cups?" Lily repeated. "Don't you mean—?"

"Yeah, 'cause with a tipsy cup, you could just lift it and go to town, right? Then you grabbed a regular cup, and it would spill all down your body. A couple of more years, you grew up, and now you're able to deal with a drink pretty good. But then you get my age and go back to pouring it all over yourself! I think older people need to revert back to tipsy cups. The only thing, though, is that my cup is going to have *special* stuff in it. It ain't gonna be that disgusting crap you all drink. Red Harbinger? Nooo thank you. My stuff is gonna be the good stuff." He leaned in to whisper. "*Whiskey.*"

Lily and I glanced over at each other as we laughed with the rest of the class. *So much for Alcoholics Anonymous.* I immediately remembered the night she had pulled me over and kissed my cheek, then leaving as if that was the norm—and maybe it was for her, but it certainly wasn't for me. I couldn't think about that, though. We'd broken up, after all.

"Have I offended anyone yet?" Kukowski asked. "No? We'll work on it. Anyway, you and your lab partners are going to take the hydrochloric acid and fill it up with water to about—"

73

The phone rang.

"Well, maybe I got fired. Let's see." He answered it. "Hello? … You need who? All right, can do—wait, who is this? … Oh! Hey, Tulip. Maybe I can come by and get some snacks, if you have any? I have a real hankerin' for some of those little vanilla… Wait, really? Sweet! Later, gator." He put the phone down, reached into his desk, felt around, and took out a plastic bag filled with cookies.

"Murch," he said to me with his mouth full. "Your insane but wonderful Spammish teacher wants to chat with you."

Besides his whiskey, I didn't know what Kukowski would have to drink to cause him to believe Mrs. Beckham was the crazier teacher. Nevertheless, I took the pass he wrote for me and smiled when he called out as I was leaving, "Make sure to tell her that *señor este este el Kukowski-o* said, um, hold on." He paused to think, then typed something into his computer. *"Mustache grassy-ass!"*

———————————

I got to Mrs. Beckham's room a few minutes before her next class started. Her first-hour was her planning period, so when I opened the door, she was sitting at her computer and listening to a pop anthem at full blast.

"Oh, you scared me!" she said, turning down the volume. She shuffled a pile of papers on her desk and took out an orange flyer, handing it to me. "I figured you weren't doing anything in Mr. Kukowski's class, so I thought I would give you this." Lab preparation days were actually pretty important, but I skimmed both sides of the flyer, anyway. It was for Student Council, and it listed all the different positions one could apply for.

"You want me to join StuCo?" I asked, flipping the paper over.

"I want you to consider running for Student Council class president," she answered. "I had my doubts about you, to be honest. Nonetheless, now that I have seen you read literature other than that science fiction series my son is into, I definitely believe you should consider running in May." She smiled. "I know that is two months from now, but we teachers talk, and Mr. Kukowski agrees with me. We think it would be... *interesting*... to have someone else run this year, instead of an unopposed election again."

I looked it over for a second time. "I just don't think I'm qualified."

Some juniors walked in and sat in their seats.

"Think it over, all right?" Mrs. Beckham asked. I nodded, though I didn't truly mean it. Why would she ask me, an absolute nobody, to run for class president? And Kukowski, too? *Was this some sort of joke?* Regardless, I took the flyer as I left her room to retrieve my things from Chemistry. I didn't want her to see me throw it away.

Lily and Ethan were talking outside of Kukowski's as I walked up the stairs to the science wing. I couldn't hear all what they were saying, but I got most of it.

He asked her, "What about San—?"

"Oh, God, no," she said. "Gag me with a spoon, why don't you?"

"Well, then who else?"

"I don't know—it's your party."

"That you want me to have!"

"Everyone has a party for their sweet sixteen!"

"It's only called that for girls," he told her. "It's just one more year until legal R-rated bloodbaths and sex scenes with nudity for guys."

Lily spotted me walking toward them. "How about Jay?"

"Yeah," Ethan said, approving her suggestion. "He's cool."

"Why am I cool?" I asked. "I mean—what's going on?"

"Ethan turns sixteen on Friday," Lily explained. "So we're going to have a party for him at his house! And you are most certainly invited."

"Awesome!" *First party!* "Who all's coming?"

"Let's see." She took out her phone and scrolled through her messages. "Megan and Ty both replied saying they can come. Plus you, me, and our wittle birthday boy—" She pinched Ethan's cheeks, and he pushed her hand away. "—that makes the five of us until I can think of more people to text."

"Not exactly the size of one of Darian's parties," Ethan admitted.

"I suppose," Lily allowed, "but she's a cheerleader. You're just adorable." She glanced down at the flyer in my hand. "What's the piece of paper for?"

"Oh, this?" I gave it to her. "Mrs. Beckham wants me to consider running for Student Council class president in May, as if."

"Well," Lily said, looking over at Ethan. "The flowers *are* pretty in the spring." He rolled his eyes. She turned back to me. "I think you'd make a great president, if it means anything."

"So anyway," Ethan said to me, "I'll text you my address, but right now I really should get to class. Can't be late to this one."

Lily and Ethan proceeded to kiss, so I took that as my cue to go. This was similar to how Aunt Nancy would tell everyone to leave her house after a Christmas Eve party: She'd take out the vacuum cleaner to start tidying up, and we would all get the hint sooner than later.

I went back into Chemistry and grabbed my backpack and spiral notebook. Kukowski asked on my way out, "Did she talk to you about StuCo?"

"Yeah," I said in the doorway. "I'll think about it."

"De piñata!" he tried as I left the room.

one hundred days ago

Lily sent out Ethan's invitation via CoffeeFolder later that week.

<u>Lily Carswell</u> (to you and...)

Hey everyone! So. Guess. What. YOU are invited to a very awesome PARTY! Why? Because Ethan has FINALLY decided to join us old people and turn 16!! It's going to run from 7 to 11, and gifts are totally optional. (Guys are so dumb. All they want is cash.) His mom has kindly provided us with drinks (no alcohol, as I know how you are about that, Meg) and popcorn for when we watch a movie or whatever. Ethan says he doesn't want a cake. Again, I don't know why boys are weird. SO NO CAKE. Boring disclaimer: his folks won't be there, so if that's an issue then have your parents get in touch with his mom, etc. Address is below. (It's the house with the new pickup in the driveway, BUT THAT'S A SURPRISE!!) Call me if you have any questions. <3

I explained the situation to my parents. While Dad was happy to see me socializing, my mom overreacted, as always—pretty much the normal good cop/bad cop parenting routine (and other fine entertainment). Dad eventually got her to OK letting me go by saying, "He actually has some friends, Karen! Let him be a teenager!" I guess she felt she couldn't argue with that.

Ethan lived in a neighborhood where the houses were one-story and closer together, but the yards were bigger, front and back. His house was made of red brick with blue-gray shingles for the roof. The porch lights were tall with dull, yellow bulbs, which revealed the cracks in the sidewalk and hedges in need of a major trim. The house to the right was already decorated for St. Patrick's Day, as the front door sported a wreath made out of four-leaf clovers while large and inflatable Patricks were lined across the property, all but one tied down to nearby bushes and tree branches. The exception was a smaller leprechaun, who had popped and was seemingly waving a giant shamrock at us as he fluttered in the light wind.

"Say what you want about the Cunninghams and their spastic dog," Dad told me in the car, "but I'm sure glad we have them for neighbors and not Mr. and Mrs. Holiday over here."

"I wonder what they do for August," I said.

"They probably sit at home and cry all month." He laughed at his own joke. "But *damn*, that is a nice truck in your friend's driveway."

"I think it's his big birthday gift," I explained, watching the light reflect off the shiny red hood of Ethan's brand new, four-door pickup.

"And to think all we got you was a cell phone." Dad admired the truck for a few more seconds before sighing, long and deep, and whispering, "Goddammit, Karen."

He let me out of the car. I walked up to the porch and knocked on the door.

"Jay!" Ethan said as he opened it. He was wearing a red and blue-striped party hat on his head of hair. "You're the... Let's see." He turned around. "Second person to arrive! Come on in."

I handed him a twenty-dollar bill. "For gas money. Oh, and happy birthday—again!"

"You shouldn't have," he said, although he took my money, anyway. "But I'm glad you did!"

Megan was sitting on an old, burgundy couch in the living room. She adjusted her own party hat before greeting me.

"Hey, Jay!" she said, smiling. "Glad to see you both don't hate each other. Ty and I were worried after Carl flipped out."

"Is Ty not here?" I asked.

"He's probably with the rest of his baseball team out on the fields," Ethan answered. "Lord knows what they're up to."

"Playing baseball?" I guessed.

"This late at night?" He laughed. "If I ever commit a crime, I hope you're the only witness."

"For the record, that is what Ty's doing," Megan assured me, then frowned at Ethan. "He said he's sorry he couldn't make it and left some money in the card we gave you."

"Put it on a t-shirt, and then I'll believe it," Ethan said. "Either that, or Jesus'll have to show up with some ID and tell me Himself. I actually used to play baseball back in the day. Well, it was called tee ball—"

There was a knock at the door. We got up as Ethan strode over to answer it. I saw him smile when he saw Lily, but that soon faded when he saw that she was being accompanied by none other than Nick Behr, Speech & Debate Captain and Student Council President of the sophomore class.

"Hello, Ethan," Nick said, holding a small box with a red bow on top. "Happy birthday."

In one swift movement, Ethan pulled Lily inside (knocking her over), slammed the door in Nick's face, and ran over to the windows to shut the blinds.

"What the hell, Ethan?!" Lily shouted from the floor. Megan and I helped her up.

"Why did you invite pubehead to *my* party?" he asked, putting a chair in front of the door.

"You told me to invite anyone I could think of!" She picked her phone off the rug. "I thought you both were friends—and don't call him that!"

"The *flowers* are *pretty* in the *spring!*" Megan said, enunciating again.

"Yes!" Ethan said, pointing to Megan. "What she said! About the flowers!"

"Oh, my God. You both are seriously not—"

"Yes, Lily, I am." He put his hands on her shoulders. "And after you both—"

She pushed him off. "Don't put this on me! Nick and I are nothing more than friends. You invited Jay, and me and him—!"

"Jay isn't a *weirdo!*" he told her. That was good to hear.

"Really, Lily," Megan interjected. "I'm with Ethan on this one."

"For the love of—" I could tell that Lily was running out of excuses. "Nick apologized, dammit!"

"He *blamed* Ty!" Megan shouted. She looked me in the eyes. "I kid you not: Nick Behr is the most antagonistic person I have ever met."

There was a knock at the door.

Lily gestured for Ethan to open it, mouthing for him to *get the damn door*. Ethan made a dramatic scene of picking up the chair he was using as a blockade, putting it aside, looking through the peep hole, and finally opening the damn door.

"Hey, Nicky B!" Ethan said with sudden enthusiasm. He put his arm around Nick as they walked inside. "How are ya, buddy?"

Nick looked down. "You're wearing your shoes? Indoors?"

Ethan shuffled toward the door, closing it. "Well, yeah, don't we all?"

"Mom says to never trust a guy who wears shoes inside his own home," Nick said, grinning.

"Then maybe you should go," Megan muttered, but I didn't think he heard her.

"Relax, Ethan!" Nick said, patting him on the back when he returned. "I'm just screwing with you, birthday boy."

Ethan leaned toward Lily and whispered, "Bad choice of words," in response to which she punched him in the chest.

"Don't be difficult!" she told him, then turned to us. "Nick, you remember Megan, and you know Nick, of course."

"Yep," Megan said, running her middle finger down her left cheek. "Scarred for life."

"How cute," was his response to that.

Lily motioned toward me. "And this is Jay—"

"Murchison, yeah," he said. "I know Jay."

"You know my name?" I asked.

"Of course," he continued. "Lily wouldn't shut up about you for the week you both went out."

"Dear God," Megan said, her hand now to her forehead.

I was going to say something until a small dachshund waddled into the room and plopped down on the floor next to Ethan. Nick honest-to-God shrieked, which I thought was sufficient enough.

"I didn't know you had a... a *dog!*" he wailed, standing on the couch.

"His name's Mr. Scary," Ethan said with a smirk.

"Not funny!"

"No, that's actually his name," Lily said, confused at Nick's antics. "Ethan's family got Mr. Scary last month for Ethan's little sister's birthday. I thought it was a misnomer, but *clearly* I've been mistaken."

Megan and I laughed, which Nick didn't seem to like.

"Just get it out of here!" he commanded. Mr. Scary was panting by Ethan's side as he pet him.

"Nicky, please," Lily pleaded. "Why don't you put your gift on the table, and I'll go get us all a board game or something."

Nick obliged—as soon as someone took the dog outside. While Lily picked up Mr. Scary and left, Ethan took out his phone and quickly started typing. I felt a buzz in my pocket and pulled out my own as Lily returned with an armful of activities.

Ethan: We have to get this guy. Just follow along ok? It's me and you against the world and I need to know which side you're on. The flowers r prett

Ethan nodded at me.
Nick noticed.

———————————————

"I accuse you, Colonel Mustard, with the lead pipe in the conservatory—"
"BULLSHIT!"
"Ethan, honey, calm down!"
"Come on! Somebody prove him wrong!"
"Jay, what does it say?"
"Um... Yeah, Nick's right.
"Goddammit, Jay."

———————————————

"Hmmm... Yeah, give me another card."
"That's your fifth, baby."
"You should've stayed."
"From the look on your face, Ethan, I believe you've busted."
"Son of a... Man, that hand was bad enough to make an onion cry."
"You've said that before."
"Goddammit, Jay."

"Megan, got any fours?"

"Yeah."

"Yes! Jay, you have any sevens?"

"..."

"..."

"..."

"..."

"Go fish."

"GOD-FUCKING-DAMMIT, JAY!"

"*Ethan David Bradford!*"

"I thought we were a team, Murchison!"

"..."

"..."

"We're... We're playing Go Fish!"

"Yeah, yeah."

Approximately two hours into the party was when Ethan gave in and flipped the table, calling the games to a halt. The final scores listed "Saint Nicholas" as the clear winner of all three, followed by "Daddy Longlegs" (I suspected that was me), "Nutmeg," "Tiger Lily RAAWR," and "Sexy B-boy." Lily had written the names, but Megan was in charge of tallying.

"Wait, why didn't that one there count?" Lily asked.

"Because we caught you cheating," Megan replied.

"I was not!"

"You kept a one-eyed Jack in your bra," Nick pointed out.

"And how do you know that?" Ethan asked, fists readily clenched by his side, looking for any opportunity to give a good swing.

"Blackjack is not a game of friendship," Megan noted.

"Tell me about it," Lily said. "Anyway, we should probably start the movie now, if we plan on watching one. Ethan?"

"Oh, right. I'll make sure it's ready."

Ethan left to get the movie set up while Lily poured everyone root beer and started the popcorn. As Ethan described it, we were watching a "1950s classic," titled *The House on Haunted Hill*, starring Vincent Price as the eccentric millionaire.

"What's the movie about?" Megan asked, sitting next to me on the couch in the den. She brushed her leg up against mine.

"Well, there's this house," Ethan explained, "and it's haunted—"

"Never would have guessed," Nick whispered.

"—and this rich dude, Fredrick Loren, has invited five seemingly-random people to stay the night at the house, which he's rented for his wife's party or something. If they live 'til morning, they'll get $10,000 each."

"Is this going to give me nightmares?" Megan asked, fidgeting with her cup.

Ethan grinned. "You can cuddle up with Jay if you get scared."

She put her head on my shoulder and looked up at me. "I better warn you, though: I'm a total screamer."

I laughed nervously. "Same here." Nick snorted.

"Aww, how cute!" Lily said as she walked back in, causing me to blush. "Unless Ty beats you up, of course." She sat to the right of Megan, and Ethan sat next to her, blocking Nick. Lily held onto the popcorn bowl in her lap.

———————

Around the time when all the characters were both paranoid and horrified, Lily left to use the bathroom. Ethan got up after her, but he merely went over to my end of the sofa and crouched awkwardly on his tiptoes so he could try to whisper into my left ear.

"Nick drinks when he's scared," he told me.

"Fascinating," I said. "Now let me watch Nora run off screaming again."

"He's gotten *six* refills, Jay!" He held up his fingers to emphasize whatever point he was trying to make. *"Six!"*

"Shush!" Megan demanded, shooing us off with a hand, as her eyes were focused on the flat-screen.

"What does that have to do with anything?" I asked him. He was about to speak, but stopped and took out his phone, instead.

Ethan: Nick will have to get up for the bathroom at some point. I will distract Lily when he does. His phone is under his cushion. You need to get it and unlock it ok???

I was going to shake my head no, but that's when Lily started walking back in. Ethan then took his seat, and she sat down beside him.

"I'll be back," Nick said as he got up, walked in front of the TV—to Megan's annoyance—and went off into the hallway.

Ethan picked up the empty bowl. "Think we should make more popcorn?" he whispered.

"Yeah," Lily agreed. "The bags are in your garage."

"Can you show me?" Ethan asked. He raised an eyebrow suggestively.

Lily laughed and stood up. "I'll make sure you don't get, um, lost this time," she said with a wink.

Then there were two.

I towered over Megan a good six inches or so. Sure enough, I could see Nick's phone with a lime-green cover sticking out between two pillows. I wanted to be as inconspicuous as I could, so I stretched my arm around Megan in an attempt to reach it. She leaned back and into my arm, then turned to me, surprised.

"Are you trying to put your arm around me?" she asked, though there was no hint of anger in her voice.

"Um, well, I—"

Ethan rushed back in, turned off the TV, and quickly put a finger to Megan's lips. "I have Lily looking for the popcorn bags," he told me. "Did you get it?"

"Get what?" Megan asked skeptically, brushing his hand away. She turned to face us both, and in doing so released my arm. I reached around her, lifted Nick's phone out with my thumb and forefinger, and handed it to Ethan.

"Good, good," he said, turning it on. "Shit. Passcode. Needs four numbers, zero through nine." He looked to me for answers.

"Wait, whose phone is that?" Megan asked.

"It's Nick's; we're trying to get inside of it; it's locked," he said, more or less answering her questions. "And we need to hurry, 'cause us guys pee fast."

"It's true," I told her. "The peeing thing, I mean. I'm taking his word for the rest of it. I don't know what he's—"

"Try Lily's birthday," Megan told him.

"One-zero-one-one," he said as he typed, and the phone buzzed negatively as its response. "OK. Um, one-two-one-eight."

"My birthday?" I asked, recognizing the date.

"No, Nick's." The phone vibrated. "Maybe… Zero-three-zero-six." It vibrated again.

"Today?"

"*My* birthday," he replied. Megan laughed. "What? It was a possibility!"

"Don't flatter yourself," she said. "He's into Lily, not you."

He looked down. "As far as we know."

Lily returned with two popcorn bags in her hands. "They were behind the garbage can, of all places," she said, and then noticing the TV was off: "Is it over already?"

"Wait," I said, taking the phone from Ethan, who I could tell was trying to think of an excuse for having it. "What if it's not four numbers, but four letters? Like, A, B, and C are under the two, so…"

"What are you guys talking about?" Lily asked. "And isn't that Nick's—?"

85

"You're right!" Megan said to me. "Try five-four-five-nine."

"L-I-L-Y," Ethan said to himself as I typed it in. The phone chirped in response. It worked.

"Oh, God," I said upon viewing the picture Nick had chosen for his wallpaper background.

"Wait, let me see."

"Is that her…?"

"What's going on?!" Lily shouted, dropping one of the popcorn bags on the coffee table and throwing the other at Ethan. I hesitantly passed her the phone.

Nick re-entered the room, flicking his hands to the side to get the water off. He smiled, then noticed the TV.

"What did I miss?"

The phone's background was a side view of a completely naked Lily leaning over a bathroom sink and staring into the mirror. Her nipples were hard and erect as she stared at herself, both hands on the edge of the countertop. It looked like she was laughing.

"HOW COULD YOU?!" Lily screamed at Nick, hitting his shoulder repeatedly with the bottom of her fists. Megan pulled her back, disgusted at Nick, but not wanting Lily close to him. "I TRUSTED YOU!"

"What are you talking about?!" he asked.

"YOU'VE VIOLATED HER PRIVACY, OUR TRUST, AND BASIC HUMAN MORALITY!" Megan yelled at him. "CEASE TO EXIST, ENEMY OF WOMEN!"

Nick opened his mouth, then wisely shut it. Ethan held up the phone, and the confused look instantly disappeared from Nick's face.

"Oh, fuck me."

In a fit of rage, Ethan pushed past me and Megan to get to Nick, who took that as his cue to run from the den, across the living room, and out the front door. Ethan chased after him, yelling, "I'M GOING TO RUN OVER YOUR TINY DICK WITH MY LAWN MOWER, YOU LITTLE SHITBIRD!" He turned to us, hesitated, grabbed his keys, and slammed the door behind him as he ran after Nick.

Megan helped Lily into Ethan's room and onto his bed. She sat there quietly, and Megan rubbed her back sympathetically. I didn't know how to handle the situation, so I stood in the door frame and admired the contrast of Ethan's wall decorations: Western-themed furniture, a couple of *Annihilation!* posters, and a Car Babes calendar above the tiny TV in the corner, a gaming chair in front of it.

"That picture of me... on his phone... was from the last time I was at Nick's house," Lily said slowly. "It was a pool party last summer, and I used his bathroom to change into my swimsuit. I can't believe him." She closed her eyes. "That... *pervert!*"

"I hate to say it," Megan said, "but Ethan and I so told you so."

"I know," Lily said. She didn't seem too angered by the comment, but more as if she had come to terms with whatever Megan and Ethan had been trying to warn her about.

A phone chimed. Megan scooted back and reached into her pocket.

"Dad's out front," she said. "Says he saw a red truck chasing a silver car around the neighborhood." She turned to me. "It's almost eleven. Keep her company, all right?"

"Yeah," I said, then a little too quickly: "Of course."

Megan frowned. "Not *that* kind of company." That wasn't what I had meant, but I guess it could have come across that way.

Then it was Lily and me, alone in the room. Just the two of us. I moved from the doorway and sat beside her on the bed.

"I feel so stupid," she told me. "Inviting Nick. What a joke. I knew Ethan didn't like him, and I'm not using this as an excuse, but I didn't know why until tonight. Nick's made a couple of mistakes—though none like this—and I thought, you know, forgive and forget."

"What are you saying?" I asked.

She fell back onto the bed. "I don't know. I guess I invited him to get on Ethan's nerves. To bug him. To see if he really does still care." She paused. "Sometimes I think I'm a heartless bitch. I left Ethan and led you on, I broke up with Nick because he got boring... That's actually what I told him. Like, when you and I watched *Together Forever*, I didn't cry when both Marine and Xavier died, but everyone else did.

Even you! The only time I ever cry is at funerals when everybody else does… but I don't feel it. That's terrifying."

"It's understandable."

"It's disheartening," she said softly. "Anyway, thanks for listening. It means more than you know."

We looked at each other. And just like that, she shifted upward, latched onto my shirt, and pulled me in for a kiss. I didn't know how to react, but I kept my arms very stiff by my side, as if I were supporting all my weight onto them. But then I relaxed and gave into her, moving a hand to her soft face as she pushed herself on top of me. Our tongues started to move in after that.

Lily was above me. She took off my shirt—which momentarily got caught around my head—threw it across the room, and then did the same with hers. Her bra was blue and magnificent and generous in what it revealed to me. She reached for what she thought was my belt buckle. It wasn't. She laughed in between kisses, grabbing my actual buckle and undoing it. I didn't realize how far she was willing to take this, and I would've stopped her if she hadn't done so herself after pulling down my jeans.

"Oh, my God," Lily said, not looking down, but around.

"What is it?" I asked. "My—?"

"Shut up!" She waved me off and moved toward the window in Ethan's room that looked off into the backyard. She grabbed my shirt off the hardwood floor and tossed it to me before covering up as well. I didn't understand the necessity of the situation, as I had already seen her naked once that night. She put her shirt on despite this (or maybe because of it).

A low rumble came from outside.

"That's Ethan's pickup," she told me. She walked over and punched my shoulder as hard as she could. "What were you thinking?!"

"Me?!" I said, standing up. "It was you who—!"

We heard the truck pull into the driveway.

"We can never, ever talk about this," she said, a finger to my lips. "Understood?" I nodded. "Good. OK. Crap." She put her hands to her head, rubbing her temples. "God, I'm such a screw-up."

I finished pulling my shirt over my head right as Ethan walked in. He was sweating and collapsed on his bed, spreading his arms out.

"I chased the fucker for a good couple of minutes before I lost him," he told us. "Then I started circling around." He turned to Lily. "I can't believe you invited him—"

"I know, I know," she said. She was facing the wall and still trying to calm her aching head. "I can't believe a lot of the things I've done."

"Well, anyway," Ethan continued, "I don't know when your folks are coming to pick you up, Jay, but you can spend the night, if you want. You can even help me beat *Annihilation!*" He made his fingers into guns and pretended to shoot at me. *"Pew-pew!"*

I didn't understand how Ethan was acting so relaxed about all this, but that was when Lily's mom drove up to the house. Lily didn't say good-bye to me, and he walked with her outside. In the meantime, I texted my dad about staying over, and he replied with a simple, "OK."

A small, redheaded girl stood in the doorway.

"What is it, Meatball?" Ethan asked from behind her.

"I just wanted to say hello," she said quietly.

"Well, hi," he told her. "Anything else?"

"I'm telling Mom and Daaaaad!" she both sang and giggled as she ran down the hall.

"Tell them *what?!* AND HE'S NOT YOUR—ah, forget it." He took a deep breath, let it out in frustration, and shut the door behind him. "That's my little sister Maisy. She's eight and annoying as hell. I call her Meatball. Somehow I manage."

"Somehow," I repeated.

There was a knock on the bedroom door, and a plump woman with red hair and a matching plaid shirt opened it. She then turned to me and introduced herself as Ethan's mother. I awkwardly waved at her from beside the Car Babes calendar, which featured a young woman in a bikini spreading her legs on the hood of a Privateer SUV.

"Before I forget," she continued, "I was gonna tell you, Ethan, that George and me are about to go to bed, and Maisy's trying to get some shut-eye, so if y'all could keep it down tonight, I'd appreciate it."

"You got it, Momma."

"Great," she said, closing the door. "Sleep tight, you two, and don't bite the horse flies!"

"Close enough!" he hollered back to her. "Sorry about that," he told me. "My mom's weird."

"I, uh… Aren't all moms?"

"Yeah, man." He dropped something into the metal trash bin beside his door. "Nick's birthday present. Can't be too careful."

While I put my phone in my pocket, Ethan took off his shoes, surprising me as he instantly shrunk about four inches, which made him almost a foot shorter than me.

"Oh," was all I could say.

"Yeah, yeah, Goliath," he said. "You gonna make fun of me, too?"

"N—No! It's just that… Wow, I did not see that coming."

"I'm five-four with muscle. You're a six-foot-something with bones for arms." He tossed his shoes in the corner. "Need we say more?"

"Fine," I said, then smiled. "But I don't appreciate the Goliath joke."

He laughed, and so he wouldn't suspect anything, so did I.

The final battle was over. It appeared that Ethan and I had won, but I'd seen the end cutscene many times before: Victoria sends William Strong off in a space pod so he can escape, and it is revealed she was impregnated with his genetically-altered offspring and is in love with him. She then shoots Commander Thunderbolt in the chest with the Annihilator—Strong's mega-weapon—before killing herself, as she already gave birth to the baby. The game finishes there, and Ted Errikson's name is the first listed in the credits.

After we finished *Annihilation!* (and Ethan yelled at the screen over Victoria's death, prompting his mother to come and check on him), he got me a sleeping bag from the closet so I wouldn't have to lie on the floor. It was well past midnight, and my mom would have been furious if she knew I was up this late, but I figured what she didn't find out wouldn't upset her.

It was dark outside, save the porch lights and the nearly-full moon. I could hear the crickets chirp, which was something I had never heard from my second-floor bedroom. I felt strangely relaxed by this—up until I remembered the sounds I was hearing were really crickets having sex (their copulatory song, according to QuickSearch). I believed them to be lucky, as crickets didn't have to worry about social norms when it came to relationships. Sure, they had to watch out for hungry birds and falling into swimming pools, but they had a good, short life other than that.

"Those bugs never seem to shut up," Ethan said. "I wish they'd have the decency to get a room or something."

"Do you have sleepovers often?" I asked.

Ethan laughed. "'Sleepover' makes it sound like we have sexy pillow fights in lingerie and do each other's makeup." He shuddered. "No, not too often. Occasionally with Ty, I guess. A couple with Nick, a year ago. Oh, until he took his dick out."

I sat upright. "He did *what?*"

"Yep," he said dismissively. "This was last summer, after he and Lily broke up. They dated at the end of freshman year, but Lily dumped his sorry ass and wanted to 'just be friends' with him because she totally had the hots for me. But anyway, he just randomly whipped out his boner and tried to put it inside my mouth while I was sleeping. Fucking weirdo."

"Whoa. So what did you do?"

"I did what any sensible person would do and told everyone he was gay. But with that picture he had... I think that guy would fuck anything." He paused. "That wallpaper? It was a screenshot from a video. That means he filmed Lily changing, the damn cocksucker."

"Where is his phone, anyway?"

"I'm holding onto it." He sighed. "When it comes to love, people want what they can't have."

"And Lily?" I asked. "What does she want?"

91

"Not Nick," he answered promptly. "Meatball—Maisy—was playing with her dolls on the floor the other day, and I heard her say in a deep voice, 'No, I'm talking about *love*. True love!' Then she asked herself, 'What is true love?' and answered in the other voice, 'Believing in something you know nothing about.' Pretty accurate for an eight-year-old."

"Love is weird," I noted.

"Like with Mom and George, or even YMC and his wife Michelle," Ethan agreed. "'Michelle' would be the best stripper name, now that I think of it."

"..."

"..."

"How is 'Michelle' a stripper name?!"

"It's just so casual!" He laughed. "I once knew this girl in third grade named Michelle. We called her Fat Mitchy."

"That's mean."

"She transferred out, though, so it's cool."

"I don't think that justifies—"

"You know what's funny?" He rolled over on his side to face me. "We all thought you'd end up being the Suicide Kid."

"Wait, what?" I didn't know what he meant by this. "How is that even remotely funny?"

"They say one person in your grade will commit suicide, right?"

"Um, no?"

"There's some statistic on it. Anyway, you didn't seem to talk to anyone this year and the last, so we all thought it was going to be you. You were a terrible loner—no offense."

I felt both confused and hurt. "Who thought this? *Everyone?*"

"I can't speak for everybody, but I know a lot of people did, myself included. So I'm glad you found your way into our little group."

I had never in my life had suicidal thoughts. It seemed morbid and something that happened to other people. *Who would glamorize that stuff?* Besides having no friends the past year and a half, I thought I had a good life—one that was certainly not worth giving up for death.

Ethan was humming softly to himself while I thought about this. "Some kids wanna be astronauts," he said, "and every girl wants to be a ballerina or a vet or a Hollywood star. But you know what? If I had another life, I would own a small cupcake shop somewhere in Europe, with a striped awning and a display case in the front window. That… would be perfect."

And in a matter of seconds, Ethan was out, just like that. His snoring, and how people associated me with suicide—along with all that had gone on between Lily, Nick, Megan, Ethan, and me—lingered in my head long throughout the night and into my own sleep.

It was the weekend when we woke up, and Ethan was pleased to find that my belt had remained buckled, given his incident with Nick.

Although my pants were still unzipped.

ninety-seven days ago

I opened my locker after lunch on Monday to have a large mound of white, sticky feathers fall outward onto myself and the tiled floor. I was wearing a dark t-shirt, so this didn't make me happy.

"FUUUUCCCKK!" Ethan screamed from down the hall. I pushed the rest of the feathers out of my locker, put my books inside, shut it, and ran over to see what was wrong.

His top locker smelled like crap—more specifically, pigeon crap, as I would later find out. A bag of it had spilled onto the floor and down onto Ethan's pants and shoes.

"What happened?" I asked him, then Lily, who was standing nearby and shaking her head, hands on her hips. A couple of girls walked by and snickered.

"Same that happened to you," Ethan said when he got a better look at me. "Nick did this."

"You did call him a 'shitbird,' whatever that is," Lily pointed out. I found it weird how she was ignoring what we had done together, but I tried not to think too much about it. "At least you didn't make a joke about spiders or something."

93

"I'm sorry, are you *defending* him?" Ethan asked, stepping closer to her. She stepped back, not because she was intimidated, but the stench was just too putrid. "Look at Jay, for Christ's sake! Who else would have done this?!" He shuffled through his belongings in his locker, then cursed under his breath. "The phone's gone."

"What phone?" she asked.

Ethan pounded against the wall beside him. "*Nick's* phone, Lillian! *He* did *this* and took his phone back!"

I was confused as to how Nick had gotten into our lockers without anyone noticing, but now I understood why he had done it.

"With the pictures and video of Lily—?" I started, but she glared at me. I stopped myself.

"Nah," he said. "I got rid of them, thank God." He looked from his shoes to my shirt, then back to his locker. "Still, this is pretty fucked up humor when it comes to revenge tactics. And to top it all off, I had to drive Mr. Scary to the vet this morning. He must've ran into a raccoon or something that scratched up his left side when we let him out that night." He closed his eyes and took a deep breath. "Stupid Nick, telling me to put the damn dog out."

"So what do we do?" I asked. "About the locker situation, I mean. Tell a teacher?"

"Nope," Lily said simply. "We don't do anything right now."

"The hell?" Ethan stared at her in shock. "I know Jesus says to turn the other cheek, but you can't be serious! Nick filmed you changing and terrorized me and Jay today with his... *his literal take on insults!*"

"I know," she agreed. "He completely objectifies me. I'm his Manic Pixie Dream Girl, and I'm just as mad as you both are—maybe even more! But we'll get Nick back, so don't you worry your pretty little red hair off, baby." A sure smile was on her face. "We'll hit him where it hurts." She turned to saunter off. "You'll see!"

"Well," I said.

"Damn straight," Ethan agreed. Although we weren't referring to her plan, we did abide by it. In fact, I didn't see Nick at all that week.

I texted Saphnie about it when I got home.

Me: I think I've made a huge mistake.

Saphnie: No one's fully happy with what they've done. What's up?

Me: Lily kissed me, and I let her. We went further than I thought we would.

Saphnie: How far?! (o_O)

Me: Not *that* far, but almost! We stopped when Ethan came back. This was on Friday (his birthday).

Saphnie: That's not cool. I thought you didn't have any feelings for this girl?

Me: I don't! I mean, not more than a friend.

Saphnie: Want my advice? The truth's going to come out eventually. It always does. If you want to keep your new friends then you're going to have to tell Ethan, but make sure he's in a happy mood first. If I ever have bad news then I make sure to tell my dad after he's gotten his paycheck and my mom when she gets home from shopping.

Me: You don't know Ethan. He'll get reeeaallyy mad.

Saphnie: He has every right to be! You shouldn't be making out with his girlfriend! That's a universal understanding. Trust is a fragile bond, but the sooner you tell him the better. Not to keep Latin-dumping on you, but Ovid's "Adde parvum parvo magnus acervus erit" means, "Add a little to a little and there will be a great heap." These things build up after a while.

While I could admit Saphnie made some good points, I couldn't bring myself to risk it. I had seen Ethan and Megan's hostility to Nick, and I definitely did not want that anger directed toward me. I figured I'd wait a while for a good time to tell him, if I ever did, and maybe by then, we would've become such great friends that it wouldn't matter.

I thanked Saphnie for her help, put the phone on my desk, and then browsed Lily and Ethan's pictures on their profiles. They looked happy together. I didn't want to damage that again—I didn't want to be like Nick.

ninety-three days ago
Friday was our last day before Spring Break, and it went by fast. Some teachers like Mrs. Beckham gave plenty of work to keep us busy, while others such as Kukowski couldn't care less, as he didn't bother showing up to class.

I was on the bus—mentally planning my week of staycation—when I got a text from Ethan.

Ethan: You going to Darian's partay tonight? Me and Lily are. It's gonna be EPIC!!!

Ethan was referring to Darian Burroughs, the cheerleader at Hennigan High most commonly known for having taken sexual pictures of herself in the eighth grade. She had sent them to her then-boyfriend during Spring Break that year, and he sent them to his friends, who in turn mass-texted them to every other boy at our middle school. I didn't have a phone at the time, but I got a look as a group of guys passed around their own TSC and snickered at Darian's facial expression in one of the pictures. It was captivating, to say the least.

Nevertheless, Darian—the only child of professional tennis player Adrian Burroughs—would never invite me to anything, as I doubted she even remembered me. I suspected Ethan got invited on account of Lily, who was friends with her and seemed to be on good terms with just about every high school clique.

Me: Wasn't invited. But you both have fun!

Ethan: Woah woah woah. All work and no play makes Jay a dull boy! I'm not gonna let my best friend who got me back my girlfriend miss out on Darians Spring Break Party! One sec

"One sec" turned into an hour, as I had already gotten home and was working on Mrs. Beckham's verb sheets when I got another text. It wasn't from Ethan.

UNKNOWN NUMBER: Do you know Lily Carswell?

Me: Um, yeah. We dated for a week. Why?

UNKNOWN NUMBER: Your Jonah, right?

Me: Jake. Or Jay, I guess. Who is this?

UNKNOWN NUMBER: Cool. This is Darian. I live in greenland hills, 2415 queen Elizabeth lane. Party's from 7 to whenever. Bring beer &RH

I couldn't believe my luck. Not only had I gotten invited to Darian Burroughs's Spring Break party, but she lived on the street perpendicular to mine, *four houses down*. While I certainly wasn't going to bring alcohol, I did need a plan, as Mom would never agree to let me go. So after a late dinner of lasagna and broccoli at seven, I went to my room and started putting clothes underneath my blankets and turning the fan on high to make some noise. I then staggered toward my mom's office and leaned on the wall.

"Something wrong?" she asked, her attention focused on me.

"I think…" I moaned, trying to sound convincing. "I think I got the stomach virus that's been at school."

"Oh, goodness!" She reached for a bottle on her desk. "Do you have a headache? Would you like some medicine?"

"Sure." I held out my hand, and she gave me two little red pills.

"Take those with some water," she instructed. "Go lie down, and I'll come by later to check on you—"

"No!" I said. "It's fine, really. I'm gonna try to go to sleep."

"If you wake up and need me, come knock on our door, all right?"

"Yeah, will do. Thanks."

I hugged her to convince her of my innocence and headed toward my room. Instead, I turned the corner into the bathroom, where I brushed my teeth, changed into some jeans and a polo shirt, and then tossed the two pills down the drain. I crept downstairs, avoided my mom and dad's bedroom, and quietly slid open the glass door to the backyard—shutting it cautiously—and by that point, I was already off and into the night.

Cars were lined up and down the street when I arrived at the party, the low bass sounding from what felt like all directions. I noticed two couples noisily making out on either side of the open door as I approached it, a group of wild teenagers within.

Darian's place looked the same as my own, but the obvious difference between our houses was that hers was *packed,* as I struggled to move through the crowd once inside. It was different from the get-together of five the weekend before at Ethan's, whom I spotted in an armchair with Lily in his lap—the both of them laughing and sloshing their red drinks around in their matching, plastic cups. I managed my way to them, eventually.

"Hey, Jay Jay!" Lily called out and raised a cup to me. "We *thought* you'd never come *back* to church!"

"Pssh, with Jay gone *you* probably thought you'd missed the Rapture," Ethan said, his eye now fully recovered. Noticing her glare, he added: "No offense, Lily-pad—er, Water Lily."

"Yeah, yeah, whatevers," she said, tilting her head to the left as she slurred her words.

"Isn't this party g-great?" he asked me, laughing for what seemed like no apparent reason.

"It's very LOUD, if that's what you mean," I said, looking around.

"Here," Ethan said, passing me his cup. "Stuff's the best!"

I peered in. "What is it?"

"Cran-*berry* juice, duh!" Lily said with a giggle as she struggled to get up from her seat. She turned slowly toward me, either for dramatic effect or because her usual nimbleness had been slowed by the booze. "It's something called Red Harbinger."

"Beer?" I asked.

"Experi-*mental* alcohol," she replied, followed by a loud laugh.

"S'very *interfesting*," Ethan noted. "Now, I don't usually drink, un-like this chick—" He pointed a finger at Lily. "—but this shit is real good, Murchi-*mansion!*"

I frowned. "I don't think that's such a good idea."

"But partyin' never *killed* nobody!" he insisted, lifting his cup for me to take. "Come on, Blue Jay!"

"I'm not coming on!" I told them, pushing his cup away. As her defiant response to this, Lily gripped my shoulder with one hand—the other around her drink—and pressed her slender body against my chest.

"Pleeeeaase?" she begged, sticking out her bottom lip. "Li'l bit'll *do* you some good!"

I don't know whether it was seeing the fun everyone seemed to be having, the fact that I had snuck out of the house for the first time, or having Lily that close to me again, but I grabbed Ethan's half-full cup of Red Harbinger and drank it all, earning me cheers from Lily, Ethan, and random others. The drink was bitter, and the aftertaste was so bad that I had to swallow some more to rid my tongue of it. It was ingenious, actually.

The room began to spin soon after.

Lily jumped on an inflatable alligator. The crowd pushed them both into Darian's heated swimming pool. Ethan cannonballed in pursuit of her. The saltwater's spray was warm. Steam rose from their bodies as they swam. Green and orange bottles of different shapes and sizes were passed around. I crashed into Sandy Goldsmith.

I didn't know who she was, but Sandy was wearing a sapphire party dress to match her indigo eyes, and her long, dark hair curled down to her waist. I wasn't watching where I was going, and although I avoided tripping on her foot, I ended up spilling Ethan's twice-refilled cup all down her neck and dress.

I started to apologize, but she stopped me, instead—laughing and pulling me down to her height. "Tell me I'm pretty!" she commanded, her breath hot against my cheeks, and I told her she was. So we spent the rest of that night together, as we danced and kissed under the half-moon behind the clouds.

I ended up falling asleep on a couch with Sandy in my arms long before the partying was over. Her hair tickled my face, although I was too enamored and oblivious to mind.

ninety-two days ago

I woke up to find my fingers interlaced around Sandy. Her dress was stained and unzipped, which revealed a white lace bra and a birthmark that had an uncanny resemblance to the shape of Ukraine.

Lily and Ethan were both asleep on the floor. Ethan was without his t-shirt, and drawn on his stomach with bright red lipstick was an arrow pointing down, and written below that: BLOW ME. Lily, meanwhile, was face-down and wasn't wearing pants. I took a double-take at her GOT YOUR HEART ON? underwear before I wiggled my hands out of Sandy's dress to reach for my phone. Three unanswered texts. It was 7:02 in the morning. The sun had not yet risen, but barely.

I carefully slid out from underneath Sandy and winced as I stood up. My body was weak and ached all over, so trying not to wake the sleeping drunks on my way to the propped-open door took extra effort. I struggled walking around and over the multitude of bodies slumped against the walls, furniture, and each other, all littered with red, plastic cups. Only once I got outside did I realize I had lost my socks.

I peeked over our neighbor's fence and made sure the Cunningham's yappy Yorkie was still inside their house. I climbed over into their yard, went across and over into mine, grabbed onto our old willow tree for support, got to the house, removed the loose panel covering up our large and long-since-used dog door, and then carefully crawled inside so as not to make a sound.

"Did you go to that Darian girl's party last night?" my dad asked without taking his eyes off the business section of the morning paper. He was sitting at the kitchen table, one leg crossed over the other.

I nodded. He took a long sip of his coffee and faced me.

"Sometimes we all need to have a little party in our lives," he declared. "'Life's one grand, sweet song, so start the music.' Not to be your typical Republican, but that was Reagan. He wants you to enjoy your life—to not stay inside the house all day before someone or something causes you to be unable to leave. So I won't tell your mother."

He looked to the headlines, me toward the staircase. Each step sent shockwaves to my head. *Was this what it felt like to have a hangover?* With my head throbbing and making it near impossible to walk, I got on my knees and inched my way up, finally collapsing at the top.

The sound of someone flushing a toilet awoke me sometime after. I forced my way to my room, locked the door behind me, and peeled off my polo and jeans to find that my boxers were backward. Regardless, I soon fell asleep on the pile of clothes that was supposed to be me. I was tired and nauseous, though I thought to myself that even if I couldn't remember half of it, I'd just had a pretty amazing night.

"Honey?" One-second pause. "Jakob, are you all right in there?"

I squinted in the dark. "Wha—?"

"Can you open up?" Mom asked, rattling the door handle. I wiped the drool from my cheek, put on some shorts and a t-shirt, and unlocked the door to see my mother's worried face.

"You threw up on your bed sheets," she pointed out.

"I'll… clean it up," I managed. "What… time? What time is it?"

"It's two in the afternoon. Did you have a hard time sleeping, too?" I nodded yes. "Adrian's kid had another one of her parties last night. I'm just so glad I've raised you better."

We stared at each other until she smiled and left.

I rolled up my sheets and clothes and took them down to the laundry room. I rubbed my tired eyes, went back into my room, sat on my bare mattress, powered up my laptop, and then logged onto Coffee-Folder. All across my homepage were pictures of the night before, each one more bizarre than the last. I wasn't in any of them, but it seemed Darian had had a repeat of eighth grade's picture frenzy (seventy-eight "likes" that afternoon, and with Ethan's later, seventy-nine).

My phone buzzed with a new text. I checked the ones from the previous night as well.

UNKNOWN NUMBER: Heyy this is Sandy, making sure this works! Do you have a SextMe?

UNKNOWN NUMBER: I see yeeew!

UNKNOWN NUMBER: Oh my goodness, I'm so sorry about that. I wasn't supposed to be there! My dad's going to FREAK! I'm deleting these messages.

Sandy was the girl I had been with at the party. Sandy was the girl I had made out with under the shrouded stars for an intoxicated audience. Sandy was the girl who I had recently met and with whom I had shared the night of my life. Sandy and I must have exchanged numbers at some point.

Me: I'm hoping this wasn't a one-night sort of thing, so to speak. Maybe we can start over? I'm Jay. :-)

Sandy: Sure! Hi, I'm Sandy. =)

After some back-and-forth texting between Sandy and me, Coffee-Folder indicated that Ethan wanted to have a video chat. I accepted the invite and saw two separate screens: one with Ethan, who appeared to have recently gotten out of the shower, as his hair was dripping wet; and one with Lily, who was still in her party clothes. From the camera's angle, I couldn't readily tell if she had found her pants.

"I've got *such* a headache," she announced, rubbing her temples and trying to relieve the pain. "My throat tastes like I got drunk off California wildfires instead of RH."

"Yeah," Ethan said, then winced. "Worst. Hangover. Ever."

"Same," I said, wondering how many times they had done this before. "When did you guys leave?"

"Some idiot's shitty, stupid, loud..." He put his head on his desk.

"Someone's phone woke us up," Lily finished for him. Her eyes were closed. "Sooo many drunk people. I got beer all over my foot... We must've looked like a pile of dead bodies." She took a deep breath. "When did you leave?"

"Around seven," I answered. She then looked down and made some odd facial expressions, as if she was miming, ooh, aah, ooh, aah, ooh, aah. "Um, what are you doing?"

"I'm. Excer. Sizing. My. Facial. Muscles." She over-emphasized each part with her lips.

"Her grandma did it while she was alive," Ethan said, seeing my blank expression. "Kept her face young or something."

"Wrinkle free! 'Cause your face is made of muscles, and if you don't exercise muscles, they become flabby."

"I thought the more you move your face, the more wrinkles it gets?" I asked.

"I may or may not still be drunk," she added.

Both Ethan and I joined in on Lily's facial weirdness, the three of us unable to contain our laughter at how silly we looked on-screen.

"By the way, Jay," Ethan started, "was it me, or were you totally getting laid by Sandy Goldsmith? Pastor Goldsmith's gonna be pissed!"

"I don't..." I struggled to remember. "Why? Who is she?"

"Sandy's father is the pastor of Redbud Avenue," Lily explained, giggling. "He's an uptight dad. I'm surprised he even let Sandy go to Darian's party."

"She mentioned she wasn't supposed to have gone," I recalled.

Lily shrugged. "Strict parents create sneaky kids."

"You both aren't, like, dating, right?" Ethan asked me.

"Well, I don't know... I—"

"Sandy Goldsmith is a very controlling girlfriend," he continued. "We've heard her talk about that Dunmire baseball player she went out with recently, and it didn't sound too pretty between them."

"She also gets jealous easily," Lily added, "so I hope you don't meet any hot celebrities between now and whenever she breaks up with you!"

"Wait, what do you mean, 'and whenever she breaks up with you'?" I asked.

"Well," Ethan started, "you can't break up with her, obviously, unless you want to face *the wrath of Pastor Goldsmith!*" He wiggled his fingers in front of his face and widened his eyes as if he were scared. "Even the devil's afraid of that man. Seriously—as soon as you get the chance, you need to let her squash it before it lays eggs."

"I don't get it. She and I aren't going out, are we?"

"Are you?" Lily countered. I had to think about it.

"Be right back," I answered, then logged off.

Me: Sorry if this is a weird question, but are we dating?

Sandy: We can be, if you want. You seem nice and cute. =P

Me: Well, I know we're on Spring Break and all, but... Do you want to go out with me? :-)

Sandy: Sure! =D

Me: Cool! :-D

I logged back on. "We are in fact going out."

"Shit, man," Ethan said. "This is bad."

"Why?" I asked to no response. "Why is everyone so scared of her dad?"

"The flowers are pretty in the spring," Lily only half-answered.

"No, the flowers are just gay," Ethan added.

"Don't be so narrow-minded!" she exclaimed. "There's nothing wrong with being gay!" She shook her head. "It's tough being a blue in a red state. Just the other day—"

"Guys," I said. "What does it mean when you say, 'The flowers are pretty in the spring'?"

She sighed. "It's silly code for something that happened, like, a year ago."

"The Bake Sale Incident!" Ethan said, again with the fingers.

"It doesn't even relate to the story," she admitted. "We only use the code because we're not supposed to talk about it."

"And I distinctly remember suggesting, 'Better take the cookie to the doctor.'"

"So the church was doing a bake sale last May to promote a local charity or something," Lily began, "and Ethan, Meg, Ty, Sandy, Nick, a couple of others, and I were all in charge of the actual baking."

"Wait, Nick *Behr?*"

"Perm boy," Ethan said. I could see him cross his arms. "God, I hate that guy."

"Anyway," she continued, "we made and sold our pies and cookies in the parking lot all afternoon. Megan's mom was supposed to pick us up in their SUV after it was over, since we were all carpooling, but she was running late. Long story short: Ty found some extra dough, and we figured, after all our hard work, we should make some cookies for ourselves. Megan pointed out that there wasn't enough time, but Nick suggested we could put it in the microwave for fifteen minutes and see how it went.

"Unfortunately, along with the dough, Nick put the tray in, too. Oops, right? Next thing we know, we smell smoke and hear banging sounds coming from the microwave. So we run over to stop it from blowing up. Nick grabs the handle and—not noticing Meg—throws the door open, which hits her pretty hard across the face and leaves her with that scar under her eye.

"Then Pastor Goldsmith showed up and was totally outraged for the lack of parental supervision, as it was just us, since YMC was out sick. Megan was crying because of the pain, so Nick tried to shift the blame onto Ty. Not a good move. Keep in mind that this was soon after Pastor Goldsmith's wife passed away, and he already resented us for having both our parents—"

"Which is stupid 'cause my real dad is somewhere off in Alabama," Ethan added.

"—and so he basically told Nick to never come back, and there's no point in arguing with an overprotective father," Lily finished. "Now I need some water."

"Well, that certainly clears up a few things," I said. "I had no idea Nick went to your church before."

"That's just how the cookie crumbles," Ethan joked. Lily frowned.

"But anyway," she went on, "you dating Sandy's not all that bad. Maybe she'll be good for you!"

"Or the other way around?" Ethan suggested.

"Maybe." She paused. "So long as he doesn't do anything stupid."

"Yeah." Ethan laughed. "Don't screw it up, Jay!"

"Easier said than done," I admitted. They smiled sympathetically.

Sandy and I texted for a few hours after that. She told me she was leaving for a mission trip to the Dominican Republic the next morning, which I was fine with, as I needed time to recover from the Red Harbinger and its side effects. Then she told me to tell her she was pretty, so I did.

As we said our good-byes, I wondered what exactly I had gotten myself into. Here was a girl I had known for fewer than twenty-four hours, and yet I had asked her out so willingly. But *why?* Because I had seen her bra? Because of her pretty eyes? Because we had kissed? I decided to ask Saphnie for some advice, as she always seemed to know what to do.

Me: I asked a girl out, and she said yes, but now I'm sort of unsure. What should I do?

Saphnie: I'm not in the mood.

Me: What?

Saphnie: IT'S ALWAYS ABOUT YOU, DAMMIT. LEAVE ME THE FUCK ALONE.

Me: I didn't mean to upset you, honestly! I don't know what's wrong, but if there's anything I can do, let me know, all right?

I wondered what could have possibly happened. Had her three-legged, one-and-a-half-eared cat Minerva passed away? Had her father lost his job?

Saphnie: Valerie died last night.

"Oh, my God," I said aloud. I wouldn't know what to do if I got news that Elena had died. We'd always been close, even after she had left for college—although nowadays, most of our contact was through CoffeeFolder and regarding *Annihilation!*

While I was thinking about that, I got another text.

Saphnie: I'D COMFORT YOU IF IT WAS YOUR SISTER.

Me: I'm just confused! You told me before not to feel sorry for you, but I *am* sorry! What happened??

Saphnie: It was only Valerie, my mom, and me at our house. I

was getting Val's bath ready and Mom had to leave real quick to get something she left with her former boss. I was supposed to keep an eye on Val. Then I got a text saying there was a party at someone's house down the street, so I left her alone for FIVE MINUTES while I fixed my hair in our shared room with the hairdryer on. I couldn't hear her. I thought it was her usual gar-bled bullshit. She drowned. She drowned in that bath I prepared for her because she hit her head on the faucet. It's my fault. It's all my fault and there's NOTHING I CAN DO ABOUT IT.

Me: God, that's awful. That's really, really horrible.

Saphnie: Please stop. I don't want to hear it right now. I know.

Me: OK... When's the funeral?

Saphnie: The service will probably be next Thursday. Anyway, tell me about this girl you asked out so I can get my mind off my sister.

Me: Are you sure? We don't have to.

Saphnie: Yes. Please. I need to think of something else.

I told her of my debauchery: getting invited to Darian's party, how I faked an illness, snuck out, watched the intoxicated versions of Lily and Ethan, got drunk myself, spilled Red Harbinger on Sandy's dress, kissed her, woke up to find everyone asleep, snuck back inside the house, asked Sandy out, and learned about Pastor Goldsmith.

Saphnie: Don't do anything you'll later regret, but I doubt Mr Preacher would do anything to you if you did break up with her. Maybe it's good she'll be gone this week. The Roman poet Sex-tus Propertius did note that "semper in absentes felicior aestus amantes," a.k.a., absence makes the heart grow fonder.

The blinds were drawn in Elena's room, but when I walked over to open them, I could see the blue sky turning a pleasant, peach color over the neighborhood of Greenland Hills. I imagined the previous night's events in my mind and saw how the sun created a sort of glow on the lone willow tree in the backyard. So I went downstairs and slid the glass door open to examine it, remembering to cover up the dog door, which I did.

I approached the willow and took out my phone to take a picture. The branches swayed lightly in the evening breeze, and I admired the intricate details highlighted by that certain sunset. I captioned the image "Nature's Beauty," sent it to Saphnie, and waited for her response.

Saphnie: Ego contemno meus vita.

Me: What? Did you get the picture?

Saphnie: I didn't. It's blank.

Me: It was of a pretty tree.

Saphnie: That's nice. I should get going. Bye.

Me: Bye.

eighty-seven days ago
The rest of Spring Break was uneventful. To pass the time, I listened to Pulsar Skies, watched some *$tore Wars: Florida*, and browsed Coffee-Folder. Everyone seemed to be uploading pictures of themselves either tanning at the beach or skiing in Colorado, as the low cost of living in Oklahoma allowed for the occasional excursion. I didn't necessarily envy them, but with Ethan driving to Texas, and Lily flying to Chicago, I couldn't help feeling a little lonesome.

Rainstorms brought green grass and blooming redbuds, replacing the yellows and creek browns from winter. When cousins from Europe stayed at my house during Spring Break the year before, they admitted to having enjoyed the quiet life of Arminster more than the theme parks on the Gulf Coast. I asked them why, and they said it was because they saw our city as the "true American lifestyle." While I didn't fully agree, I couldn't dismiss the truth in it—that Arminster was about as urban as it got before reaching countryside.

On Thursday evening, I texted Saphnie to see how she was doing.

Me: What's the weather like over there? It's been raining all week here. The storms were so loud, I could hardly sleep last night!

Saphnie: I remember Oklahoma having ugly St. Patrick's Days. I wish it would rain here. It's been too sunny lately. Hate is a strong word, but I do hate this peaceful weather.

Me: How are you?

Saphnie: I'm fine now. Tired. Listening to WHVB. I was crying so much this morning it hurt. My eyes are red and I have a bad headache. It sucks to attend a funeral you caused. Only my parents know. I think the sad truth is we've simply accepted it. I'm going to sound real inhumane by saying this, but maybe this is what she would have wanted?

Me: It's possible.

Saphnie: You know you're in a rough spot when you find yourself praying to a god you don't believe in. Sometimes you could look into Val's eyes and the way she looked back at you was almost as if she remembered what her life used to be like before it was taken away.

Me: Tell me about her.

Saphnie: She was amazing at the piano. She had best friends. She had the biggest crush on Laine Geier from $tore Wars. She had a strong dislike for Taco Kick and she really, really wanted to own a Privateer for its safety features. Valerie's the one who introduced me to Amos Metres books and Pulsar Skies songs. She knew all the lyrics. It's just not fair.

Me: No, it's not, and you shouldn't be having to go through this. No one should.

Saphnie: I know, I know.

Me: Who all attended the burial?

Saphnie: Everyone you would expect. My parents, obviously, some of Val's old friends, teachers she'd had before she was forced to drop out, neighbors. It made me wonder who would show up at my funeral when I die.

Me: I'm trying hard not to say this because I know you don't like it when people do, but I'm sincerely sorry this happened to you, Saphnie. And when others say it, know that they mean it, too.

Saphnie: It's all fake pity. Only the creatures of the sea know what it's like to be a fish out of water, not the waterfowl who live off it. I know because I have to live with the fact that I killed my sister because I was so goddamn conceited.

Me: Valerie's death wasn't your fault. It wasn't anybody's fault!

Saphnie: THEN TELL ME WHAT WILL BRING MY SISTER BACK! TELL ME SO I CAN STOP DIGGING THIS HOLE DEEPER

Saphnie was looking to me for advice—a first in our relationship.

Nothing against her, as it was she who always had the answers. But with Valerie dead, and the grieving that came with it, her mind was just as confused.

Me: You'll go crazy trying to change things beyond your control. I think it was you who told me that. Ronald Reagan once said, "Life is one grand, sweet song, so start the music." According to my dad, he means that we need to live life now while we have it before something unfortunate occurs, like with Valerie.

Saphnie: My cousin hates Reagan with a passion. Wasn't he the president who talked about how you can tell a lot about a person's character by their way of eating jellybeans? Didn't they find out he was crazy? He's overrated anyway. He was oblivious to the needs of the lower class, whom he was trying to help.

Me: His Alzheimer's was slowly destroying his memory, but he said both quotes before that. Regarding the jellybeans (which he was famous for liking), I think he was just making fun of people who say, "You can tell a lot about a person by the way they…"

Saphnie: I guess you can come up with some answers if you think about it, like how some people will eat handfuls while others carefully pick and choose their flavors and sometimes refuse to eat a certain one.

Me: I'm pretty sure he was joking.

Saphnie: To each their own. People are complicated, sort of like ghoughpteighbteau.

Me: What?

Saphnie: I knew you would ask that. (^_~) It illustrates the complexity of the English language by being another way to spell "potato." Ghoughpteighbteau: gh- from hiccough, -ough-

from though, -pt- from ptomaine (as in various organic bases), -eigh- from sleigh, -bt- from debt, and -eau from bureau. There's also "ghoughphtheightteeau," but both are essentially "potato."

Me: And I thought Spanish was difficult!

Saphnie: Please, you've got it easy. Latin's a dead language.

Me: Yeah, I suppose so. But anyway, if you get the chance to go out, you should. I hear the ocean air is good for you!

Saphnie: Good times to replace the sad ones, right? That almost sounds too perfect, but talking about jellybeans and potatoes was nice enough. Thank you, Jay. You're a good friend.

Me: I try my best! :-D

Saphnie: That you do.

Me: Have a good night, OK?

Saphnie: Okay. Good night.

Me: Sorry about everything.

Saphnie: So am I.

eighty-three days ago

Sandy came back on Sunday with many stories from the Dominican Republic. Most were about how she and her group were in charge of a Vacation Bible School, which included activities for impoverished children such as puppetry, music, performances, and devotionals. She said that she and her group also separated into smaller groups and did arts and crafts with the kids, played soccer with them, and gave each of the children candy and little presents from the United States. I wanted to ask how candy was supposed to help those kids, but instead, I told her what she did was good, as that seemed easier.

She waited for me by my locker on Monday morning.

"I didn't know you wear glasses," I admitted when I saw her—the first time since the party.

"I wear those blue contacts for special occasions," she said, sounding disappointed. I thought then of my own contacts, which I always wore, which made me wonder if that meant every day was a special occasion for me or that I never had any. Perhaps I had given up entirely. I decided the latter was the most likely of the three.

"I mean, you look great!" I added, laughing nervously. She smiled.

"Oh!" she exclaimed. "I got you something *de la República Dominicana!*" She reached into her sky blue backpack and took out a small box covered with teal duct tape. She handed it to me, and I opened it to find a keychain shaped like an ornate cross with what I assumed to be the country's emblem in the middle and the red, blue, and white-crossed flag of the Dominican Republic as the background.

"Very cool," I said. "Thank you!"

"The red stands for the blood of heroes," she explained, "the blue for liberty, and the white for salvation. The *'Dios, Patria, Libertad'* on the emblem means, 'God, Fatherland, Liberty.' The Bible is opened to John 8:32. 'You will know the truth, and the truth will make you free.'"

"That's the motto of the CIA," I said, then added: "I learned that from QuickSearch."

"Oh, that's neat."

"Yep."

" . . . "

" . . . "

She pushed her cheeks with her fingers, pursed her lips, and smiled.

"Tell me I'm pretty!" she said, looking like a fish up against glass.

"What?"

"Tell me I'm pretty!"

"You're pretty!" I said, confused.

She laughed. "Try again."

"Your eyes..." Brown. They were naturally brown. "Your eyes are the color of... the soil that flowers grow from?"

She smiled again. It was a pretty smile. I should have complimented it, instead.

"I could plant kisses on your jaw like flowers," she told me, then stood on her tiptoes to do so. But I was too tall, so she went back down, and we stood there. "Well, class is about to start."

"Uh, right," I said. "And again, thank you so much for the gift!" I opened my arms, and we hugged. Then we parted ways, with her looking back to wave, and me to check the mounted clock on the wall.

Kukowski was late to Chemistry, so I spent some time trying to clip the keychain onto my backpack. When I finally got it on, I noticed there was a piece of notebook paper in the box she'd given me. I unfolded it.

> *Me!*
> *I hate being confused or frustrated, though I get like that sometimes. So if that happens, I need your support, or a listening ear, or sympathy, Jay. I will try not to project bad feelings onto you, but bear with me, as I'm not perfect!*
> *Believe it or not, I am still new at this whole relationship-thing. This time will be different, thankfully, and it already is. I'm super excited about this, and I foresee it going well. Anyway, this concludes my note!*
> *The first of many letters, Sandy*

I'd never been the person to write someone a note. I preferred email, texting, or CoffeeFolder, as my handwriting was "chicken scratch," to quote Mrs. Beckham. Despite this, my email account primarily consisted of junk mail: Canadian pharmacy Rock Solid wanted to sell me testosterone pills, CLICK*4*LOAN provided life insurance for as low as $13.04 per month, and both Hairy Gurlz and BDSM site for anglers Rods'n'Reels offered "free pictures of thousands of busty women in the Arminster area." That said, I wasn't much of a writer.

"At least she's being subtle," Lily whispered from behind me, then laughed all the way back to her seat.

I walked Sandy to her white convertible at the end of the school day, hand in hand, and we hugged for the second time. It felt different than with Lily—Sandy's didn't feel as special to me. But then again, I wasn't giving her a chance, as Lily and Ethan had tried to scare me into thinking she wasn't worth the supposed trouble. But what did they know? When I had first met Sandy, we'd had a good time (under the influence of Red Harbinger, admittedly).

I managed to get inside the bus to my neighborhood right before it drove off. When I arrived at my house, I logged onto CoffeeFolder to find a relationship status request from Sandy pending approval. I hesitantly accepted, and it was official.

In a Relationship with **Sandra Goldsmith**

APRIL

seventy-three days ago

A little over a week after the CoffeeFolder relationship update, I walked down the stairs for some water before bed to find my mom reclining on the couch in the living room. She was using her laptop.

"Jakob," she called out to me. "Did you change your CoffeeSmolder password?"

I sighed. "You mean Coffee*Folder?* Yes, I did."

"Well, then what is it?" Her reading glasses were on, and her fingers were ready to type.

"Twenty ones and an F," I muttered. "Uppercase. Why—?"

"It won't let me tag you in this picture," she explained. "It says you need to approve it. Repeat your password?"

"1-1-1-1-1-1-1-1-1-1-1-1-1-1-1-1-1-1-1-1-F. No spaces." I left the room, retrieved the water, and then went back toward the stairs, waiting for the inevitable.

"YOU'RE DATING SANDRA GOLDSMITH?!" she exclaimed, then called out to my dad: "NIGEL, GET OVER HERE!"

Dad walked out of the kitchen and into the living room. "God, Karen, what's with all the yelling?" he asked her. "We could get into the ranching business with all the cows you've been having—"

"HE'S DATING PASTOR GOLDSMITH'S LITTLE GIRL!"

"You're *what?!*" he shouted at me, and they both looked away.

"He'll have to break up with her," Mom declared. "Right now!"

"No, he can't do that!" Dad said, grabbing her shoulders. "Not with the pastor…" They both turned to me.

"You have to be as nice to her as possible," Mom commanded. "And you can't break up with her—*she* has to break up with *you*. No kissing!"

"And no sex," Dad added.

"No sex with anyone, for that matter!"

"Right, exactly!"

"When did this even happen?!"

"Was this at that Darian girl's party?"

"Wait, what?!"

Eventually, they were just arguing with each other, so I snuck away with the water I came for and started my homework in my room. My phone buzzed a few minutes later.

Saphnie: I reread Rudderless at Sea!

Me: Nice! How was it the second time?

Saphnie: Good. I noticed some things I didn't before. The plot thickens! I still think the Island's metaphorical, but now I also believe it's a living entity on its own entirely.

Me: Yeah… What?

Saphnie: I think it brought Edward to the Island to teach him a lesson or to punish him for getting his daughter killed and then later for shoving O'Rourke to his death so he (Edward) could be with Paluure. Maybe they were all brought to the Island to be judged for one reason or another. Even Mercer said that "this Island knows me better than I know myself." I'm only speculating here, but the Island was definitely messing with Edward's head and I think his suicide was proof of that.

Me: I still don't think he jumped off that cliff, though I don't know if I already told you that.

Saphnie: Remember when Edward returns to the beach and finds everyone gone after he kills O'Rourke? The next paragraph is almost the EXACT SAME as the one before he first saw the survivors after the shipwreck. Mercer drops his fourth seashell onboard the Apricity, remember? Edward then finds it in his pocket after they crash on the beach and throws it into the ocean before he sees Paluure, Mercer, and Basil (Requiescat in Pace). Then they later find O'Rourke, who gets back together with Paluure. Edward's jealous and power-hungry, so he murders the ex-captain after the raft is finished. When Edward returns to the beach, everyone and the supplies are gone. What does he do? He reaches into his pocket and throws the shell AGAIN into the water. Get it now?

Me: Edward throws the same, missing seashell twice. What does that have to do with anything?

Saphnie: I think it means it was all a mirage of sorts created by the Island to give him a false sense of control while isolated, meaning Edward is suffering for failing to realize the truth of his actions. Either way, I think Mr Metres was right when he said it was meant to be open for interpretation. It's crazy how many outcomes there could be, all the more reason why that contest is stupid.

Me: I guess you're right in that it could be a number of things. But shouldn't you be in bed by now? It's getting late on the east coast!

Saphnie: Sleep is the only thing I stay awake for. (=_=) Bye!

Me: Good night!

Thus concluded our discussion on *Rudderless at Sea*. While I didn't agree with all of Saphnie's observations, I did enjoy the fact we were examining the book. The robotics team said they played *Annihilation!*

for the gameplay, but I actually enjoyed it for the story, as I was interested to see what would happen next during Commander Ace Thunderbolt and Binary Jack's crazy adventures together. While I doubted I'd ever be able to convince Saphnie to play as Mysti in co-op, it was nice to be analyzing a story—any story—in such great detail.

I went online, changed my password to "ghoughpteighbteau517," and saw the picture my mother had tagged me in. I wasn't anywhere in it, and neither were the other people she'd included, and it was then when I realized she had merely wanted to make sure we saw her post. It was a photo of a Julius Caesar statue inside the Jardin des Tuileries (next to the Louvre museum, as the caption noted). On top of his likeness was a large and actual bird with its head cocked at the camera.

Elena's comment: "Sometimes you're the pigeon, sometimes you're the statue."

sixty-five days ago
A week later, I logged onto CoffeeFolder before school started and found a friend-related update on my homepage from the day before.

Saphnie Kane-Tachibana is in a relationship with **Luke W**.

There was a comment from him saying, "You're my drug, Saph. Not a bad drug, but an awesome one filled with fiber and vitamins." Below that, someone said, "This is the cutest comment ever and all the other comments can go home… INTERNET OVER!" which made me laugh. I didn't know who Luke was, so as every curious person does, I checked his profile and discovered that he was sixteen, blond, spoke both Japanese and English, and had over a hundred comments on his profile pictures with other girls. I felt a little jealous of him, but only a little. That was all I could allow.

I was putting some things away in my locker when Lily ran up to me, waving her phone in her hand.

"You did it!" she yelled. "You won!"

"What did I win?" I asked, confused.

"The *Rudderless at Sea* contest! Your entry is at the top of the page!" She threw her arms around me, and although I felt that familiar bulge against my jeans, I hugged her, anyway. She then said that she was extremely happy for me, but she had to go her next class, so she did.

Sandy promptly appeared seemingly out of nowhere. Her arms were crossed, and she was tapping her foot against the tile.

"Why was Lily Carswell hugging you?" she asked.

"I won a contest on CoffeeFolder," I said, smiling.

"But you were hugging her back."

"Well, yeah, I was glad that—"

"Just remember who your girlfriend is, OK?" She swung her heavy backpack over her shoulder and walked off. I didn't know if I was supposed to go after her, but I wasn't in the mood for her sudden trust issues. Lily and I were only friends, and we were both excited I had won. Why couldn't she see that?

When I got home and opened my laptop in the living room, lo and behold, a new CoffeeFolder post was waiting for me.

Rudderless at Sea (Official)

And the winner is... Jay Murchison! His winning submission to what he liked about the book is as follows:

"What I enjoyed most about 'Rudderless at Sea' was that the character Mercer may not have been who he appeared. In the beginning, he told Edward there was no reasoning behind the jangling of the seashells, and I believed him. But as we later find out, Mercer [spoilers redacted], which makes me wonder whether he was lying and there was indeed a story behind his odd mannerism.

"Since discussing Rudderless with my friend, I have wondered whether the Island was real or imagined, and I continue to question it. At this point, I think the controversy over the Island is anyone's guess, which seems to have been the intention of Mr. Metres. One thing is for certain: Everyone can have their own way of interpreting the story, and I believe that's my favorite part about it."

Congratulations, Jay! Information regarding your signed copy and an answer to any single question has been sent your way. Stay subscribed to our page for more info on #RudderlessatSea.

In my inbox was a message from Rudderless at Sea (Official) asking for an address to ship my free, signed copy. In return, they listed the publisher's contact information so I could send mail to Mr. Metres. They also provided some advice: "Remember: The best way to write to a writer is to write the way a writer would write."

The thing was, I didn't see the point of getting another copy of a book I had already purchased and currently owned, signed or not. The signature might be worth more to some, but anyone could scribble "Amos Metres" onto a page in the front and people would think it looked legitimate. Nevertheless, the answer to any one question was kind of cool.

The front door opened, and in came my mother with groceries. I picked up an orange that fell from her arms as she locked the door, and I helped her bring the bags into the kitchen. While we were unloading an electric apple peeler, of all things, she gave me a look of concealed excitement, as if she were about to start laughing, but for whatever reason wouldn't.

"What's so funny?" I asked as I put the milk in the fridge.

"Oh, nothing," she said, looking away.

"Well, OK then."

"All right, I'll tell you, goodness!" She laughed again. "Guess where we're going the first two weeks in June!"

"Is it an amusement park?"

"It's not an amusement park."

"Fine," I said. "Where to?"

"We're staying with Elena in *Windhaven!*" She announced this in a sing-song voice and with a big smile on her face.

I hesitated. Elena didn't live in Windhaven. At least, I didn't think she did. But Saphnie sure did.

"Elena lives in Windhaven?" I asked, seeking confirmation.

"In North Carolina." Mom tilted her head quizzically. "We visited her two summers ago. You rode on the Ferris wheel by the beach, remember?"

"I thought that was in Florida."

"You're thinking of Aunt Nancy, bless her soul." She sighed momentarily. "But anyway, isn't this going to be fun?!"

"As long as we're not driving the whole way again," Dad said as he walked inside with an oversized blender. "That was *real* fun." He noticed my confused look. "Your mother's asked me to make dinner tonight," he explained, though Mom hated it when he referred to her as "your mother" to me. Dad, in turn, did not like cooking, especially the night before his morning flight to Chicago for a work conference.

My phone buzzed then, and I excused myself to go to my room. Halfway up the stairs, I heard Dad exclaim, "Karen, come look at this! We have a *spoon drawer!*" I unlocked the phone and read the text.

Saphnie: YOU WON THE CONTEST! \(^o^)/

Me: Thank you! But I thought you didn't care for it?

Saphnie: I don't, but I'm still happy you won!!!

Me: I'm not sure what I'm going to do with two books, though. Anyway, I actually have a question for you! Who's Luke W? :-P

Saphnie: Luke Wilbourne is a cutie pie and he's super awesome. (^-^) I actually met him at a party you unintentionally told me to go to after we talked about Reagan and jellybeans, so THANK YOU for that!

Me: Really? That's cool.

Saphnie: Ginger Jenny introduced me to Luke at her party. He wouldn't stop talking to me and would do anything to sit next to me. Not saying it was bad, just obvious he liked me. Then he kept texting me afterward.

Me: And then he asked you out, I guess?

Saphnie: Luke was going to wait until the next time we hung out, but he "couldn't stand it any longer." He texted me while I was in Latin, but crazy Professor Gramen (who may be the reincarnation of Hitler or even Satan himself) has this all-seeing eye, so he always knows if you look at your phone, which meant I couldn't reply right away. Luke kept sending texts for the entire hour and basically asked if it was official. Of course I said yes!!!

Me: I have good news, too! My parents and I are going to visit my sister in Windhaven at the beginning of June. :-D

Saphnie: Awesome! We might see each other if you ever end up on Windhaven Beach. (>^o^)> <(^_^<)

Me: We have to see each other! And I've always thought that if I ever lived by a beach, I'd eventually get annoyed by it. The sun makes me sleepy, haha.

Saphnie: Spring and autumn are rather nice with the warm weather and gentle breezes and blooming flowers where there isn't any sand. The temps are better in July, but there are always ups and downs. In more literal terms, the grass is only greener if you take good care of it. It really depends on which part of the coast you live by. Not all beaches are fun and sunscreen.

Our conversation ended soon after. I went back to my inbox and re-read the note from Rudderless at Sea (Official), which asked for a shipping address. I then opened up QuickSearch, typed, "tallarico bay high school windhaven nc," and entered in that address, instead, along with special instructions.

I closed my eyes and thought of Saphnie, a stranger-turned-friend, and Sandy, a stranger-turned-girlfriend. Would it have been wrong of me to wish to exchange one for the other?

sixty-four days ago

On Saturday, Sandy invited me for a late lunch at a coffee house. Mom dropped me off outside, which was furnished with wooden tables and had a large sign reading CROSSED FLINTLOCKS. The interior was similar, save a couple of couches, signed posters of bands I didn't recognize (aside from Pulsar Skies), and teenagers either reading books on their tablets or messing around on their phones.

I sat next to Sandy at one of the tables. She had already received her raspberry iced tea and a salad. I ordered a chicken sandwich.

Our date mostly turned out to be her interviewing me.

"What's your favorite movie?" she asked.

"Uh... *The House on Haunted Hill* was pretty good."

"Oh, gross," she said in disgust. "That sounds like a horror flick. I don't like those. What makes you scared?"

"Ceiling fans, actually."

" ... "

" ... "

"Are you being serious?"

"I'm six-foot-three—those things are terrifying!"

"Because you're tall? Is anything else a downside of your height?"

"Finding the right pair of pants, but that's about it."

"What's been your greatest accomplishment so far?"

"Huh? I'm sixteen, I don't—"

"Just think about it."

"I can... bake a frozen pizza."

" ... "

Pastor Goldsmith called. While he and Sandy talked on and on, I had to wait for either their conversation to end or for my mom to pick me up—whichever came first. Sandy was even talking about how our date was going *while we were on the date*.

She eventually hung up, and then it was back to the questioning.

"Any idea on where you want to go for college?" she asked. I was a sophomore in high school, so I didn't have any plans just yet.

"The Farmer's University of Central Kansas," I told her, getting tired of whatever this was that we were doing.

"You want to be a, um, farmer?"

"It's a Christian school, too," I added for fun.

"Oh!" Sandy instantly brightened up. "That's good!" She put her hands below the table, where I imagined she was flipping through various notecards with questions such as *How's the weather?* and *How's life?* written on the back. "So how many relationships have you been in besides me?"

"Including Lily? Two."

"Why do you have to put it like that?" She took another sip of her iced tea. "I didn't even know you both had gone out until last week. Speaking of which, how did you end up meeting her?"

"Lily and I have the same first-hour together. She saw me reading a book in there and came over to my desk to talk about it—"

"Which book?"

"*Rudderless at Sea*. Have you—?"

"By Amos Medlock?"

"Metres. Have you read it?"

"Yeah." She drew lazy circles with her fork. "It wasn't necessarily bad, it just didn't make sense to me."

"What didn't make sense?" I asked.

"The ending! Everything's contradictory, and nothing adds up. It was lackluster and had too many critical plot holes that ruined the experience."

"The narrative is like that so you can think about Edward's story and interpret it however you choose," I said, defending the novel that had aided in my friendships. "Like, the question of whether Edward committed suicide or—"

"That's stupid," she declared as she stabbed at her lettuce. "Who in their right mind would kill themselves? How selfish is that! Anyway, it all sounds like a really lame excuse to not have a concrete ending. Sure, it's interesting for a while, but then the symbols are overused so much that it loses all the meaning it's been struggling so hard to obtain, and it ended up falling flat because of it. It's fine some people enjoyed the story. I just wasn't one of them."

She finished her drink, then narrowed her eyes.

"That contest you won was for the book, wasn't it?" she asked. I nodded, unsure of what she meant by this. "Of course it was. That's when you hugged her."

Mom texted me then, saying she was around the corner at Taco Kick. I told this to Sandy, left a twenty-dollar bill on the table, got up, went behind her, and then kissed her on the cheek. I didn't want our date to end badly.

My mother had an insecure smile on her face when I opened the back passenger door.

"How'd it go?" she asked as I eased my way into the car.

"It went well," I lied, and she accepted it. I watched the setting sun as she drove home.

Since my date with Sandy had happened so late in the day, I didn't eat a proper dinner. Besides, I couldn't stop thinking about how she hadn't liked *Rudderless at Sea*. I was biased, sure, but I wasn't convinced she'd taken the time to try and figure the novel out.

I was going to text Saphnie about all this—maybe get her opinion—when I noticed she had texted me thirty minutes before.

Saphnie: I heard it, Jay.

Me: Heard what?

Saphnie: A couple of us had planned on going to the beach to-day, but it's been raining all week, on and off like the tide. We got there when it was sunny, but then the clouds came and the sky was white to match the waves. It started pouring and nobody wanted to get out of the car, but I did anyway. So I'm walking along Windhaven Beach by myself as all hell's letting loose and then BAM! I hear the ocean.

Me: The ocean?

Saphnie: I heard the ocean SIGH, Jay, on that beach in the mid-dle of a storm. Think about it. All the ocean ever does is brace itself and slam against the rocks over and over again. It's been doing that since the beginning of time when your Someone or Something created the gathering of the waters. How would you feel if you had to do the exact same thing over and over again?

Me: I imagine it would get boring after a while.

Saphnie: EXACTLY! The ocean's tired. It wants change. It's a caged bird longing for freedom, an escape, anything! Quod me nutrit me destruit. What nourishes me destroys me.

Me: So what does that mean?

Saphnie: Don't you get it? I was the only one who got to experi-ence it. That downpour was crafted SPECIFICALLY for me. Not my friends, not my parents, not Valerie, not you. I heard the ocean sigh. I did. It was my own private deluge.

Me: I'm not following, Saphnie…

I sat on the edge of my bed, waiting for her reply and trying to think of what it all could mean. But Saphnie didn't responded to that text, so I messaged her on CoffeeFolder, which I had attempted a few other times. But they always went unanswered, as she was never online. I then looked over her profile and realized its entirety was made up of images and posts by other people—never her own—and not once did she leave a comment.

But I had homework to do, and since I didn't understand her epiphany, I ignored it, and life continued.

sixty-three days ago

The next day, I got a phone call after lunch. I heard mostly crying.

Me: "Hello?"

Lily: "You have to do something about your... *girlfriend*."

Me: "What did Sandy—?"

Lily: "She confronted me at the end of Carl's sermon and said to leave you alone and to not talk to you anymore. Ethan told her she was being a controlling girlfriend, and she called him a... a 'stupid ginger,' and said that redheads are 'an endangered species, like the Indians and the polar bears,' and if Carl hadn't stepped in... I'm sorry. I didn't mean to cause any trouble between you and her—"

Me: "No, this is my fault. She saw us hugging in the hallway and asked me about it yesterday. I told her we had discussed *Rudderless*, and then she told me how she didn't like it, and... I shouldn't have gotten *you* into this."

Lily: "I thought you both might be good for each other, but some people don't change, I guess."

Me: "You're right in that she's being too possessive. I'm sorry this happened."

Lily: "If she tells her dad—"

Me: "Ethan won't be allowed back? I don't think you can deny... Oh, I see."

Lily: "Yeah." (Pause.) "Be careful with her, OK?"

Me: "Will do. And thanks for taking the time to call me."

Lily: "I'm sure you'd do the same. And before I forget: Carl's dad—
Carl asked us to stop calling him YMC—um, he died in the
hospital on Friday. It's sort of complicated. Anyway, Carl said
you're invited to the funeral service this Wednesday. It's during
school hours, though."

Me: "Don't you think it'd be awkward if I went? I mean, with what
happened last time?"

Lily: "Suit yourself. Bye."

She hung up, and right then, I got a text from Ethan.

Ethan: Dude our girlfriends totally had a fight this morning!!!

Me: I heard. What happened?

**Ethan: Sandy was getting all bitchy at Lily for idk what and so
then they started girl fighting with their words or whatever and
then she called me a dangerous animal. Me and Ty had to stop
them from clawing each other's eyes out and damn I wish Megan had brought some popcorn cos that was some pretty entertaining shit lol**

Me: Wow… I don't know what to say to that.

**Ethan: I thought Lily was gonna rip Sandy apart. Total BA! Not
to have a competition between girlfriends or anything**

Me: Good, 'cause I definitely would have lost.

Ethan: Yeah, no offense

Me: None taken.

Sandy's attitude wasn't cool, and I told her this on Monday. But
she only denied it, saying I should've been defending *her* and not Lily

and Ethan. Things were tense between us for a while after, but we still made the effort to see each other whenever it was convenient. Some days, I just wanted to forget our arguments and go back to the night I had drunkenly bumped into her.

I didn't attend the funeral for Carl's father, and like my thoughts, that was inexcusable.

fifty-six days ago

Sandy and I were due for a movie date a week after Lily's call. I had first offered to take her to see *Mary Had A Little Lamb*, but she didn't want to watch a horror movie, as it turned out Mary had the little lamb for dinner. I then suggested *Seventh in Line*, but she told me her dad didn't like her seeing fantasy movies, despite it being contemporary.

We eventually decided on an animated children's movie called *Polar Opposites* about a clumsy polar bear and the ruthless penguin out to get him. There were a couple of problems, however, and not with the film:

(1.) I got to the theater fifteen minutes before the previews started to get us some snacks, but inside the lobby were Sandy and two other young women. Sandy introduced the one on her right as Madeleine, her older sister, and the one on the left as her cousin. She had brought two of her family members with us on our date, and I seriously doubted they were there to merely watch the movie.

(2.) Not only was I expected to buy popcorn for Sandy and me to share, but now I had to pay to buy food *and* drinks for these other two (which I did because I wanted to leave them with a good impression of me to tell the pastor).

(3.) Lastly, when I had purchased all their stuff and followed them into the theater, first went in the cousin, then Sandy, then Maddie, and finally me. I wasn't even sitting next to Sandy—I was sitting next to her sister. Whether this was to prevent me from making out with Sandy or whatever, I didn't know. It wasn't like I was going to, anyway, with the slapstick comedy on-screen and all the parents and little kids surrounding us.

Other than these small setbacks, my time was well spent if I ignored the fact that I was supposedly on a date. I saw a surprisingly funny film I probably wouldn't have seen otherwise, I got a bucket of popcorn to myself, and as Saphnie had said, *Absence makes the heart grow fonder.*

When the movie was over, the four of us emerged from the darkness with smiles on our faces, even though I had every right to not be happy. Sandy and I had an awkward good-bye hug—with a glare from Maddie and the cousin—before she left in their car. I stayed behind, waiting for my mother.

I sat on a bench outside the theater and decided to count the cigarette butts in the grass to pass the time. There were eight total. I noticed all the spilled popcorn and how the birds hiding in the bushes would dart in and out to pick at some. I saw an older man wearing a fedora and a trench coat, as the sky was still cloudy from the recent rain. I saw a large mother and her children, who passed her phone back and forth and squealed as they did so. I saw two girls my age holding hands as they walked inside before one of them stopped to kiss the other's cheek. I wondered what had brought them all here, besides presumably wanting to see a movie. I wondered what their friends and family were like. I wondered who they talked to when they needed advice. Did they have their own equivalent to my relationship with Saphnie?

A silver coupé pulled up, and Nick got out from the passenger seat. He was wearing dark skinny jeans and a light jacket, which got caught in the door as he struggled to get off the curb.

He looked my way for a moment. I stared back. He raised his middle finger at me and walked toward the self-service kiosk. Mom arrived soon after.

May

forty-four days ago

The first week of May ended the stormy month of April. The grass was noticeably greener, the birds were out and singing, and there were only twenty-two days until school was out and summer began, at least as far as I was concerned.

Instead of preparing us for our final, Kukowski decided to tell us about the time in his life when he used to be a nurse. He always had the craziest of stories, which was probably because he was always in odd places doing odd things with the odd people of the world. It was clear he enjoyed this.

"Well, technically, I wasn't *permitted* to be a nurse," he told us, "but in the gorgeous state of Arizona, they don't give a damn. Anywafers, here I am, a fake medical expert with a full head of hair, and I'm rolling an older man—probably in his late forties—down the hallway to the surgery room. He's still awake and on a buttload of meds, staring up at the ceiling as I'm pushing him along, and he tells me, 'Nurse... Nurse, do you see it?' And I look up and say, 'See what?' and accidentally crash into a doctor, but he doesn't seem to notice. The patient, I mean. The doctor definitely noticed."

"Mr. Kukowski, what about the study guide for our—?"

"Oh. My. God. Sherman, for once in your lifetime, SHUT UP ABOUT THE GODDAMN FINAL!" The kid, Sherman—whom I recognized from the robotics team—lowered his hand. "Where was I?

Oh, yes! So anyway, he's still asking me, 'Do you see it, nurse?' and I'm, like, 'What am I supposed to be looking at?' And he tells me, 'The lights, nurse, the lights! There's a certain rhythm to 'em!' And before I know it, I'm rolling a loopy man in his late forties to his impending doom while he's humming some crap to the rhythm of the lights!"

We all laughed at this. Kukowski was happier telling us stories than teaching us Chemistry, which, in truth, I was fine with. We liked him too much to care, as warped as he was.

"Another time, I was wheeling this elderly woman," he continued, "strapped to a catheter—you all know what a catheter is, right? This won't be on your final, but it's a very uncomfortable tube that doctors shove up your urethra when you can't get up to urinate. The urine then travels from the tube into a bag, and from my experience, doctors seem to get off on that kind of stuff.

"So yeah, I'm pushing this patient from point A to point B, as I did so often in my years of nursing, and her eyes widen as she looks at me and says, 'My purse! We left my purse in the room!' I say, 'Ma'am, you didn't bring in a purse'—which was a lie because I had rifled through it just that morning, looking for gum—but then she says, 'No! My big, yellow purse! We must go back and retrieve it!' I'm confused, as you'd probably be, but then I remembered she was doped up, so I pull up her colostomy bag and say, 'Oh! You mean *this* purse?' You should've seen the look on her face—as happy as a clam, she was! So I give it to her, even though I know I'm not supposed to, and she's hugging and cradling and squeezing that baggie so hard, it *pops!*" He clapped his hands for effect. "That woman's piss is all over her face, and she's so mortified, she can't speak, and I'm laughing so hard, I can't clean her up!"

We were all in hysterics by this point.

"My sides were hurting so much, I could hardly move!" he told us. "But thank God I could, because I hightailed it outta that place and quit my job as a nurse right then and there, leaving the helpless woman behind—"

He stopped. Kukowski was glaring at two girls talking to one another near the back of the room.

"Yo, girl in pink and girl in blue," he said, waving his hands and trying to get their attention. "Hey! How many times do you have this ruggedly handsome, good looking of a man telling you a story? Huh? Have you *seen* the other teachers in this frickin' school? Some of you young women are saying, 'I will never date a prick as big as this.' Yes. Yes, you will. Because he'll look like me." There were a handful of laughs, and Kukowski turned to me. "Honestly, can you believe them, Murchison? Talking during *my* story? I'll never understand the deceptive beasts that they are—the female species.

"Did you all know," he went on, "when you're sixteen years old, you can legally quit high school with your parent's permission? By all means, bring the forms by, and I'll sign off for Chemistry. In fact, I'm going to recommend that to three young ladies in my next hour because the first thing I'm going to suggest to their folks during the inevitable email exchange asking why their grades are so low—because they copy their homework and do shit on my tests—is to *ground them from their damn phones!* Period. They don't need them! I mean, really, who wants to be in touch with you all? Or are y'all just playing Tap-Tap Whatever? My kids are at the age now to where they're ignoring my calls, so I'm constantly ringing them up just to bug 'em. Sometimes, I'll leave little messages, like, 'If you had answered, I would've taken you out to buy you steak, booze, and maybe hookers!' I don't say that to my daughter, though.

"But anyway, tell me, dear students, what the moral is behind both these stories?"

We thought about it for a moment. "Doing drugs is cool?" asked the girl in blue.

"Have you ever paid attention to a thing I've said?" Kukowski asked her, noticeably angry. "Some of you have treated Chemistry like this for three quarters, and soon, you'll get your grade and go, 'Huh. Maybe I ought to treat it differently? Nah, let's learn the hard way one more time! Yay!' You're barking puppy dogs, is what you all are, and you wouldn't make it in my kingdom. You'd be the moat people. In my kingdom, I would cut the livers out of your dogs and eat them in front of your children. I'd also use your female children's hair to wipe it off my face, and all my knights would all be women, 'cause they're heartless, anyway.

"Here's my advice: Whatever class you all decided to enroll in next year, please, take it seriously. You are no longer in the freshman I'm-gonna-color-in-an-alligator league, 'kay? Now, sometimes, we get motivated to do something, so it comes easier, and we listen better. When you're interested, you connect dots in your head. The real academic person—who was born without sheer brilliance—can take something they're not interested in and still do well. And what I'm talking about up here isn't even Chemistry!"

The class was silent. He took a deep, long breath.

"The lesson to be learned here is that *perspective is the key to everything.* I wouldn't have noticed that lights have a funky rhythm to 'em if it weren't for the tipsy man lying down, and I wouldn't have known that colostomy bags make such highly fashionable purses if it weren't for the abandoned woman and her delirium. Life's all about perspective, kiddos, and when your perspective breaks expectations, you'd be surprised at what you can discover."

Mrs. Beckham called me over to her desk while the rest of the class did group work and attempted to talk to each other in Spanish. She then reached into a drawer and took out her surprisingly-worn copy of *Rudderless at Sea.*

"It's a wonderful novel, don't you think?" she asked me. "My son and I spent hours discussing the book after I had finished reading it. Who was Mercer? What happened to Edward's daughter? Was Edward being punished?"

"Was he?" I asked. "I read the story and have my own opinions, but I've heard so many different theories."

"I have my own," she began. "When Edward returns to the camp, he finds the raft, the supplies, and the crew gone, correct? Furious with them for leaving him behind, he tosses both himself and Mercer's sea-shell into the waves—the ocean laying claim to the both of them. As with *Rudderless at Sea*, the real world also dissolves in water."

I thought about this for a moment, then asked, "But what about the Island? Is it real? Is it penalizing Edward for his stubbornness or for whatever happened between him and his wife and daughter? I can't imagine it would, but I'm not sure of anything, at this point."

She pondered my questions for a moment. "Could it be a metaphor? Absolutely. Metaphors are always present in the world outside of fiction, and it is important to identify these same symbols and figurative language we see each day. If the Island was trying to teach him a lesson, I personally think Edward failed to understand for what he was being punished. With that in mind, maybe he will have to live on the Island in a state of purgatory until he comes to terms with whatever demons he is unwilling to face—if you interpret it that way."

"When perspective breaks expectations," I noted. "Kukowski was talking about that today during his, um, lesson."

She laughed. "When I taught a literary seminar for high school students last year, one of our tasks was to come up with a short story revolving around life on a farm. We decided to pick a word relating to our topic and branch out from there. We were on the word 'tractor,' and the students each gave wonderful responses, but when I got to a girl who had been quiet throughout the exercise, she suggested 'potato chips.' The other children mocked her, saying, 'What on earth do potato chips have anything to do with tractors?' I was curious and asked her to expound on her approach to the activity. She told me she had visited her uncle's farm every summer until she was nine. While she rode with him on his tractor, he would always have the same, empty bag of potato chips on the floorboard. So when I said 'tractor,' potato chips came to mind.

"Was her answer wrong? It was her own interpretation, albeit an unexpected one. Your teacher was right: When our perspective breaks expectations, there are no limits to what can be accomplished." And as I turned to leave after thanking her, Mrs. Beckham smiled and said,

"Even if all someone ever reads is fanfiction, any form of writing is a beautiful thing, and we must not waste precious time trying to understand the intentions of the author. Rather, we should decide what the story means to us."

I was surprisingly free that night, despite finals coming up shortly. I used this time to my advantage and caught up on past episodes of *$tore Wars: Florida*. Laine was about to buy a seemingly-deserted thrift shop in Orlando when I got a text from Saphnie.

Saphnie: Hey, I'm back.

Me: What happened?? You totally disappeared on me!

Saphnie: I got grounded for going to that Pulsar Skies concert in Raleigh. My parents have been more protective of me since Valerie died.

Me: Oh. So how was it?

Saphnie: It was good! They played some of my favorites as well as their new single, The Sun Sets on Me Now. The band was taking payment in either cash or jars of bees, which I should've taken as a hint that something weird was going to happen. They released the bees in the middle of Demon Drink! It was both dangerous and breathtaking. Thankfully my knight in shining armor was there to protect me!

Me: How are you both, by the way?

Saphnie: We're great, thank you for asking! Luke was my first kiss. I was laying my head on his lap and he looked at me and I looked back at him and he leaned down and kissed me and I just

took it and was like, "Hey, this kissing thing is cool," and we kissed a lot.

Me: You're making me a little jealous. ;-P

Saphnie: Don't flirt! You've got a girlfriend! How are you and Miss Sandy?

I was going to tell her that Sandy and I were fine, but that wasn't true. So I told Saphnie everything that had happened since, from the Crossed Flintlocks Coffee House discussion to Sandy and Lily's drama at church and even our alleged date at the movie theater.

Saphnie: Rudderless certainly isn't for everyone. I would even say a lot of people might agree with her lack of satisfaction given the amount of contest submissions. As for Lily and the movie fiasco, you have a controlling girlfriend and friends who don't trust her. Hell, she doesn't trust YOU, Jay! You two should totes break up. That's my advice.

Me: I think I'm more likely to break up with her, but everyone, including my parents, is telling me to wait for her to break up with me.

Saphnie: Because of Pastor Daddy Goldfish right?

Me: Goldsmith, but yes, haha.

Saphnie: Love is a hungry drug. She doesn't sound healthy for you, but it's really your call. Our limits are what distinguish us from animals.

Me: I'll see what I can do.

Saphnie: Good for you! Anyway, I should be doing homework or studying. Sweet dreams!

Me: You, too! Good night!

In a little over a month, I'd be in Windhaven to see Elena. I wondered if Saphnie would be there on the beach with Luke. I wondered if I, too, would be honored with the apparent privilege of hearing the ocean sigh.

forty-three days ago

On Saturday afternoon, Lily, Ethan, Sandy, and I went to Mistletoe Park by Ethan's house. Sandy wasn't too happy with the idea of going, at first, but after some persuasion—and reminding her that *Lily had a boyfriend*—she was fine with it.

Ethan threw me a Frisbee, which I caught and tossed to Sandy. She caught it, and when she threw it to Lily, I could've sworn that Sandy was trying to throw it in a way that would have Lily running after it. But she caught the disc, only somewhat annoyed with Sandy's aim, and Lily threw it back to Ethan. I might've caught his throw, but my phone vibrated in my pocket then, and moving my hands toward the Serenade resulted in a Frisbee to the head.

"Jay, you OK?!" Ethan shouted. I put up a hand, signaling that I was fine. I tossed the disc to Sandy so I could check the text.

Saphnie: What word means "happy accident" or "sudden luck?"

Me: Serendipity?

"You playing, or what?" Lily asked from ten or so yards away.

Saphnie: Yes! Serendipity. Thank you very much!

Sandy walked up to me and pointed at my phone. "Who are you texting?" she asked.

"Nobody," I said, about to put it away, but Sandy grabbed my arm.

"She must be a pretty important 'nobody' to stop a game with your friends."

I laughed and tried to move my arm, but Sandy wouldn't let go. "Let me see it."

"What?" I asked. "Why? You don't trust me?"

"You don't trust *me?*" she countered.

I gave her my phone, and she started fiddling with it. "Why do you have a passcode?" she asked. "Nevermind. What is it?"

"Zero-five-one-seven," I told her.

"Does that spell out a name?"

"No," I answered while she typed it in, scrolling through my texts.

"Are you both gonna be a while?" Ethan hollered.

"Just a second!" Sandy shouted back. "So who's this 'Saphnie' person?"

"She's only a friend—"

"You're not cheating on me, are you, Jay?" she asked, and before I could respond: "Oh, my Lord. You *are* cheating on me! Who is she?!"

"I'm not cheating on you, San—!"

"I'm calling her—whoever she is—right now." I could hear the dialing of the phone, and before I could stop her, she said, "Hello? Hi, my name is Sandra Goldsmith, daughter of... What? No, Gold-*smith*. Not... I was just here with my boyfriend, and... See, you texted... Uh-huh... Well, how do you know him? ... Wait, who? ... *Really?*"

Sandy was laughing. Lily and Ethan eventually got bored of waiting and started throwing the Frisbee to each other.

"Yes, he's here," she continued. "I understand. Small world, right? Sorry about that." How Saphnie got Sandy to apologize for something, I didn't know. "OK, will do. Bye."

She ended the call and gave the phone back to me.

"What was that all about?" I asked.

"Turns out we dated the same Jason," she said, reminding me of Saphnie's initial text. "They went out their eighth grade year, but then she moved. He and I were dating when she sent you that text in December. We broke up in March."

141

"Oh, OK," I said, still confused. I returned my phone to my pocket. "What happened between you and Jason?"

"I don't know. I guess we were cherishing how things were in the beginning, and we sort of… drifted apart." She sighed. "Tell me I'm pretty." I did.

We went back to throwing the Frisbee.

thirty-seven days ago

"Before I'm done talking for today, we need to discuss the concept of dispersion," Kukowski said on Friday toward the end of his lecture. "Now, how many of you unfortunate beasts in here are allowed behind the wheel of a two-ton killing machine? Put your hands down. Follow up request: Do not drive on Saturday. I want to ride my motorcycle in peace, 'kay?

"Have y'all ever been on the road, almost at a dead stop in a traffic jam, crawl about a hundred yards, and then you speed back up like it's nobody's business? This actually happened to me while I was on the expressway this morning, going about eighty, flippin' people off, and drinking beer on my bike. There's three violations for ya.

"Let's imagine an Okie mother on the road: She's drivin' all over the place in her Privateer with a tribe of children in the back, all of which are yellin' and screamin' and one just poopied his diaper *real bad*, and she's chawin' tobacco in her lips, spittin' in a spit cup. You females in here—'I can't wait to have a child!'—you're crazy. Get another dog, and let it bark, instead! At least you can take the pup out back when you're tired of it and probably not get in too much trouble. DHS knows about you, so you can't lock those babies in a closet. But anyway, her phone rings—one of those TSC types—and this isn't one of those fancy SUVs that picks it up for you. So what does she do? Taps her brakes. Why? 'Cause she's a woman, and women are terrible drivers, but they can't help that." He paused. "No one's mad yet? I think I've properly educated *and* offended you all today. Anyone not feeling either of the two?"

The two girls in the back both looked at each other before raising their hands. Kukowski shrugged.

"As I was saying," he continued, "because the road is crowded, that mom taps her brakes for one reason or another and causes the next four cars behind her to slow down, then the next sixteen, and before you know it, no one's moving. But if the road isn't crowded—say there's six people on the road—and that one person puts on her brakes, what do we do? We go around and carry on. So the more crowded it is, the greater the effect. That's what dispersion force is. That's what dispersion force is. If I say it twice, that means you should probably write it down. And the more electrons, the greater the dispersion effect. Any questions?" He ignored Sherman's hand. "No? Good. *Do not hit a man riding his green motorcycle this weekend!* 'Kay, I'm done talking to you."

Chairs started scooting as people began talking and pulling out their phones. I felt a tap on my shoulder and turned to see Lily, who pointed to Kukowski's desk. I didn't know why we were walking over to him, but whatever it was would have to wait, as Sherman was busy negotiating his grade with Kukowski.

"But I can't have a B in Chemistry!" Sherman told him. "I'm an all-A student!"

"Obviously not," was Kukowski's response to this. He then laughed at his own cruelty.

"I wasn't here the day we took that quiz because I was at a robotics competition. That's an excused absence! Instead of a zero, you could've maybe given me a fifty percent or—!"

"I'm not some mainstream teeny-bopper, but I'm seriously LOL-ing!" Kukowski said as he laughed. "You can't stand by your popped tire and wish it was only half-popped, or sit by your dead dog and wish it was only half-dead. That's how everyone and their mother was taught, so the world must've forgotten to inform you."

"But—!"

"You're a mammal, for Pete's sake! Mammals are supposed to explore their surroundings! I got one B in college, and that was my ex-wife, so don't bitch to me about Chemistry."

"What about, 'Peace on Earth and goodwill to mankind'?" Sherman asked.

"Yeah, I have no idea what the crap you're talking about," Kukowski admitted. "'Now begone!' said the sweet baby Jesús in response to the drummer boy. 'I have kings to see!'"

Sherman left, clearly upset.

"There's always a broom you could be pushing!" Kukowski shouted to him before turning to us. "If that boy keeps running around like a yard ape, he's bound to hurt himself. Either that, or I'll do it for him." He laughed again. "How can I help you both?"

Lily smiled and put an arm around my shoulder. I tensed up a bit.

"Weren't you going to tell Jay about *you know what?*" she asked him.

"Oh, yes!" he exclaimed. "The 'springtime flowers,' or whatever silly code you use!" He took out of his desk the same orange flyer that Mrs. Beckham had given me two months before. "In order for someone to run for any StuCo position, they need to have a teacher's backing. Luckily, Beckham and I think you'd be a great candidate to run against Behr, as it seems he's the only one running, once again." He considered this. "Well, Sherman's trying, but I don't think any teacher's going to support him."

"Why would I run for class president?" I asked them both. "No one knows who I am, and I don't know a thing about Student Council."

"You could use that to your advantage," Kukowski suggested. "Student Council doesn't mean too much—all it really does is look good on college applications. We can petition for a garden or a prom or better air conditioning in this frickin' building, but unless the parents and the administration vote for it, there's nothing StuCo can really do. We don't touch that money."

"Then why does Nick care so much about being class president?"

"He likes the feeling of having power," Lily said. "That's why he's captain of the Speech and Debate team."

"Exactly," Kukowski continued. "I, as a teacher, have caught on to who Behr is: a manipulative, power-hungry, brown-nosed slime ball. You, on the other hand, are a nobody. Not a loser, just someone who's gone by unnoticed these past two years. You're about as clean of a slate as it gets! You're an everyman, a representative, the face of the students! They'll see your name on the posters for class president, and they're going to ask, 'Who the fuck is Jay Murchison?' And that allows you to be *whoever the fuck you want*."

I thought about this. "But I like who I am."

"So be you!" Kukowski cried out. "Be Jay Murchison! You're intelligent, funny, and though you confused gold and silver on your polyatomic ion test—something a woman would never do, I might add—you can win this election. *You can be Jay Murchison*, president of next year's junior class!"

I remembered what Ethan had said about people labeling me as the Suicide Kid. Perhaps this would change their outlook on me.

"Huh. All right, I guess I'm convinced."

"Great!" He handed me the form. "Give it to me filled out by the end of the day. The election's next Thursday, so you should make some posters this weekend to hang up on Monday." He looked to Lily. "Carswell can help you with that, I'm sure."

She nodded. "I'm the queen of arts and crafts."

"And these are troubling times in the kingdom, for sure," Kukowski told us, then spun in his chair to face me directly. "But anyway, the effect is greater the more crowded it is, right? If you can kick Behr's campaign right in its ass, then that'll definitely be a force worth reckoning with."

Ethan was excited about me running in the election—more so than Lily, even. When I got home to video chat with them on CoffeeFolder, I saw on my homepage:

Saphnie Kane-Tachibana went from being "in a relationship" to "single."

145

I put took out my phone to text her, forgetting the video chat.

Me: I saw you and Luke broke up. Mind if I ask why?

Saphnie: He says he doesn't have enough time for me, which is bullshit since I've run into him like 50 times or so this week. I'm exaggerating, but whatever.

Me: He sounds like a jerk. Did you, for lack of a better way of phrasing it, "like-like" him?

Saphnie: Yeah, I "like-liked" him. I still kind of do, even if he did lie to me about everything. (o_o) It's okay. I could probably do better. I guess in real life the boys don't come running back, climb up to your window in the middle of the night, and sneak you a kiss. They take off and never speak to you again.

Me: Well, I don't think that's particularly fair. Something similar happened to me with a girl about two years ago. Sure, you could assign gender roles to this, but I think it's the unrealistic expectations we have of the other's capabilities. Maybe that's why we're so surprised when it finally does happen. When they finally leave, I mean.

Saphnie: What happens when the wrong people care?

Me: Maybe you need to reevaluate your priorities?

Saphnie: Maybe.

Me: Did something happen?

Saphnie: Luke never had the energy for me and stopped sending cute messages. I think I gave him a cold, but if he's mad at me for that I'd be like, "You kissed ME. Get over it." His adorableness is why I forgave him for being an asshole.

Me: Did you both break up after that?

Saphnie: Yes. He did it. I was crying. A lot of people wanted to hurt him and they were blowing up my phone with messages like "ARE YOU OKAY?!?!?!??!?" which made me feel a bit better, but I hardly told anyone because I didn't want to give him crap. I was okay, but then he texted me saying he was so incredibly sorry, and that kind of made me think, "Hey, he still likes me!" and gave me hope even though I knew it would be stupid to go back to him. "Hold out for summer," they say. Hold out for summer. I think I'm going to go lie down. Have a good night, Jay.

Me: Same to you. And sorry for Sandy's behavior last Saturday.

Saphnie: You can't judge a movie by its poster, just the marketing team. It's fine. Bye.

thirty-six days ago

Lily, Ethan, and Sandy all showed up at my house around two o'clock the next day. It was a clear-sky Saturday, perfect for throwing a Frisbee in the park, but we were all tasked with trying to get people to vote for me, which would not be an easy feat.

Dad was out running errands, so it was Mom who opened the door to greet my friends. She smiled at Ethan and Sandy, but frowned when she finally met Lily, who didn't seem to mind.

"Jay," Ethan said, looking around. "Your house is a *mansion*, man!"

"It's very nice," Sandy noted.

"Well, thank you both!" Mom said, blushing slightly. "If Arminster was a coastal city, there would be no way we could afford it. The house was fairly cheap compared to other areas, considering no one wants to buy a home in Oklahoma. Anyway, you all run upstairs and go, um, do whatever it is you're here for. I'll go get some snacks." She marveled at me. "This is the first time he's had anyone over in ages!"

147

Lily and Ethan both started to laugh. All I could do was give Mom a stern look before she smiled and headed off.

"Did I ever tell you that your mom added me as a friend on Coffee-Folder?" Lily asked me.

"No way," I said. "Tell me you didn't accept!"

"I felt obligated!" She laughed again, and Ethan and I joined her.

Upstairs, the four of us gathered in the second living room. We surrounded ourselves with a bunch of different-colored construction paper and the markers Lily had brought in a storage tub, which had to be hauled in the bed of Ethan's pickup. After Mom brought up a plate of cookies—and I almost left the room due to sheer embarrassment—Lily stood up, and the meeting began.

"All campaigning parties need a slogan," she told us. "What's Jay's going to be?"

"I sway Jay?" Sandy suggested. "Like, 'I like Ike' for Eisenhower?"

"Don't be a Behr and vote for... Murchison?" Ethan tried, leaning back against an ottoman.

"I like bears," Sandy replied.

Ethan frowned. "Not this one."

"Vote Jay Murchison for junior class president?" I added in an attempt to contribute.

"Too simplistic," Lily said.

"Who the fuck is Jay Murchison?" Ethan said with his mouth full.

"Swear," Sandy pointed out as Lily kicked him hard with the point of her shoe, causing him to spit out bits of cookie onto Sandy's lap.

"What?!" he exclaimed while Sandy cringed and tried to scoop the pieces with a napkin. "They're going to be asking that!"

"That could work, though," I said. "Well, change it to 'Who the *eff* is Jay Murchison.' People don't really know who I am, and maybe this could emphasize that I'm not in it for the wrong reasons—that I'm not Nick or anybody."

Lily considered this. "That's actually not bad."

"Great," Ethan said. "Y'all start working on the posters, and I'll go to the bathroom to release myself."

"You mean, 'relieve'?" Sandy hoped.

"Different strokes for different folks," he said with a grin, and we left it at that.

Lily and Sandy had already printed out a dozen or so decent pictures of me to glue onto the construction paper by the time Ethan had returned. He and I started cutting out the images while the girls wrote WHO THE EFF IS JAY MURCHISON? on the posters in their neat, legible handwriting.

"The slogan or whatever should be, 'Flush the Shit out of Hennigan High,' instead," Ethan said.

"Swear," Sandy noted.

"I don't get it," Lily said. I was just as confused.

"Next to Jay's bathroom is a pillow that says, 'Life Begins with a Single Flush,'" he explained. "Like, a fresh start. So the shit—"

"Swear."

"—as in Nick, gets flushed away by Jay, the newcomer. You flush the shit away."

"Swear."

"I *swear* to God, Sandy, this is the reason we don't invite you to anything," Ethan told her. She frowned and looked to me. I shrugged, which probably didn't help.

"While that's a, uh… *interesting* observation," Lily allowed, "I think we'll stick with the other one. Capisce?"

Sandy opened her mouth, then thought to herself. "Is that a bad word?" she asked us. "I was told not to say it when I was little."

"I thought it was a pizza topping," Ethan said. I laughed at them, bickering over the little things. I was happy to be a part of it.

I got a text from Saphnie half an hour later, but I ignored it. Despite my infatuation with her, I was busy having fun and—to my mistake— figured she could wait another day.

thirty-four days ago

"—but I don't know how to make Mexican food!" Ethan said while Lily, Sandy, he, and I were hanging posters by the second-floor stairwell of Hennigan High. We were discussing Mrs. Beckham's Food Day assignment, for which each of her students needed to prepare a dish that her classes would sample on Thursday, which also happened to be the day of the elections. It was going to be an eventful week.

"Mexico isn't the only Spanish-speaking country, babe," Lily said as she taped a poster farther down the hall.

"Yeah," Sandy added. "There's Venezuela, the Dominican Republic, Costa Rica—"

"Costa Rica?" Ethan asked. "I'm no expert, but I don't think that's a Mexican city."

I was going to say something until I saw another poster about four times the size of mine: a large, high-quality picture of Nick hugging a big, black hound in a forested area. The caption stated: NICK BEHR WILL MAKE H.H.S. THE DOGGONE BEST IT CAN BE.

"Thought that dumbass was afraid of dogs," Ethan noted, and while Sandy pointed out his swear, I took another look at the photograph. It did look strange, and if it weren't for the smiles on both their faces, I would have thought Nick was putting the dog in a headlock. Its collar read: ANDY JACK.

"In the background..." Sandy started. "Are those... *socks* nailed to a tree?"

"Speak of the devil," Lily said. I followed her eyes to the actual Nick Behr, who was passing out honest-to-God buttons to anyone within arm's length. They were designed in a similar fashion to his poster— dog bones and canine colloquialisms alike.

"Hello, Jay," he said to me, then to the rest: "Lily. Ethan. Sandy."

"My daddy doesn't want you near me," Sandy said to him.

"Yes, I remember," he replied, then stage-whispered to me, "Some days it's like common sense isn't so common anymore!"

"What do you want, Nick?" Lily asked him, her hands on her hips, subsequently creasing my posters.

"I should be asking you that, as it appears we're no longer on speaking terms." He looked to me again. "She's so amusing."

"You know what you did, perv."

"Ah, but it was curiosity that did you all in, not I."

Ethan stepped forward. "Maybe we should let it do some more."

"Oh, I'm *so* scared." He laughed, then turned to me for the third time. "Been there, done that, and got the t-shirt that burned in the house fire, am I right? Even so, I suggest you be careful with this one, Jay. You guys can be the best of friends, but if you so much as forget to bless him after a sneeze…" Nick paused for dramatic effect while he slowly smiled without showing his teeth. "Well, let's just say you might as well have made out with his girlfriend."

Ethan looked at first to me, then Lily. "What's he talking about?"

"I dunno," she said so calmly I almost believed her myself.

Nick handed me a flash drive. I took it with uncertainty.

"Drop out of the election," he said to me. "This isn't your burden to bear."

And with that, he turned around and walked off. Sandy watched him with unease. "What a creep," she said, and that was one thing we could agree on.

Lily agreed to help Ethan and me prepare some rice and chicken (or *arroz con pollo*, as she called it) and *gallo pinto con natilla*—rice, beans, and sour cream—for us to bring in for Mrs. Beckham's Food Day, respec-tively, so long as we got the ingredients ourselves.

I went to the school's library to print off a recipe. QuickSearch brought up several, so I printed them out and waited around. Curious, I took out Nick's flash drive and plugged it into the appropriate slot.

I waited, suspecting the old computer didn't recognize the device. I tried to move the mouse, but the screen was frozen, so I couldn't do anything. Then the screen turned black, and the tower started whirring loudly as if it was overheating.

A countdown started in the upper left-hand corner, beginning at three seconds, two seconds, one.

Nothing happened, and the computer shut itself down. Despite my best efforts, I couldn't boot it up again. I decided to leave the flash drive by the keyboard, as I had no use for it. I wondered, though, what Nick was trying to tell me. I wondered how much he really knew.

Food/Election Day

Ethan and I carried our individual dishes into Mrs. Beckham's room early Thursday morning. The week had gone well, so far, and some people had even stopped me in the hallways to say that they were going to vote for me.

"I couldn't believe it!" I told Ethan as we walked in. "Darian Burroughs—you know Darian Burroughs?"

"Do I?" he asked in a manner of answering. "She's public_vagina on SextMe."

"Wait, what?"

"Well, yeah." He shrugged. "Nothing's private when it comes to that girl!"

I shook my head. "Anyway, she told me that I have her vote, and we haven't talked since middle school! We're only friends on Coffee-Folder!"

"Jesus, Jay, calm down," Ethan said, laughing. "It looks like you're about to blow a gasket, what with all the excitement you have."

Our laughter came to a halt when we saw Mrs. Beckham talking to Nick by her desk. They seemed to be having a good time, which was no surprise, as Nick was friendly with all the teachers—except Kukowski, apparently.

She noticed our dishes, smiled, and urged us to her desk.

"How wonderful, Mr. Bradford!" she said to Ethan. "I thought you would fail to complete this assignment."

"Uh, thanks," he said as he handed her the plate of rice and chicken. "It's Ross con polos."

Nick grinned at Ethan's mispronunciation. *"Arroz con pollo?"* he suggested. "Judging by the smell coming off yours, Jay, I'm guessing… *gallo pinto?"*

"—*con natilla,*" I added.

"Of course," he said. "How silly of me." He turned to Mrs. Beckham. "Those need to go in the fridge, right?"

"Yes, though my mini one is full." She tossed him her set of keys, which he caught in his left hand. "Here. Take their dishes to the teacher's lounge, would you? I'm sure you know where that is—with you being the class president, after all." She smiled at me. "Though maybe not for long!"

We all laughed awkwardly as Nick took my bowl and Ethan's plate.

"Be sure not to spill the beans!" Mrs. Beckham called out to him as he opened the door.

Nick stopped and turned around. "Wh—what did you say?"

"The beans." She pointed to my bowl in his hands. "Don't spill them. *Gallo pinto es mi favorito.*"

Nick nodded, no longer worried with whatever he was concerned about.

Everyone was hungry during seventh period. Whenever they weren't talking about the elections in an hour, my fellow classmates were eating meats, soups, and desserts of all sorts. One kid had even brought cups of gelatin in the colors of the Mexican flag. As expected, there were also the typical bean burritos, tacos, and nachos for trying, but Mrs. Beckham ignored them (along with the purchased goods from Taco Kick, still wrapped in the bag—*"¡La Buena Loca!"* and everything).

Another unpopular food choice was Ethan's *arroz con pollo.*

"Try some!" Ethan urged me. "Lily helped me make it!"

"That looks like mold on the side."

"Nah, it's supposed to be like—oh, wait a minute." He took a piece for himself, then ate it. "Nope, it's all good! Just don't look at it."

"Why are your hands red?" I asked.

"What?" He glanced down at them. "Oh, the restroom was full, so I used the one on the third floor, which was a mistake, since the water's boiling hot while you're washing your hands." He laughed. "Today's just not my day."

I hesitantly scooped a spoonful of his meal off the plate and onto mine. We were the only ones to do so.

Me: So I ran for junior class president today.

Saphnie: This is news! It's good to get out of your comfort zone. How did it go?

All two-hundred and ninety-five sophomores of Hennigan High showed up in the school auditorium at three o'clock that afternoon. Lily and Ethan were sitting in the front row, saving a seat for Sandy. With all those eyes focused on the stage, I didn't know if I could present my speech, after all.

"How're you feeling?" Kukowski asked while we were behind the curtain.

"My stomach hurts," I told him.

"That's normal," he assured me. "You know what else comes with fame? Broads. Women. Girlies. Class president's a long way from any important stuff, but it usually can't hurt, right?"

"I beg your pardon?" Sandy asked. She was standing beside me and was obviously annoyed.

Kukowski snorted. "And you are?"

"Sandra Goldsmith. My father is the pastor of—"

"Yada-yada-yada, don't care." He grabbed my shoulders. "You can do this, kiddo. You can beat his ass all the way to—"

"Swear."

Kukowski turned his neck slowly to face Sandy. "Excuse me?"

"You swore," she told him. "Swearing is a sin."

He rolled his eyes. "I am at peace with the Lord and my surroundings, but thank you for your concern. Anyway, Jay, just remember to swallow so the spit doesn't build up in the back of your throat, don't be intimidated by him, don't piss—"

"Swear."

"—your pants, and don't be distracted by the song in your head." He clapped my back, picked up a microphone, and gave me a thumbs-up. "You got this! Break a leg and bust a nut!"

"Swear."

"JESUS-FUCKING-CHRIST, SANDY, WILL YOU SHUT THE FUCK UP?!" Kukowski yelled at her. But the mic was on, and the whole auditorium laughed while Sandy ran off to either cry or to pray.

Saphnie: Ha! What happened next?

Kukowski fixed his collar and walked out onto the stage, the whole audience clapping and cheering. He was a popular teacher, and I'm sure everyone was willing to pretend nothing had happened behind the scenes to retain his position as a faculty member.

"It's so nice to see such bright and chipper faces," he said once he had reached the podium. "You should've seen my second-hour when I gave them a pop quiz this morning—oof!" The crowd laughed with him. "I am not a happy human. I say, 'Gosh, I wanna strangle them,' but I only have two hands, and there are thirty of 'em! I swear, if one more kid pushes me over the edge, I'll go homicidal. I mean, what's a teacher to do?

"Anyway, for some reason, in America, we think if we moan, groan, whine, scream, and pout, we'll get our way eventually, right? If you did that in my house growing up, you'd get hit with a concrete highway divider. But I can't do that to you all. I think. I'll check my contract.

"Like I was saying," he continued, "this is the reason we have a class president: You complain to him or her so us teachers don't have to hear it. Sound good? Great. Yes, I see your hand, Sherman, but I'm skipping over you. Sorry. For those of you who don't take my class, that was a man's sorry, by the way, which signifies I didn't really mean it." He laughed. "I don't know why they thought it'd be a good idea to give me the microphone. As I tell my kids, when it affects my paycheck, I'll start to care about it.

"But I digress—"

Saphnie: You're kidding! (>_<)

"—and so, without further rambling, here's your current Student Council class president, Nick Behr, running against Jay Murchison, the new kid on the block!"

People clapped politely for Nick as he went onstage. He was wearing a suit with a bowtie striped with orange and black, which were the school colors. It might have looked like he was dressed for Halloween from an outsider's perspective, but Nick knew what he was doing. Nick knew all along.

"Good afternoon," he said into the mic. "My name is Nicholas Roland Behr—"

"GO PERMY-O!" someone shouted from the crowd. Everyone laughed, especially Lily, Ethan, and Sandy, who had joined them in the front.

"It's all natural, really," Nick assured, not taking any noticeable offense. "I understand you all might be wondering why I've gathered you here today. Well, folks, I'm going to talk to you about a great menace sweeping our school hallways—a threat that needs to be immediately addressed." He paused, then smiled. "Just kidding. We're here to talk about Jay Murchison."

Most everyone laughed at his joke, except for Sandy (who stuck her tongue out), Lily (who booed), and Ethan (who rushed to the trash can and threw up into it).

"Wow," Nick said about Ethan. "The poor guy couldn't stomach a joke." Nick was calm, cool, and collected, as I imagined a master debater such as himself should be.

"I would like to start off by stating that, contrary to popular belief, I did not put up the posters that said, and here I quote—" He shuffled through the papers on the podium. "—'Who the eff is Jay Murchison?' Those were not mine. I don't even know how that got approved, to be honest. Nevertheless, they do bring up an interesting point: Who the eff *is* Jay Murchison? Let's be serious here: How many of you all hang out with him on the weekends?"

Lily, Ethan, and Sandy raised their hands in the front row. They were laughed at.

"Uh-huh," Nick went on. "Three out of the... two-hundred and ninety-five of us. Another question: How many of you even knew who he was before this election started?"

I saw a number of raised hands across the auditorium. There weren't a lot of them, but it did make me feel a little better. Then again, it was probably the response Nick had anticipated.

"The point I'm trying to make is that, essentially, Jay Murchison is a nobody, and his posters practically poke fun at this. This isn't any new information, people, and I hope for his sake he gives a good speech today, because we, fellow students, have absolutely no idea what he plans to do for us as junior class president.

"On the other hand, you all have seen what I'm capable of these past two years I've served. Remember homecoming's spirit week? That was us in Student Council. Winter Formal with The Orpheus as the band? I *personally* requested them myself for that event. And all the fun you had during Freshman Orientation almost two years ago? We made sure this year's freshmen felt the same enjoyment as you all did— maybe even more!

"I have the experience to run Student Council, and almost anyone can tell you that. You all know who I am. So when you vote as you leave this auditorium, really take the time to ask yourselves, 'Who the eff *is* Jay Murchison?' Thank you."

Saphnie: Nick sounds like a total dork. What did you say?

157

I was nervous as I walked up to the podium with scattered clapping to encourage me. I wasn't dressed as formally for the occasion as Nick, and I lacked the confidence he clearly had. In all honesty, I had nothing.

"Hi… there," I said to them. "My name is Jay Murchison, and I'm running for junior class president of Student Council." I swallowed. "Um, yeah."

A few people laughed. It wasn't meant to be funny.

"Nick made some interesting points," I continued. "The most obvious, I guess, is who I am. I'm not a part of any team or club, I don't play a sport, and if we're being truthful up here, I'm pretty nervous talking to you all right now."

More laughter, more smiles.

"I suppose the question is why I'm running for StuCo class president. I don't care about the power, really, if there even is any. But I do notice things—though I can be a little slow to do so, I'll admit—and I've seen how people complain about the air conditioning, or that the water from the sink is too hot in the boy's restroom on the third floor, and the computers in the library being ancient. And although I didn't personally go, I heard from a couple of people, Nick, that the rock band you hired? Was terrible."

Everyone was laughing. I didn't mean to put Nick down, but that's how it came across. I felt bad, but I was happy the crowd was starting to like me. I was sweating, less from the uneasiness and more from the bright stage lights in my eyes. I felt dizzy—as if I would fall over at any second.

Someone moved at the far right of the auditorium. Ethan was try to tell me something, though I couldn't hear him.

"You all know what Nick's done for this school—and don't get me wrong, 'cause he's done a great job, for the most part. Sometimes change is good, though. Like Kukowski mentioned, I'm here to listen to you, not the other way around. I'm not about control or manipulation or whatever. This might sound like a dumb thing to say, but I just want everyone to be happy, that's all." I sighed. "I want to be happy."

Now Lily was trying to get my attention. I looked over to see Ethan holding up a sheet of paper with three words on it in her handwriting, large enough for me to read.

NICK

TAINTED

CHICKEN

I gulped, though I wished I hadn't, as my legs gave out then, and I stumbled to the middle of the stage. I clutched my stomach—a terrible pain inside it—and felt the rice and chicken rise from my body and out my mouth, spraying the carpeted floor and first row of the audience with orange chunks of puke.

I felt *awful.*

Saphnie: Are you okay???

Me: Yeah, I'm better now. Lightheaded, sure, but that's to come with food poisoning.

Saphnie: You really think this Nick guy did that?

Me: I'd be surprised if he didn't. He was in charge of putting it in the fridge, after all.

Saphnie: So he's a lobbyist working for himself? Some people have too much free time.

"While the janitors get Jay and the, uh, front cleaned up," Kukowski said a bit uneasily, "let's give it up for our final nominee, whom I found out was running not even five minutes ago: Darian Burroughs!"

The audience clapped and whistled for Darian as she strut onto the stage while I got helped up and walked outside. She was wearing a short skirt that revealed her long and toned legs. I only heard the beginning of her speech.

"Hey, everyone!" she said in her peppy voice. "All you need to know is that I'm Dirty D, I'm running for StuCo class president, and I'm going to make sure next year is the most funnest ever! Now let's make some noise!"

Everyone cheered as music blasted from the speakers. Lily, Ethan, and Sandy were waiting for me out in the hallway.

"I think I lost five pounds giving that speech," I told them.

"From the vomit or the sweat?" Lily asked.

"Probably both."

"I hear you," Ethan said. "I lost three from listening to Nick's!"

"But you can't afford to lose any weight!" Sandy said to me. "You're so skinny!"

"Hear the preacher's daughter preach," Ethan whispered. Lily elbowed him in the gut. "Oooh, oooh, why would you do that? Aaah. A little ill, here, remember? Besides, it's not like we had any choice. This is all Nick's doing. He was supposed to put my Ross con polo in the fridge, but he didn't, knowing we'd eat it. He probably thought Jay would barf *before* three o'clock."

"I wish I had," I admitted. "Would've saved me a ton of embarrassment. I went from being 'the Suicide Kid' to the guy who puked on stage. Not much of an improvement."

"We didn't mean the whole 'suicide' crap, Jay," Lily said. I could tell she was sincerely sorry.

"It's OK," I assured her. "Think I still have a chance of winning, though?"

"Definitely," Sandy affirmed. "Your speech was better by far. Well, until you threw up, of course. But other than that and your Chemistry teacher being a jerk, it was good."

"But that was the best part!" Ethan told her as he rubbed his sore side. Sandy just rolled her eyes.

"Darian running is a surprise," I noted. "She didn't put up any posters, did she?"

"She did not," Lily affirmed. "She's never mentioned an interest in StuCo or anything like it. Really, all she wants is an excuse to flaunt her legs." She sighed. "Figures."

"Something smells funny about this," Ethan said, "and it's not me or Jay." He sniffed his t-shirt. "It's not me, is it?"

Saphnie: That does sound strange. When do you find out the election results?

Me: If everything goes well, tomorrow.

Saphnie: Did you get a vote?

Me: Yes, haha.

Saphnie: Just curious! (^_~)

Me: Sorry about not responding to your text on Saturday. What did you want to talk about?

Saphnie: Luke, but I should go now. I hope you win! Bye.

Me: Same here! See ya!

thirty days ago

"Now, the last thing we want to discuss before your final is a little thing called entropy," Kukowski told us the next morning. "This is something every teenager is keenly aware of—it's called chaos."

"Chaos?" Sherman repeated.

"Disaster. Disorder. That kind of stuff," he continued. "All things tend toward entropy, and eventually, things that are organized will fall apart, 'kay? En-*thal*-py is part of what runs a chemical equation, and the second thing is the disaster of it, or entropy.

"See, I imagine there are a couple of neat freaks in here, and the rest of you are all slobs in your bedrooms, right? Clothes all over, boogers hanging off the edges—it's just disgusting. Mom and Dad, they come

161

in every now and again, yell at you about it, I'm guessing. They may have even given up by now! Sixteen years of telling you to pick up after yourself, and they're going, 'Man, I cannot wait 'til my kid moves out. Teenagers eat like locusts and make the water bill skyrocket!'

"You guys think I'm full of BS. I know you do, and sometimes I am, but this is what you're gonna do: Every day this week, go into your bedroom, draw the blinds, and then take your clothes off—your school clothes—and throw 'em into a corner so you can put your play clothes on.

"'Bout a week goes by. Mom and Dad are going to come up and blah blah blah and nag nag nag to you about it, 'kay? Your response: 'Hey, parental units, chill. Chemistry experiment.' Not once in those seven days did you strip your clothes off and throw them in the corner to have them land folded in a neat, little pile. This will prove the second law of thermodynamics: All things tend toward entropy. And this is in kilojoules, by the way, not *kill-a-Jews*, which is both culturally insensitive as it is grammatically incorrect, as my second-hour class so kindly pointed out."

He glanced over at the clock. It was almost 9:30.

"Son of a mother!" he yelled as he ran out the door. "Nobody talk! I have to announce who won the election!"

Everyone began chatting with one another as soon as he left. Sherman walked over to me.

"Hey, Jay," he started. "That was a great speech yesterday. Are you feeling any better?"

"Yeah," I told him. "Must have been something I—"

"You didn't insert Nick's flash drive into your laptop, did you?"

"Huh? Well, not mine, but the school's computer." I shrugged. "It shut itself down, but nothing really happened, other than that."

"You didn't see the video?"

"What video? And how do you know about—?"

"Nick paid me to design a virus for him," he admitted. "Something that would basically lock a computer after showing a short message— but I didn't know it was for you!"

The intercom beeped three times.

"It's OK," I told him. "Seems illegal, but really, no harm done."

He shook his head and returned to his seat as Kukowski's voice came over the speaker system.

"—thing on? Oh! Good. Wonderful. The Student Council presidential election results for next year's junior class are in. May I remind you that the senior class stuff will occur this afternoon in the auditorium at three o'clock, et cetera, et cetera."

It sounded like he was struggling to open an envelope when something suddenly beat against the mic, sending a piercing noise through the speakers.

"Crap, sorry about that," he said. "Drum roll, please! We had two votes for a Mr. Jake Palaver—oh, come on, kids, this isn't season fourteen of *House of Love!* Anyway, two votes for him; sixty-nine, heh, votes for Mr. Jay Murchison; seventy votes for Nick Behr; and one-oh-three votes for... *Darian Burroughs?!*" Someone muttered something to Kukowski. He continued with noticeably less passion in his voice. "I can't believe I'm saying this, but sophomores, please felicitate Darian, your StuCo class president. Yay and hooplah. God, I need a drink."

Me: Nick beat me by a single vote, but Darian won. I think Ethan's taking the news the worst.

Saphnie: No! You were so close! (;_;) I'm sure you would have made an awesome president, if it's any consolation.

Me: Haha, thanks. It was a good experience, I guess.

Saphnie: That's the spirit. I need to go take care of a few things for my birthday on Sunday, so I got to go. Take care!

Me: Have fun!

twenty-nine days ago

I got a text after dinner on Saturday. I had hoped it to be from Saphnie, but when it read DARIAN BURROUGHS, I was shocked.

Darian: Heyy, party at 8 to celebrate me as prez or whatevs. Forget the beer& bring RH.

Another party at Darian's? I wasn't too enthusiastic about the idea, but I wanted to check with Lily and Ethan before I made a decision. As per usual, they were on CoffeeFolder, though this time with Sandy. I joined in on their video chat.

"Hey, Jay!" Lily said. She was holding up two sets of clothes, and I could see miniskirts and tees lying on her bed in the background.

"You get the group text from Darian, too?" Ethan asked. I nodded, even though it had been sent to me individually.

"Well," Sandy began, "the general consensus is that we're all going, but I'm not so sure how I'm going to get out of the house."

"You don't have to go if it's too much trouble," Lily said sympathetically, although I knew she was faking it. "I'm only going so I can talk with Darian."

"About what?" Ethan asked.

"Rumors," she answered.

"Well, I could pick you up, Sandy," Ethan suggested, to Lily's annoyance. "You can even tell the pastor you're going to the movies with your youth group friends. Same to you, Jay."

"You want me to lie to my father?" Sandy asked, skeptical. "And from seven to *midnight?* I'm already kind of tired—"

"The weekends are too short for sleep!" Ethan told her, seemingly proud of this philosophy, though Carl might have argued against it.

"I suppose you could spend the night with me, afterward," Lily offered to Sandy. "I got my mom to let me go to the party, and I'm sure she wouldn't mind you staying over after."

"How nice of you," I observed. Lily laughed.

"Cool!" Sandy said, excited. "But what if he calls your mom, Lily?"

"Why would he call my mom 'Lily'?"

"No, I mean, what if he calls asking about where we're going?"

"Oh." She giggled. "A lot of people say we sound exactly alike. I've called the school at least eight times this year, saying I was too sick to come. I'll handle it."

After Ethan agreed to pick her up at 8:45, Sandy logged off.

"UGGGGGHH," Lily shouted. She first looked up at the ceiling, then started exercising her facial muscles. "No offense to you, Jay, but you have no idea the irk I feel from that girl."

"And why did I offer to pick her up?" Ethan asked. "Doesn't she cruise around in that flashy convertible? Anyway, I better change and get ready if I'm getting y'all. What's the weather like?"

"It's supposed to cool down tonight," I said, "but even for Oklahoma, it's been unusually warm this week."

"Sometimes I think I'll die in this heat," Lily told us. "I don't understand how Ty can play baseball in this weather. IT'S SO FRIGGIN' HOT OUT."

"I know how you feel," Ethan assured her. "George makes me go on these forced marches called 'walks' on the weekends with wild accusations of me not getting out much. It's only to bore me. He does a lot of stuff like that."

"Aww, baby, I feel you," Lily said. "My mom gave up on me going out. The only time I will ever leave the house is during the night, but she usually doesn't let me, so it's indoors I stay. I got lucky today."

He let out a soft groan. "I left my phone in the truck. Damn, I'm falling apart."

"It's too hot to think straight," she allowed.

"I tend not to think, so that's not much of a problem," he deadpanned. I enjoyed those two.

After an outrageous amount of time was devoted to convincing my congested mother the superhero movie *Live to Rise* was age appropriate,

I got her to agree to drive me to the movie theater by Ethan's house—despite her complaining of a headache—and have him take me home after he and I went to his house to play *Annihilation!* From the theater, I waited a few minutes before Ethan arrived at 8:30 in his pickup. I was wearing a blue-gray button-up, while he wore a t-shirt with text that read: WHALING IS ILLEGAL IN THE STATE OF OKLAHOMA???

We drove to Lily's house first, a little one-story close to Ethan's. Next to get was Sandy, who lived in one of Arminster's older neighborhoods, which consisted of two-story houses with white walls, tall columns, and big windows. I texted her that we were at her house, and she walked outside and climbed in. She was wearing her contacts again.

"OK," Sandy started as she shut the door. "Let's get this out of the way: No drinking. Got it?" We nodded. "Especially you, Ethan, since you're our designated driver."

"Yeah," Lily agreed. "Not after the last time…"

"We're, like, what, sixteen?" I said.

"Fine, fine, no drinking," Ethan agreed. "I'm gonna start driving now. Feel free to yell at me if I'm going a mile over the limit. Wouldn't want to get a ticket or nothing, considering it's already illegal for me to be driving more than one of you under my restricted license."

"Wait, *what?*" Sandy asked.

"Well, yeah," he went on. "You can't have more than one person in the car for the first six months of having a license, at least in this state. It's also complete bull, and almost nobody has gotten in trouble for it." He shook his head. "Sorry. I needed to vent."

"Can't ignore everything that bothers you," Lily pointed out. I contemplated this as he drove off.

"Easy, Ethan."

"Yeah, slow down before you hurt somebody!"

"Maybe I'd drive better if you'd all shut up for a goddamn minute!"

"Swear!"

"Sandy, we talked about this!"

"I think he's doing it on purpose."

"Not helping, Jay!"

"God, this is a nightmare."

"Seriously, who issued your license?!"

"Y'all are the reason I'm—!"

"IN THE ROAD!"

"OH SHI—!"

"WHAT THE HELL, ETHAN?!"

"Just a scratch, people! Just a scratch."

Ethan somehow got us into Greenland Hills a little after nine o'clock, passing my street and parking a little farther down Darian's. Her house was still as crowded of a mess as the last time, and I could have sworn the same two couples were making out on their respective sides of the front door.

"All right," Ethan said, attempting to sound cool as he turned off the engine. "On the count of three, we're going to open our doors and all get out at the same time. Agreed?"

"Why are we—?"

"I saw it in a movie," he answered. "Work with me, people. Everybody ready? On three. One. Two... Th—"

"Wait," I interrupted. "So do you mean 'on three' or 'the one after three'? Like, 'one, two, three, go,' or 'one, two, go'?"

He considered this. "We go on three. One. Two... Thr—"

"What's the point in counting to three when three is going to take longer than it should?" Sandy asked.

"WE'RE GOING ON THREE, OK?! ONE. TWO. THREE— GO GO GO GO!"

We opened the doors as per his request, though Sandy significantly after us. Ethan was annoyed at this, but Lily and I laughed with her.

"Think anyone noticed that?" he asked, looking around.

"Not as much as we notice you wear the same pair of jeans multiple days in a row," Lily pointed out. "All right. Let's party."

It looked as if a fog machine had been turned on when we walked inside—the smoke thick and hazy and smelling of skunk. I was going to ask about it, but Lily and Ethan went their separate ways, leaving Sandy and me by ourselves. We didn't have much to talk about, though, and after some time had passed, I noticed she was gone as well. I looked around for some water, but couldn't find any, instead settling for sipping on Red Harbinger while I quietly walked around Darian's large home, every now and then making meaningless conversation with random people whose names would become inaudible over the crowd.

It was while doing this when I noticed the place had not one, not two, but three living rooms on the first floor alone. I felt there was too much space for too few people in that house, yet this was a problem Darian had fixed with obvious success. In fact, within the first two hours of my time at the party, I came across proclaimed "Internet-famous" singer-songwriters, self-published authors, paid photographers, catalog models, commercial actors, content creators, website hackers, app developers, musical prodigies, rising entrepreneurs, and one girl who had gained a mass of 400,000 followers for posting hourly pictures of beaches she'd never been to and had no interest in ever visiting. They were all my age, and yet far more accomplished than I was—and being around them felt just as rewarding as it did inspiring.

I had been going through this socializing routine for a while when I felt a tug on one of my pant legs. Nick was on the ground and gripping the neck of a beer bottle in his left hand. His hair was long and flat. He looked tired.

"You straightened your hair," I observed.

"It is... what it is," he said simply.

"I liked your posters, by the way. It's too bad neither of us won." I offered him my hand, but he shooed it away with his drink.

"Who cares?" He slouched back, noticeably wasted. "I've seen… I've seen *diamonds* cut through harder bitches than Darian. She'll come 'round, eventually." He glanced past me. "Where's Lily? She here?"

"Somewhere," I said, then quickly added: "Why?"

"She's so…" He placed his empty bottle in a potted plant. "*Amusing.*" He looked up at me. "She still going out with Ethan?"

"What's that supposed to mean?" I asked him. Nick shook his head. He got up, narrowed his eyes, and wandered off, leaving me to stand awkwardly alone in the middle of the room.

I spotted Ty leaning against a wall and drinking from a plastic cup. He looked over at me and nodded.

"'Sup, Jay?" he asked as I approached him. "Haven't seen you since you stormed out of church."

I laughed nervously. I didn't feel like causing Nick any more trouble, despite all he had done, and decided to answer Ty's question, instead.

"Oh, nothing much," I said, trying to make conversation. "I hear you're into baseball." At his nod: "So how's, uh, Michael McGinnis?"

"You mean Michael Gillenwater?" he suggested, looking off somewhere in the distance.

"No, um… Michael… Mickey…"

"Mickey Mantle?"

"Yeah! How's he doing this season?"

"…"

"…"

"Mickey Mantle's been dead since 1995."

"Oh!" I exclaimed. "I'm so sorry! I—I didn't know!"

"You don't watch a whole lot of baseball, do you, Jay?" We both laughed, though me a bit too loud and for a little too long. I glanced around for something to add to the discussion.

"Everyone seems to be acting a bit crazy tonight, huh?"

"Well, duh," Ty said, taking another drink. "We're all high."

"What?" I asked. "Wait, *everyone?*"

"Yeah, dude. Dope, weed, pot, marijuana. That stuff."

"But you don't mean *everybody*, right? Like, you... you haven't—"

Ty laughed, cutting me off. "I don't know what Meg has you believing, man, but it's not that uncommon. Look around! Most of these guys are from your school, and I'd go as far as to say at least half the sophomore class there smokes weed—there's a reason they call it 'the Hennigan High!'"

I thought back to the night of my first party at Darian's with Lily, Ethan, and Sandy.

"Anyway," he went on, "it's not as bad as teachers and parents say it is, assuming you do it moderately." I'm sure he meant responsibly, but those were his choice of words. "This coming as a shock to you?"

"I never thought you guys did that stuff," I answered, following Ty as he took another cup from the kitchen countertop. "I mean... *Why?*"

"Dude, it's like having sex," he said in such a casual manner my body went stiff. "Why the fuck wouldn't you?"

"I... I don't know. I thought—"

He was laughing really hard. I felt like I was going to puke again as the voices got louder around me.

"—Reagan has her physical tomorrow. She said she'd pay me thirty bucks to piss for her—"

"—I need to post this selfie so people actually know I did something tonight, or else it's, like, I didn't even go—"

"—Yeah, we got to third base in the backseat before school started, but that's all I'm gonna say—"

"—No, you have to take *double* what the doctor prescribed if you want those pills to work, dumbass. Everybody knows that—"

"—This year won't be complete until there's some scandalous teen pregnancy. Oh, wait a minute—"

"—He's sending nudes, but not to his girlfriend. Those pics end up everywhere. I thought everybody knew. That's how I found out—"

I thought about the deceit, the gossip, how superficial it all was, but Ty's ceaseless laughter soon brought back my attention.

"The first time Lily had some was in the SUV back in March," he said. "Beginners get real paranoid. We had the windows up and the lights off, and she started freaking out and panicking. Stuff like, 'Omigosh, omigosh, my mom is gonna find out and call the cops, and I'll go to jail,' or some bullshit. Sex and stones and weed and bones, right? But then you start seeing everything as super funny. Like, Ethan and I would be watching TV, and something that normally wouldn't be entertaining, we'd find *hilarious!*"

I had no idea what he was talking about, but he continued, anyway.

"The feeling you get when you first wake up? That's what it feels like—the best damn feeling in the whole goddamned world. There's nothing like it. Sure, your throat gets real dry, and you get hardcore munchies—like when Ethan practically cleared out my fridge this one time at the lake—but it's really not that bad. There's no hurling on carpets, too, so that's a plus."

He stopped momentarily, sensing my worry.

"Hey, I'm not trying to peer pressure you into this. I'm not like that. But if you ever want to try it—"

"No," I told him. "No, I don't think I... I don't want to—right now, I mean. I—"

"I get it. Lily gave me one helluva phone call when she found out." He smirked. "Now we're toking together every weekend. Sure, we're high as kites with our pipes, but what you have to understand is that pot takes the stress away for a while and makes life so... enjoyable. It relaxes you. It's a whole new perception."

I felt dejected, hanging out with people my mother would have labeled as bad influences, drinking when I knew I shouldn't, and breaking every rule and going against all my beliefs in order to be with the in-crowd—to be accepted.

"Hey, J-man, I gotta go," Ty told me. He finished his drink and crushed the plastic cup in his hand before tossing it elsewhere. "Think about it, all right? And don't tell Meg, 'cause that'd be bad. She's too pure. We're way past that, you know what I'm saying?"

He gave me a sly smile before disappearing into the crowd.

I turned around to go and find Sandy when I slammed into a guy and accidently spilled his cup of Red Harbinger all over his white V-neck. He was about my height and wore a white baseball cap with the green Dunmire emblem over his shaggy, dirty blond hair. On his left wrist was a large gold watch with a blue face. I recognized it as a Julian Morrissey collector's edition only because Meredith had discovered a similar one in the back of a store she'd won against Laine on an episode of *$tore Wars: Florida*.

"Look where you're going, asshole!" the guy yelled at me.

"Sorry," I said, slightly intimidated and feeling much shorter than I was. But before I could finish apologizing, my eyes glanced behind the stranger and toward a girl with long and straight black hair. She was wearing a backless dress and heels that made her almost as tall as the both of us.

"Courtney?" I asked the girl. She turned around.

"Jake?" she asked in a sharp, almost accusing tone. "What are you doing here?!"

"Jason?" Sandy asked from behind me. I was about to correct her when I realized she was referring to the guy I had bumped into.

"*Sandy?*" he asked, pointing a finger from me to her, then back to me again.

"And I'm Lily Cars-*well*," said, well, Lily, with Ethan following her as she stumbled into our little circle. "And I swear to *drunk* I'm not God!"

The stunning blonde known as Darian Burroughs walked up and put one arm each around Courtney and Jason.

"What's going on?" she asked them, and then to me: "Oh, I didn't know you were here, Jake."

"You invited me," I reminded her. "You sent me a text—"

"I don't have your number," she told me. "At least, I don't think I do. Have I added you as a partner on SextMe?" She gasped. "Are you gatsby5459?!"

"Hey, Darian!" Lily said, raising a cup to her. "Can I talk... we talk for a second? I heard the *craziest* things about you and—"

"Yeah, you've lost me," Jason said, who was just as bewildered as I was. "How do y'all know each other?"

Courtney and I were a couple toward the end of middle school. We had both been in the same classes—with Darian—though we had only started dating in April of eighth grade, when popularity and social skills didn't matter as much. She was my first girlfriend, my first kiss, and the cause of my first instance of emotional misery. At least, that's what I thought when she broke up with me over a phone call while I was on vacation. I never saw her again after that, as she chose to be a cheer-leader at Dunmire Preparatory School, rival of Hennigan. So seeing Courtney there that night—and the young woman she had become—left me in a state of awe.

"Jake and I dated in eighth grade," Courtney simplified it for him.

"You went out with this guy?" He laughed, but she didn't join him.

"And now I'm going out with 'this guy,' jerk," Sandy said, defend-ing me.

"Wait, you and Sandy hooked up?" Darian asked Jason. She mim-icked gagging while he nodded.

"Worst three months of my life," he answered. "Dumped her right before Spring Break started." Sandy looked down at her shoes.

"Let me get this straight," Darian continued. She pointed at me. "You went out with Courtney while we were in middle school. This year, you went out with Lily and are currently dating Sandy, who was with Jason before he went out with Courtney, which is now... right?"

"Isn't that, like, one step forward, two steps back?" Jason asked me regarding my relationships with Courtney, Lily, and Sandy. "But any-way," he said to Courtney, then pointed at me, "I still can't get over the fact that you went out with this scrawny, little French fry."

"I'm clearly not a French fry," I told him. "Besides, my name's—"

"Whatever, French," he went on. "I just hope you're prepared to deal with the sack of shit this one carries around." He gestured toward Sandy. "'Tell me I'm pretty! Tell me I'm pretty!' Jesus Christ."

I wanted to punch him. I was seriously going to punch his face with my fist. But Ethan grabbed my shoulder, and when he saw me tense up, whispered, "This jerkoff's not worth it, man." I quickly shrugged him away. I could still smell the weed.

"At least his penis isn't as small as his brain!" Sandy shouted at Jason.

"At least Courtney's not a 34A!" he countered.

"Wait, she saw your *what?!*" Courtney yelled, punching Jason hard in his arm, though he didn't even flinch. "And you—?!"

"It was only a shitty dare from a couple of the guys, babe," Jason said, but she put up her hands and left.

"ONLY A DARE?!" Sandy screamed. "YOU HAD YOUR HAND ON MY ASS FROM DECEMBER TO MARCH, AND YOU HAVE THE BALLS TO SAY IT WAS *ONLY A SHITTY DARE?!*"

"Swear," Lily—sitting up against the wall—struggled to pronounce, apparently having forgotten whatever she was going to talk to Darian about. "And *Jay* thinks you're a con-*trolling* girlfriend, but that's simply ridicu-*lousy.*"

"Now is really not the time," I muttered to her. Sandy gave me a sad and disappointed look.

"THANK YOU!" Jason shouted, then to Sandy: "At least Saphnie wasn't a little bitch like you and your dad!"

I punched him. Maybe it was the mentioning of Saphnie—as if he had any right to bring her up—or maybe it was calling Sandy a bitch. Perhaps I had needed to release my anger toward Nick and his actions. Whatever it was, I'd had enough, Courtney was fed up, Lily was drunk, and Ethan knew not to restrain me. Unlike with him, this punch had been intentional, and all he could do was stare and mumble, "Whoa."

"Don't talk about her that way!" I exclaimed as Jason grasped his face. "Don't talk about anybody like that! You think muscle and nice hair and clothes and a fancy watch make you better than us?! You think that gives you the right to treat people like they don't even matter?!"

"Jesus, Jay!" Ethan yelled, holding my arms back. Jason had fallen to the wooden floor. "I'm all for beating his ass, but he's bleeding, god-dammit!"

"GET OVER YOURSELF!" I screamed at Ethan, my whole body trembling. Blood dripped from Jason's nose and onto his fallen cap, right down the Dunmire emblem.

"Will you both shut the fuck up?!" Darian shouted at us.

That's when we heard the sirens.

"You called the cops?!" Ethan asked her, shaking his head in disgust.

"This is bad," she told him. "This is, like, really bad! Some neighbor must've complained. Daddy's going to *freak* when he gets back from his tournament!" She looked around. "I've got to get out of here."

"Wait," Ethan said to her. "Lily's been acting weird."

"It's whatever, Bradford," Darian said. "You're not the only guy with pics of me masturbating—and their girlfriends are just as pissed off." With that, she left him and re-joined the crowd.

People were running left and right to get out of the house, causing a commotion in all three living rooms. Lily and Sandy had disappeared, Courtney had already left, and Darian had fled her own home, leaving Ethan and me with Jason, who was covering his left eye.

"You... *pussy*," he groaned, but we ignored him.

"Dude, what the hell was that back there?!" Ethan asked me, then looked around. "Forget it. I'll go find Lily and Sandy, then we'll meet you by the Mother Trucker." Seeing the confusion on my face, he added: "That's what I named my pickup."

"Since I live down the street and past a couple of houses, I can—"

"That's right! Wait, then why did I have to get you at the theater?!"

"Just take them home before midnight!"

Ethan shook his head, smiling. "You really shake shit up, don't you, Murchison?" He looked down at Jason, then back at me. "Of course, guys who wear stuff on their wrists are only trying to cover up their tiny dicks." He laughed. "All right. *¡Lo siento!*"

"Huh?"

"'Good luck?' Mrs. Beckham says that before we take all our tests."

"What? No. That means, 'I'm sorry.'"

"..."

"..."

"Well, that makes more sense."

He left with the party as the sound of police cars got closer.

I turned to Jason on the floor. "You dated Saphnie, right?" I asked him, despite having little time.

He nodded, then winced. "She was really hot, man."

I kicked him hard in the side, then almost regretted it. My punch and the quantity of booze he had consumed were a bad combination for Jason, so I slowly helped him up. I wasn't insulting, arrogant, and muscular like Jason, but I wanted to get out of Darian's house just as much as he did.

I struggled to help him outside as he limped past the backyard gate and in the direction of Queen Elizabeth Lane. He then pointed to a large, black, customized truck that could have easily blended into the dark, lucky for him. We walked toward it, he unlocked the door, and I helped him inside.

"French," he began as he started up the engine.

"Jay," I told him with confidence.

"Whatever, asshole," he finished before speeding dangerously off into the night.

I heard the police vehicles driving into the neighborhood, so I instinctively ran for the Cunningham's house. Their energetic Yorkie was already yapping away, so I figured I was safe as I hopped their fence, ran across their yard, and jumped over into mine. Mr. Cunningham—in his bathrobe—shouted to a couple of teens: *"Put some pants on, you fuckers!"*

I leaned against my side of the fence and allowed myself a minute to breathe. It took me a while in the darkness to notice Courtney was crouching beside me.

I screamed. She threw a hand over my mouth, muffling the noise.

"Why are you—?!"

"Shhhhh!" She waved a finger in front of her mouth. "You'll wake up the whole neighborhood!"

"As if the sirens haven't already!" I pointed out. "What are you doing here?!"

"I figured this was a safe place to hide until things settled down," she told me. "The Murchisons are a respectable household, so I didn't think anyone would come looking over here."

I thought about this for a moment. "Where's your car?"

"My friend drove me to Darian's. I don't have a ride home." She noticed the Cunningham's barking dog. "They still have that thing? It never shuts up."

Courtney and I sat in silence for a while, looking not at each other, but toward the stars.

"I'm sorry," she said. "About before. I shouldn't have—"

"It's OK, Courts," I told her. "I know."

We continued to admire the yellows, pinks, greens, and blues in the sky. I turned my body to face her. She looked sad, as if she was nostalgic for a happier time. I wondered if we were thinking of the same thing.

"No one's called me that since middle school," she said, then sighed. "I think you were the last. God, the last place I wanted you to be at was one of Darian's parties. I always imagined you sitting at home or doing something better than... than *this*."

"That's what I did for a long time," I admitted. "I sat around. It was boring. I wanted to be with the popular people."

"And drink with losers like us?" she countered. I didn't answer. It wasn't the kind of question that needed a response.

I looked over to the willow, its branches and leaves moving back and forth with the pollen in the wind. I closed my eyes and thought of middle school, when two kids could simply look at each other, smile, and be the best of friends—and it really was that easy.

"Do you remember our first kiss?" I asked her.

"We were sitting underneath that tree—" She pointed. "—and listening to your music while your parents were in Hawaii. The song stopped, and you asked me to pick a new one." I could see her white teeth in her smile. "I found your sister's *Annihilation!* soundtrack and chose 'Kiss Her, Thunderbolt.' You got the hint, though the repeated line helped."

I reached into my pocket and took out my phone. It was 11:56, and while I could get inside my house, Courtney had no place to go.

"Tell you what," I said. "I have to be home in four minutes, since my mom's probably still up to make sure I actually get in at midnight."

She laughed. "Oh, yes. I remember Ms. Karen."

"Once she sees I'm fine and goes to bed, I'll open up the dog door, and you can stay here tonight. Sound good?"

Courtney looked as if she was about to say something, but she refrained from it, as she was out of options, and I had to get inside. While she stayed in the backyard, I went around, knocked twice, and waited on the porch until my mom opened the door.

"What's with all the cops in the neighborhood?" I asked her. "Is everything all right? I thought they were tornado sirens going off."

"Adrian's... kid... had—" Mom sneezed into her hands. "These allergies will be the death of me. Anyway, Adrian's kid had another one of her wild parties." She frowned. "Those kids should know nothing good ever happens after midnight. I'm just glad I called the police and put a stop to it! Now maybe we can all get some sleep."

"Well, that was, um, nice of you."

"Yes, it was!" She clasped her hands together. "It will be nicer when that dog quiets down. What's its name? Chico? Fido? Dildo?" Pause. "I think dildo's a bad word."

I snorted. My honest, outspoken mother.

"Anyway," she carried on, "how was the movie?"

"It was good. A lot of superheroes fighting bad guys... and stuff. Anyway, I'm going to bed. G'night."

"Sleep your finest," she said, turning off the lights as she went upstairs. I lingered in the foyer for a while, then pretended to get a glass of water from the kitchen. Courtney quietly slid aside the panel in front of the dog door, and I held it open while she crawled inside. It was hard not to watch as her body brushed against the tile.

We crept up the stairs and into my room. I locked the door behind us, not wanting my mom to open it to find my ex-girlfriend sleeping on my bed. Courtney stayed there while I was on the floor. We discussed how school was, who our friends were, stuff like that. It was a sleepover with lots of sexual tension, though we had been separated too long for that to happen.

So Courtney and I only talked. We talked about things that didn't matter then and still wouldn't the next day. Yet it was nice spending that time with her, as even if it all meant nothing, I felt it was somehow necessary for both of us.

twenty-eight days ago

I woke up to the sound of the shower across the hall, looked over at my bed, and then stood up when I saw that Courtney had disappeared. I quietly left my room, trying not to look too suspicious, and peeked downstairs to see a note from Mom on the dining room table. It said that she and Dad had left for the farmers market and would be back by eleven. It was 10:21.

I went back to my room and found Courtney on the edge of my bed. She had a towel wrapped around her head and was wearing one of my old t-shirts. Some might have believed this to be sexy—and I did—but I was thinking more practically and wanted to ask when I'd get my shirt back. Instead, I got her a banana from the fruit bowl, and we left.

The day was warm, and the sun was out, shining its rays on Courtney's hair as we walked around the neighborhood. She thanked me once we got to her friend's house. I told her it was no big deal. "You would have done the same for me," I said.

She smiled. The birds chirped. There was no hug and definitely no kiss. Not even a handshake. I didn't attempt to contact Courtney when I got home.

10:50. I went to the kitchen to make myself some breakfast, and in my peripheral vision, I noticed it was May 17th on the wall calendar.

Saphnie's birthday.

I was going to send her a text when I noticed I already had one waiting for me.

Sandy: Ethan got us to Lily's house. We're at church now, and I think she's a little hung-over… She keeps mentioning she needs to see Ty, but he's not here, and neither is Ethan. Just us girls. Hope you got home okay.

I didn't respond to Sandy right away, but instead redirected my attention to Saphnie and wished her a happy birthday while thanking her for being such a good friend to me. She didn't reply, and I suspected this was because she was busy with other texts. So I went on CoffeeFolder to post it on her page, but similar Sweet Sixteen! messages were coming in too quickly, and I didn't want my own underneath them. I suddenly got very frustrated with these people and had no desire to be a part of this supposed group of besties, deciding instead to patiently wait for her to respond to my text.

I thought of how similar Courtney and Saphnie were: both were admittedly popular (although Courtney wasn't when we had initially dated); both were having boy trouble; and both were beautiful, young women. And then their differences: I had dated Courtney, whereas I'd never gone out with Saphnie, who I frequently communicated with, whereas I hadn't heard from Courtney since the angry email I'd sent her. Curious to what I had actually written, I turned on my laptop, opened up my account, searched, and found a message sent to Courtney Brooks on June 14th, two years before.

Courts,

I was your friend before you opened your mouth and were labeled as popular for it, but apparently, I'm not good enough for you. Now all the jerks who called you a bitch are the people you hang out with, instead. What the hell is that about, anyway?! You can't be with me because I'm the same old Jake, whereas your new friends and clothes and haircut suddenly make you better than the one guy who defended you?!

You used to be really quiet, you know, and lots of people misinterpreted that as you being hateful. But I'm more forgiving, so I denied it, saying, "No, she isn't. You just have to get to know her." They would say, "How?! She never talks to anyone!" and I'd respond, "Exactly—you have to talk to her!" That's all it ever was, even now: me talking to you. You never talked to me. Then you gained your confidence and became the very person they made you out to be. I guess I've learned my lesson, but I don't think you care. I'm not sure you ever did.

Fine. Whatever. Good luck with your new popularity status. I hope it makes you happy.

Although I had meant everything I'd said, I regretted pressing send. But that was then. She had made her choices, and I guess I wasn't one of them.

I checked Saphnie's profile again after a dinner of salmon and fresh vegetables. I found the same scenario as before, but this time with people adding pictures by the minute, tagging their friends and Saphnie. Her party had been on a beach, from what I could tell, and although everyone in the pictures had blue lips from the cold, it still looked like they'd had a fun time.

There was one of Saphnie that really stood out to me: Her hair was much shorter, and she had her head turned toward the pale ocean waves. Her fingers—nails painted white—were around her left ear. The half of her smile I could see was wide. She looked happy.

For a cloudy day in North Carolina, Saphnie had a great tan and the curves to complement it. More important, though, was her perseverance, as she continued to smile wide, despite the circumstances. I thought back to the night when I had first kissed Sancy, and Saphnie had lost Valerie. How opposite those days were for both of us. How opposite our *lives* were. Yet we were still a part of each other's, and that made me smile, too.

twenty-four days ago

My sophomore finals week at Hennigan went by easily enough, as I did well on all my tests and ended the year with good grades to please my parents. Mrs. Beckham's final was unsurprisingly the hardest, while

Kukowski's was open book, and he was gone for most of it. Darian came to school wearing a diamond necklace, and it was announced that she had left Student Council, handing over the position of junior class president to Nick.

Like most afternoons of the school year, I rode the bus home the second-to-last day—a Thursday. It was a hot week, and everyone appeared to have given up their pants for shorts. This was unlike Nick, who walked onto the bus in tight jeans and took the seat next to me. His hair was still straight.

"I thought you drove that silver car," I said.

"Oh, but I can always make an exception for you, Jay." He laughed, and I looked away from him. "Now, now. Don't be a child. I won this popularity contest fair and square."

"Fair and…?" I couldn't believe what I was hearing. "You gave me food poisoning and tried to destroy my laptop!"

"So what if I forgot to put Ethan's crap in the refrigerator, paid a dork twenty bucks for a simple virus that didn't even work, and got Darian to run last minute and give up her title by bribing her with a fake necklace—as if she'll ever find out." He shrugged. "Chin up. People know who you are now, and you aren't a total loser like Ethan. Isn't that what you've always wanted?"

The driver pulled away from the school.

"Why do you have to be such a jerk?" I asked Nick. "What have I ever done to you?"

"I could write a whole damn book on all the shit you've made me go through," he said viciously, then calmed himself. "When I was nine or ten years old, I saw this little girl in my neighborhood crying on the curb. I rode my bike over to her, sat there, and asked what was wrong. She didn't want to talk about it, she said. Being the romantic I am, I told her that I would live with all her sadness for the rest of my life if she took that one day to be happy—"

"Yeah, I'm not following…"

"—and then she grinned up at me and ran off down the street. I never saw her again, and I've been unstable since." He sighed. "Lily and Ethan were my best friends before they were yours, you know. Then I messed up at their church and couldn't see them as often. I'm an atheist now, so I suppose that wasn't for nothing. It's all fool's gold, anyway.

"So Lily, Ethan, and I continued to hang out every now and again, though never with Megan and Ty. Then Lily and I started dating, and God, that was amazing. But do you know why she broke up with me?"

"Because you got boring?"

"She's so amusing," he stated. "We remained friendly, but Ethan didn't like me very much after that."

"Because you put your penis in his face."

"Is that what he told you?" Nick asked, frowning. "You're not as astute as I'd made you out to be. I know I'm not the most trustworthy person, but believe me when I say that Ethan had absolutely no reason to tell people I'm gay except to make Lily believe it. He's just as controlling as I am, if not more! Remember how he got you to take my phone for him and convinced you to break up with Lily? Now you're with Sandy, whom he told you not to break up with. Being tied to Miss Goldsmith, there's no way you can fall for Lily again, right? How convenient. Ever think of that? No, of course you didn't, but now you are. Does it feel like there are cold hands squeezing your heart? Or is it more like your stomach is endlessly dropping? I get that sometimes."

He continued on as I considered what he was saying. "Lily tells me one day at my pool party that she's starting to like Ethan—just casually mentions this about a week or two after she breaks up with me. So yes, I film her changing, and yeah, I keep the cup with her name written on it in permanent marker. It's still on my desk, actually. I even started wearing the same brand of deodorant as Ethan. I knew if she liked him, it would be a long time before I saw her again. When a girl gets a boyfriend, you see, she puts all her other guy friends on hold indefinitely. It's like they're no longer of major concern! You're lucky to have only known her while she's dating someone. We were inseparable. She would text me every morning when I woke up and tell me all about her day before she went to bed. Now? Not so much.

"And then you came along," he went on. "I admit I had tried other girls—like that one you saw me helping in December. I took her home and felt her up, but it wasn't the same as with Lily. I needed her back, so after she dumped Ethan, I snuck into their church on talent show night or whatever to ask her back. And do you know what happened just as I was about to approach her? I missed her by mere seconds. *You* showed up. *You* kissed her. *You* ruined my chances, *she* was singing to *me*, and I had to make you *pay*.

"I told Ethan this—oh, boy, did I tell him. He was furious with you! But then they got back together, and hey, I didn't think anything of the name 'Jay Murchison.' Well, that was until I saw you again at Ethan's party and you took my phone, violating my privacy. How did I retaliate? I broke into both your lockers and put the sticky feathers and pigeon shit inside. I was done with you. You were nothing to me—no longer a threat.

"I was mad only at that redneck in the beginning, but then you started meddling and decided to run for junior class president—the only thing besides Speech and Debate I had going for me. You cannot imagine how angry I was, Jay. I knew you couldn't possibly win, but the mere thought that you had entered just to spite me? People discover what they're truly made out of once they're pushed to their breaking point, you know, and *that* pushed me over the edge. Kind of like how Darian's SextMe arrangement with Ethan is starting to get to Lily, now that I think of it, and yet they're still dating! It's going to take a lot more to break those two up, it seems.

"So what did I do, you ask? I took my uncle's stupid farm dog—the one from the pictures—*and kicked the fucking shit out of it.* I mean, sure, I wanted to chop the damn thing's head off, but that wouldn't look realistic enough. My aunt actually believed it had been attacked by some coyote. Crazy, right?"

"You're insane," I said to him. "That's... that's horrible!"

"How do you think I felt when you humiliated me in front of all our peers on Election Day, huh? Hopefully the same as what you suffered through when you puked all over them. And you have the nerve to tell *me* what's horrible? I'm the only person in this goddamn school who knows what the fuck he's doing!"

The middle schoolers had gotten on the bus at some point during our conversation, and while they had been louder than the both of us, even they heard this. We were silent for a while, then Nick regained his composure.

"Women are a many strangled thing," he said with a frown. "You know that, right? They're merely feelings, Jay... very fickle feelings wrapped in a seductive layer of skin. But I am in love with that feeling—with her. She's so amusing. And there's the irony: We use women to get the anger out, but they're the direct source of all our problems! They promise the moon and deliver frustration. Some species we are. At least the black widow eats her husband! We've been left for dead, you and I."

The bus pulled into Greenland Hills.

"I'm sorry..." I said. "Sorry that I ever thought higher of you than the sick, messed-up person you truly are."

He pointed at me.

"You are selfish, Jay Murchison!" Nick yelled, swallowing hard. *"You take all that you have for granted, you privileged piece of shit! And when she breaks your heart, it'll hurt even worse, 'cause there was nothing there to begin with—!"*

"It's over between you and Lily," I told him. "Deal with it."

He sat there quietly as the bus came to a stop at the corner. Then he lowered his finger, stood up, and stepped into the aisle. I watched him sigh deeply before he looked into my eyes.

"All in perspective," Nick reminded me. "I hope the coffee tastes as sweet as it does bitter."

He walked off the bus and toward the silver coupé he had parked on the street. He didn't take his time as he started the car and drove off without looking back.

Nick and I were finished.

end of sophomore year

Friday was the final day of school. Kukowski spent our last hour of Chemistry passing out different flavored ice pops and answering any questions we had left to ask, no matter what the subject.

Sherman's hand was raised. Kukowski called on it.

"I have an inquiry," Sherman began. "Well, two actually. One is a statement—"

"Anyone else?" Kukowski asked, looking around.

"Wait!" he exclaimed. "What would happen if an unstoppable force met with an immovable object?"

Kukowski thought about this for a second.

"Let's put on our safety goggles and find out!" He grinned. "Nope, just kidding. Sherman, if that happened, it would become an annoyingly catchy song produced by the makers of *Rehab Runway* to accompany yet another hit reality show later on, and gravity would've failed us all while human life makes no sense—ending in a fiery death toward the sun. All stories end in death. Next!"

––––––––––

Mrs. Beckham was playing a movie when I walked into her seventh-hour for the last time. I sat down next to Ethan, as usual.

"It's been one crazy year, man," he said. "I'm just sorry you had to deal with all that Nick and Sandy drama."

"Yeah." I was sort of mad at him—the whole weed and Darian situation—and was keeping my distance. "I think I'm going to break up with her today after school."

"WHAT?!" He sat up straight. "You can't break up with San—!"

"No, stop," I said. "Just stop it. I've had enough of that. Everyone's saying I can't break up with her because they're all afraid of her dad, but I'm going do it, today at 3:50."

His eyes were wide. "Wow. That takes guts. I'm proud of you!"

"Coming from you, I doubt that means much." I paused. "Still, thanks."

"No problem," he said, clapping my back. "That's what friends are for! And speaking of which, you get my text the other day?"

"I don't think so." I took out my phone and looked through my messages. Nothing. "Why? Is Darian having an end-of-the-year party?"

"Nah. Her dad was furious after the last one. He had to leave his tennis match to answer questions for the cops. He took away her phone and everything, which sucks. She's been grounded for *life!*"

I laughed. "Hey, remember that guy you said who dated Sandy before I did? Baseball player? Do you remember what his name was?"

"Yeah. Jared, or someone."

"Jason?"

"Probably," Ethan allowed. "Wait, was that the guy you punched?!"

"That was him," I answered. "And speaking of the party and Darian, is there anything going on between you and her? I'm just wondering—"

"That's not funny," Ethan said, and I could tell he was being serious. "Don't kid around like that. What I'm doing isn't wrong. It's only cheating if it's physical, like George and—" He stopped himself. "Besides, it makes me appreciate Lily more! You know I would never cheat on her, and neither would she. All right?"

"What if it was Lily and Nick instead of you and Darian?"

"Man, fuck you."

"Mr. Murchison," Mrs. Beckham called. "Can I see you for a moment?"

Ethan went, "Oooooh," and I got up from my desk and walked over to her while he reached into my backpack, pulled out my yearbook, and then started to write in it.

"I have been thinking about *Rudderless at Sea*," she said, "and what happened to Edward's family. Did he and his wife divorce? Did the daughter die?"

"Did she?" I asked.

"No, actually. I believe it was the *wife* who died." She took off her glasses and rubbed the bridge of her nose. "Let me explain: When we read a novel with such questions left open for interpretation, we do not often think for the characters, but for ourselves. When my husband passed away a few years ago… I could not bear it. Arthur was a great man, and the cancer happened so fast. All I have left of him is my son, and it truly has been difficult living off a teacher's salary. Anyway, my point is that I, without question, always believed it was Edward's wife who had died, not the child, as I could not imagine how Edward would have managed were it his daughter. I suppose that must have been self-ish thinking on my behalf.

"Do I think Edward committed suicide? Yes. Do I think that was a cowardly decision? No, of course not, because I probably would have done the same. If I had not received all the support I had when Arthur died… I don't know where I would be as of now."

She got up, took a tissue, and blew her nose.

"I'm sorry if this embarrasses you," she said. "I simply presumed you would like to hear my thoughts."

"Oh, no, thank you," I said sincerely. "But do you… do you think it was a happy ending?"

"Does it really need be a happy versus sad ending? Is there not gray in this black and white? I felt satisfied as a reader, as Edward is now free from his Island of guilt, but it really depends on how you feel about death—for me, a momentary disadvantage. Hope is the *modus operandi* of our Western culture, after all. That said, remember that I have had access to the same text as you, and your opinions and beliefs are just as correct as mine."

The bell rang, so I thanked her again and allowed her to sign my yearbook, as Ethan had already left. Afterward, I went to my locker for the last time. I found only a pencil sharpener and a couple of pens waiting for me inside, as I had cleaned it the day before so I wouldn't have to carry a lot of stuff home. I put them in my backpack—deco-rated with Sandy's keychain—as my phone vibrated in my pocket. I entered in my passcode to see the text was from my mother.

Mom: Can you mix some carbaryl when you get home and spray the broccoli and Brussels sprouts? There are some worms on

them. I don't have time, but if it doesn't get done ASAP, we'll lose our broccoli!

I received another text soon after.

Mom: Sorry, not for you. Reminder that I'm picking you up today. I'm parked by the football field. Hope you had a good last day of school!

Me: OK. Save the broccoli!

I was in the science wing door when I saw Sandy.

"Hey," she said.

"Hey," I said back.

"We need to talk."

"I think we should—"

"No," she said, cutting me off. "I need to go first."

We turned around and took the long way together.

She sighed, deep and shaky. "I'm sorry if I came across as a tyrant. That isn't me. I'm also not the girl you met while we were both under the influence. I'm the girl in that note I gave you. I like romance, I like flowers, I like poems—and I like you, too. But I'm insecure, though I don't mean to be. I rushed when I should've slowed down, talked when I should've listened..."

She stopped, leaned against the lockers, and closed her eyes as people passed us.

"When my mom died," she started, "my dad didn't know how to handle it. He took it upon himself to protect Maddie and me because we're all he has left. Since then, people have been scared of him, and they don't know how to act around us. So please don't judge me because of my dad, and don't judge him, either. We're good people. I promise."

She started to cry. I tried to put hold her, but she pushed me away.

"No," she told me. "That's only going to make this harder."

"Make what harder?" I asked.

"We're moving," she said. "To Alabama. I didn't know how to tell you. Dad says it's because Arminster reminds him too much of Mom. He needs to get away, I think. We haven't told anyone yet. We leave in a few days."

I opened my arms, and she came in to hug me. I was significantly taller than Sandy, but this hug wasn't awkward like the rest. This hug was genuine, like I had always wanted it to be with her. It was a shame it had to come so late in our relationship.

"Back at Darian's—"

"I'm sorry," I said, and she looked up at me. "I'm sorry for not taking the time to ask you about these things. I just assumed, and I was wrong."

"Tell me I'm pretty?" she asked, her head heavy against my chest. I stroked her hair, wondering how things could have gone differently.

"You're beautiful," I told her.

"I don't feel beautiful," she admitted, "but thank you. For all our ups and downs, I think I'll miss you the most."

It was a warm day. Trashcans overflowed with binders and essays no longer relevant. Teenagers sped out of the student parking lot, blaring their horns in triumph. I spotted two kids in my grade high-five and shout, "JUNIORS!" before they hugged each other good-bye.

"I'm going to miss you, too."

I could say a lot of things, but… I'm just going to say thanks. I don't know what I would've done without you this semester. Have a safe summer. —Sandra "Sandy" Goldsmith

Chemistry got so much better when I met you. Come back to church! Ethan misses you! You're a great friend, Jay. Thank you for always listening. See you around, okay? Love, Lily Carswell @LilyliciousLilypop

69 VOTES!!! Come by and see me next year, kiddo. Kukowski

H.A.K.A.S., Murchison! Ethan @JustEthanBradford (Lily made it.)

Jakob. ¡Eres un estudiante muy inteligente! Sigas estudiando español. Que te diviertas durante las vacaciones. Sra. Beckham.

I smiled. Leave it to Ms. Beckham to sign my yearbook in Spanish.

"Hey, Mom," I said as we got closer to Greenland Hills. "Sandy and I broke up."

She slammed on the brake, causing me to hit my head against the passenger seat's headrest.

"WHAT?!" she shouted, craning her neck to look back at me. "Who broke up with her?! When was this?! What happened?! Is Pastor Goldsmith mad?!"

"Gaah." I rubbed my forehead, wincing. "They're moving."

"Oh," she said, literally clutching her chest. "Oh, *phew!* Well, that's one disaster avoided. Where are they heading?"

"Alabama," I answered, and she started driving again.

Mom was telling Dad the news while I went up to my room to check CoffeeFolder, though I managed to hear his own on the way up—that he was able to save the broccoli. I logged in and saw that Sandy had already been on: Jay Murchison went from being "in a relationship" to "single."

Was I happy with what had happened? Yes and no. I was glad Sandy had apologized for her behavior, but I felt as if I hadn't gotten proper closure, like Edward in *Rudderless*. She had fought with Lily, gotten worked up over Saphnie's texts, and allowed her family members to separate us on our dates and act as if that was completely natural. But then again, I had knowingly hugged my ex-girlfriend, avoided answering Sandy's questions regarding Saphnie, and criticized her based on other people's views and not my own. Was I no different? Did I even deserve closure?

I shut my laptop, put it on my desk, and fell back on my bed. I was only like this for a few seconds before a text came through.

Saphnie: No. You. Did. Not! \(^o^)/

Me: Did what? Break up with Sandy?

Saphnie: I'll ask about that in a minute, but I was called out of class today because a package with a SIGNED COPY of RUDDERLESS AT SEA arrived for ME! I didn't win any contest! Did you do this???

Me: Haha. That would be me! ;-D

Saphnie: THANK YOU, JAY!!!

Me: You're welcome!

Saphnie: This is crazy. You've never met me. Why would you do this? You could have given it to Lily!

Me: I guess I thought you'll enjoy it more. Besides, I already have a copy!

Saphnie: Oh, whatever. THANKYOUTHANKYOUTHANKYOU!!! NOSPACESFOREMPHASIS!!! AAAAAHHH! (^3^)

Me: Not a problem! :-D What does his signature look like?

Saphnie: Neat, although not very calligraphic. At least you can read it, unlike other people's signatures.

Me: Nice. So how was your last day?

Saphnie: We don't get out for another week. I'm studying for finals from now until then. No hanging out, no parties, nothing.

Me: Well, that sounds like a good plan!

Saphnie: Thanks! How was your end to tenth grade?

Me: It went well. A lot of movies, actually. Was your party fun? It looked like it, from the pictures that were posted!

Saphnie: Surprisingly yes! I got some good gifts, too. I was kind of wishing Luke would show up, but he didn't, not that I was expecting any better of him. (I know, I know. I should be more grateful. Thanks, Mom.)

Me: Any new developments with him?

Saphnie: He posted some stuff recently about how nobody cares about him and how no one would notice if he shot himself. He has a lot of guns at his house and a whole collection in his room, which is dumb since he never locks the window by his bed, so I texted him to see if he was okay. Then he sent me a text with a smiley face, which gave me more hope. I said, "People do care about you," and he said, "Not really," and I said, "I do," and he didn't reply.

Me: Sounds complicated.

Saphnie: We're all complicated, but that still doesn't explain why he throws his life away. He's really smart, but he does drugs, drinks, and had a "fuck buddy" or something. He told me he would change, but I saw him smoking with his friends yesterday. (Am I the only teen in Windhaven who doesn't smoke or drink?!) He cheated on a lot of his past girlfriends, but I know he didn't cheat on me. He told one of his friends he still loves me but doesn't have enough time at the moment and feels bad, which is dumb because he was with his friends all weekend and not at my birthday party. Anyway, you said you broke up with Sandy? How was that?

Me: I was going to, but then she told me about how her dad is protective of her because her mom died, and that Sandy and her sister are all he has left.

Saphnie: Her dad shouldn't define who she is. It sounds like she made up excuses. How nice of her. (~_~;)

Me: Well, not exactly, but that's kind of how it came across. She's also moving to Alabama, so that made things easier.

Saphnie: She's moving?! No! That's not how you both break up! Where is the catharsis??? Where is the emotional relief???

Me: Wait, what just happened? I'm confused.

Saphnie: You and Sandy dated for seventy days on the dot. I've heard you rant about how horrible she is for two-and-a-half months now. This was your opportunity to tell her! I know she's more than a portrait of loss and innocence, but you both needed to talk this through!

Me: We apologized, if that's what you mean.

Saphnie: So you said you're sorry for dating so suddenly and without any thought of the lasting consequences? She said she's sorry for acting in the way she imagines people are meant to act and for participating in relationships in the manner in which she understands they are meant to function?

Me: Hey, not all of that's true. Besides, aren't you always talking about how people need to think of others as more than what they appear to be?

Saphnie: We text a lot, Jay. I think I know you well enough by now. You were deprived of social connections for a long time, so you latch onto any that come your way to compensate. That's why you take every available opportunity to hook up with a girl and jump in so quickly, whether it be with Lily for six days and a brief session on Ethan's bed or with Sandy after you two drunkenly bumped into each other (and despite your friends specifically warning you she was bad news). Breaking up with her today was your moment to release these suppressed emotions while at the same time asking her why she believes as if she needs to fit a certain standard to feel validated. Guess what? You blew it! It's gone. You're right: think of people complexly, but don't ignore the facts in doing so. You could really do this with all your friends. Why is Ethan so brusque? What's important to Lily? Her motives are unclear and her impulses need to be addressed. A LOT needs to be addressed.

Me: Why are you analyzing people all of a sudden?? Yeah, we have our faults. I'm aware of that. Just last weekend, I found out Lily and Ethan smoke weed, and it was our other friend who told me. I think Ethan's sexting this other girl, too, and I don't know what I'm supposed to do about that, if anything. So yeah, I might not like everything about them. But they're my friends, and I try to accept them for who they are, just as they accept me.

Saphnie: I know, I know. This isn't Rudderless at Sea. I'm sorry. Good for Sandy. You, too. I just think you both were a thorn in each other's side. That's all. As for Ethan clearly cheating on Lily, remember what I said about you and her that Sunday when there was that fiasco at the church? "After a while it becomes less of a relationship and more of a courtesy running off fumes."

Me: Yes, that's familiar.

Saphnie: It's what my mom said about her and my dad. It sucks. I think they're working it out. Anyway, before I forget: thanks for the birthday wishes. I was busy, but it was nice seeing you were thinking of me.

Me: But of course! I'm just sorry I didn't give you a gift, haha.

Saphnie: You did! If that signed copy of Rudderless at Sea doesn't count, I don't know what does! Now we're even.

Me: Even? For what?

Saphnie: For me unintentionally giving you my number, silly!

Me: Oooh, right. Thank you for that, by the way!

Saphnie: The art of baking a frozen pizza can strengthen any bond! It's a gift that keeps on giving. <3

Me: You're never going to let me forget that, are you? :-P

Saphnie: Someday, eventually!

Me: I noticed you got a haircut. It's *much* shorter!

Saphnie: It was getting too long and I figured it was time. It was annoying, all that weight on my shoulders.

Me: It looks nice! :-)

Saphnie: I'm glad at least someone appreciates it, ha ha. Thank you. Good night! (^_^)oUUo(^_^)

Me: Good night!

The only person I hadn't gotten into any drama with throughout the whole second semester was Saphnie. I couldn't help wondering if that was because she and I had never met face-to-face. If we had, how would our friendship have changed? Does absence truly make the heart grow fonder?

There was a knock at the door, and Mom came into my room with three postcards in her hand. She showed them to me, saying how sweet and thoughtful Elena was for sending them. The one for Dad was a side-view photograph of a battleship with large turrets on the front and back. It was in the middle of a bay, and in the upper left-hand corner, it read, "USS *Goodwin*." Mom's postcard was of a pink-and-orange sunset over Windhaven Beach, featuring the pier's silhouette and a bird flying over the ocean. The lower left corner: "North Carolina." Mine was a picture of an old bicycle propped up against some grass with the white sand and blue ocean in the background—this one, too, read, "North Carolina."

I flipped it over and saw Elena's inscription.

> *Hey, Jay! I haven't heard from you in a while. What's up, baby bro?? School's over, isn't it? How was sophomore year? Anyway, I can't wait for you all to come to town in June! We're going to have tons of fun, and don't worry, I'll have LOTS of sunscreen this time!*
>
> *OK, running out of room here. Much sisterly love, Elena*
>
> *P.S. Why didn't you tell me you've had not one, but TWO girl-friends this year?? You have some explaining to do, mister!*

I laughed, and Mom asked why.

"Nothing," I told her. "I just really want to see Windhaven."

"Again."

"Again."

Memorial Day

Me: I messed up.

Saphnie: Nothing new.

Me: Forget it. I didn't think it would be you, too.

Saphnie: Calm down. You're not the only one out there causing damage. I hope that knowledge can provide you with some comfort. Tell me what happened.

I let her know. I let her know everything.

Lily, Ethan, Megan, Ty, and I all went to Mistletoe Park on Monday to hang out. It was a hot but beautiful day, the sky blue and the air not quite as humid as the forecasters had predicted. Sandy wasn't with us, as she was busy packing, and that was fine with me. There was nothing more for us to say.

Ty wasn't as high as he had been the weekend before, and while I tried not to think too much of it, I was still upset about Lily, Ethan, and him doing drugs together and not telling me about it. It made me wonder what else they were doing without my knowledge.

As we got tired of throwing the disc back and forth, Lily decided to lay on her back in the middle of the field and watch the clouds blow away. Megan joined her, then Ty, Ethan, and lastly me, having nowhere else to go. We were positioned in a circle—our heads in the middle and mimicking the intros of all those friend-dramedy shows we had watched when we were younger.

"This would be a great moment to post," Lily said. "Someone take a picture! Capture all the memories!"

"More like, *revamp* all the memories," Ethan noted. "Besides, whoever takes it won't be in it."

"I'll do it," I offered, sitting upright.

"Here, use mine," Lily said, struggling to pull her phone out of her tight shorts.

She handed it to me, and I fumbled with the phone's camera while attempting to take a few pictures.

"Good?" she asked.

"I don't think it worked," I said. "The pictures aren't showing up."

"Crap." She turned to Ethan. "I need to get that taken care of before we leave for our mission trip on Wednesday."

"You've gotta treat it like a woman," he suggested.

"And how's that?" Ty asked, grinning.

"Hit it several times!" They both laughed until Lily elbowed Ethan's ribcage. That silenced him.

"Try mine," Megan said, rolling her eyes at them and handing me her own phone. I took a few pictures and returned it to her. "Oooh, very nice! You should be a photographer. I'll just make a few edits in Photofixer, add this filter, crop it a little, throw in a dash of color, make my teeth whiter—"

"I thought you said they were nice," I joked. She playfully stuck out her tongue while staring at the screen.

"Aaaand... done! I've uploaded it to CoffeeFolder, too, and tagged you all." She smiled, then frowned at something on the screen that had gotten her attention. "From *Hollywood's Highest:* 'Laine Geier, 37, died Friday afternoon on the set of *$tore Wars: Florida.* The actor opened the doors to an unlabeled storeroom in a cloth factory he had recently purchased and was immediately smothered to death when over a ton of wool scarves poured out into the narrow hallway.' Wow."

"Serves him right," Ty muttered. "Guy was a total snob."

"He had a wife and three kids!" Megan exclaimed.

"He certainly didn't deserve to die," Lily added.

"Even if he was a dickhole on the show," Ethan pointed out.

"That's all scripted," Megan told him. "You didn't honestly think that was his personality, right?"

"Well, I don't know," Ethan said with a shrug. "That's still kind of funny—death by scarves. Awful way to go out, but yeah. Do they have pictures?" Then, seeing Lily's glare: "Thought I'd ask!"

"He spent five seasons looking for that mermaid-themed boutique," I recalled. "All that work, and he never found it."

"What a waste," Ethan said.

"Also from *Hollywood's Highest*," Megan went on. "'In the shocking season nineteen finale of *House of Love*, it was revealed that the last two contestants were gay and in love with each other. They ran off together with the million-dollar cash prize, leaving the bachelorette behind in what has been described as the single-greatest twist in reality television history. This was the first season to feature a woman as the lead, with men acting as the romantic interests. Producers have declined to comment on questions of authenticity.'"

"Damn, that's great TV," Ty said. "Totally fake, but still awesome."

"I actually saw that last night," Lily said. Megan continued to scroll down. "The girl was devastated, so I don't think—"

"I read on Chipper it was staged," Ty told her. "They have the behind-the-scenes footage and everything."

"What's Chipper?" I asked. "Is it like CoffeeFolder?"

"It's faking your virtual smile behind 120 characters or less," Lily explained. "Attention spans are a whole lot shorter than what they used to be."

"CoffeeFolder-dot-com isn't even a thing anymore," Ty continued. "Megan and Ethan are about the only people who still use it, and even he has a Chipper now." Ty leaned toward me. "I'm @BaseballerStatus, by the way. I follow back!"

"It's all about SextMe and Chipper, these days," Lily went on. "I can't believe you've never heard of it!"

"He still uses TSC for his phone," Ethan pointed out. "No wonder you didn't get that text from me, Jay. You're so behind the times! I'd ask if you've been living under a rock, but with that mansion—"

"Um, Lily," Megan said. "I think you need to see this video."

She scooted over to Megan and watched from behind her shoulder. Then curiosity got the better of Ty, then Ethan, followed by me, as always. Megan played it from the beginning.

The video started pitch-black, but we could hear someone walking over fallen leaves and branches. Then the camera moved up to a window, and through the blinds were what looked like two people. It zoomed in to reveal that the figures were Lily and me—myself without a shirt and Lily removing hers. She then moved on top of me, and the view was of the back of Lily's blue bra straps. We were both laughing as we kissed and she reached for my pants.

There was a sound. The camera abruptly showed a small animal moving toward it. The cameraman yelped and kicked a dog brutally in the stomach, causing it to whimper. The camera then turned back to the window to see Lily inspecting it, her cleavage displayed for us to see. I was on the bed behind her. She reached down, picked something up, threw it at me, and crossed her arms in front of her.

It sounded like she mentioned a pickup when headlights appeared in the upper right-hand corner of the video—from the direction of the street. The cameraman struggled to stop recording, focusing on his denim high tops before turning off the video, ending my humiliation.

"Oh, shit!" Ty said, cringing. Megan gave him a much sharper elbow to the chest than Lily had to Ethan, who was still staring at the phone. He was not happy. He was not happy one bit.

"Baby," Lily said to him. "I can explain."

Ethan looked at me, his eyes wide and face twitching. He tried to swing at me, but Ty held him back.

"I THOUGHT WE WERE A TEAM!" he screamed at me, then to Ty: "THIS FUCKING FUCKER FUCKED HER, AND NOW I'M GONNA KILL 'IM!"

"Stop it!" Lily commanded. "It was a mistake!"

"I'LL TELL YOU WHAT A FUCKING MISTAKE WAS: INVITING THIS SACK OF SHIT TO *MY* PARTY AND INTO *OUR* GROUP!"

"Dude, knock it off!" Ty said, struggling to restrain him. "That video wasn't right, but—"

"HE'S ALREADY FUCKED UP ENOUGH!" Ethan continued, simultaneously desperate and enraged. "YOU HEAR THAT, JAY?! I'M GONNA RIP YOUR GODDAMN THROAT OUT AND MAKE YOU SWALLOW IT!"

"Look, I'm sorry!" I told him. "I didn't mean to—"

"SHUT UP! JUST SHUT THE FUCK UP! YOU'RE NO BET-
TER THAN THAT FUCKTARD NICK, YOU PIECE OF SHIT!"

"AND NEITHER ARE YOU!" I yelled back at him. "YOU'RE
JUST AS JEALOUS AND CONTROLLING, IF NOT MORE—
TELLING EVERYONE THAT NICK WAS GAY TO TRY AND
MESS WITH HIS LIFE! SO WHY DON'T YOU PUT *THAT* IN
YOUR PIPE AND SMOKE IT!"

"I WILL SHIT IN YOUR MOUTH!"

"BOTH OF YOU, CHILL THE FUCK OUT!" It was Lily who
screamed this. She was beyond furious.

"Come on," Megan said, taking my hand and pulling me away from
them.

"What are you—?"

"Just come with me," she insisted, somehow more calm than the
rest of us. She looked upset, though not with me specifically.

Megan led me to the small parking lot behind the field, and from
there to her blue Privateer. She took the driver's seat. I sat beside her.

She started up the SUV and pulled out of the park.

"Where are we going?" I asked.

"I'm taking you home," she told me. Ethan had given me the ride
over, so this made sense. "Greenland Hills?" I nodded.

We drove in silence for a while, but then she got tired of it and
turned on the radio.

"—that was 'Radiation Man' off Seymour and the Cancer Survi-
vor's latest track, *Malignant Tumors*, in loving memory of Barrett Carpenter. From the same album, here's 'Kimi Chemo' on Audiotherapy
FM: *Your cure through our mu—*"

She clicked it off.

"What on earth were you thinking?!" she asked me in the same voice
a mother would use to scold her child. "After all she had been through,
you would willingly kiss her like that?!"

"ME?! It wasn't like that at all! You weren't there!"

"I was trying to get your attention the entire night! I—" She stopped
herself. "I don't know. I don't know what I was thinking, either."

We continued the ride with obvious tension. I could see her starting to cry as she drove into the neighborhood.

"7497 Sir Alexander Boulevard," I told her. "The house with—"

The SUV came to an abrupt halt in the middle of the road.

"What did you mean?" she asked. "When you told Ethan to 'put this in your pipe and smoke it?' What did you mean by that?"

"It's nothing—"

"No, dammit!" A tear fell down her face. "I need to know."

I sighed. "They smoke weed. Lily, Ethan, and Ty."

She turned away from me. We were silent. I didn't know what to do or say.

"I guess I wasn't worth the truth," she said, still facing the road, still stopped in the middle of it. She rested her head on the wheel. "God, where did freshman year go?"

I'd never heard anyone sound so sad—so completely disappointed.

"So... pretentious," she muttered under her breath. "Everything's so... *fucking fake*." She sat up straight and glared at me. "Get out."

"What?"

"Get out of my car and walk." She wiped the tears from her eyes. "You've already caused enough trouble."

I left slowly, shutting the door behind me and watching the Privateer drive away.

Then I ran.

The video had been taken down when I got on CoffeeFolder, and the same could be said of Megan's picture, no matter how much I searched.

My phone rang. CARSWELL, LILY. ANSWER? DECLINE? I answered.

Me: "Were you ever going to tell me?"
Lily: "What? I called because—"
Me: "The *weed!* Why would you do that?!"

Lily: "Great. First Megan's pissed at us, and now you. Look, I didn't want to introduce you to that life, OK? I mean, God, you can be so naïve sometimes—"

Me: "Don't act as if I'm somebody less than you! I've been treated like that my whole life—the last person I need to feel that way from is a bunch of hypocrites like you all. I mean, Ethan's all about loyalty, and yet he has a Car Babes calendar *in his room!*"

Lily: "Shut up for a second. Just shut up, OK? Ethan and I... I want to feel wanted, and for that, I need his full attention. I know the stuff he does on SextMe, and sometimes I can't help wondering if I actually matter to him. I don't know what I don't know. And that terrifies me."

Me: "He said he loved you."

Lily: "You can love someone and not find them attractive."

Me: "So why did you make out with me that night?"

Lily: "I'm not going to—"

Me: "No! Why did you make out with me?!"

Lily: "BECAUSE I'M STUPID AND MESSED UP AND CON-STANTLY MAKE HIM JEALOUS TO BE SURE HE STILL GIVES TWO SHITS ABOUT ME! *Is that what you wanted to hear?!* I mean, Christ, I'm not good enough for my own *mother*, let alone my boyfriend! So yeah, I end up using the people I care about: I use you, I use Nick... Hell, I didn't think you could win that stupid election when I told you to sign up! But Ty wasn't supposed to tell you about those get-togethers. It's just—" (Pause.) "It's entropy. Things that are organized eventually fall apart, and everyone deals with their problems and insecurities in their own way. Some kids cut themselves. Some chicken out and cut their dogs. Carl's wife beats him, Sandy prays, Kukowski's an alcoholic, Nick's a creep, Ethan jacks off to other girls, and I smoke pot. That's how we don't end up Suicide Kids. You had *absolutely no right* to tell Meg—"

Me: "'What nourishes me destroys me.'"

Lily: "Huh?"

Me: "Whatever. I've heard enough from everyone today."
Lily: "No, wait, Jay—"

I hung up because I was mad at her. Like with the email to Court-ney, I felt as if I'd needed to do it, although I wished I hadn't. I was furious at Lily and Ethan for choosing *me* to be their new guy in the group. But I chose them back, which is why it hurt the most. They trusted the convenience of it all, whereas I had trusted solely them.

My whole body was shaking, I was crying, and my hands felt numb. I glanced over at the blunt scissors on my desk, causing me to drop the phone and drop to my knees, falling down and asking myself the same question, over and over again: *"Why?"* I didn't expect an answer, but I needed one. I needed *something*.

I needed Saphnie's advice.

Saphnie: I like how your friend suggested you be a photographer since you clearly need to find your focus.

Me: All of that, and you choose to comment on the most irrelevant thing you could possibly joke about?!

Saphnie: The "irrelevant" is only as beside the point as you take it to be. I'm not going to go all I-told-you-so, but you really should have listened to me when I said to tell Ethan about you and Lily. I've never understood what makes it so hard for people to simply communicate with each other. Granted, I wasn't there, just like Megan wasn't present when you made out with Lily. That's probably why I'm able to help you out so well. Sometimes the best form of human contact is the kind we make up in our head. I don't know where you would be without me!

Me: Just tell me what I should do. Please.

Saphnie: It sounds like they've all been friends with one another longer than they have with you. I'm sure they've dealt with similar catastrophes. Give them time to sort things through and wait it out. It's human nature not to think of storms when the ocean is quiet. I believe that's Machiavelli. Anyway, I'm glad you finally confronted Lily. I think she needed to say it as much as you needed to hear it. She and Ethan are both majorly in the wrong.

Me: I want to see you when I get to Windhaven.

Saphnie: That would ruin the magic. A magician never reveals their secrets!

Me: Try me, haha.

Saphnie: I'm sure it can be arranged. (^_~) Now I need to go study, remember? Take care, Jay.

Me: Will do, Saphnie.

Will do.

sixteen days ago
FRIDAY
3:10 PM

Saphnie: I never thought this year would end. Fridays truly are a blessing.

Me: Is the week over already? I can't tell anymore!

Saphnie: Very funny, Mr Summerpants. Speaking of which, how's yours treating you?

Me: It's been OK. I've been catching up on TV episodes and hanging around the house. I haven't seen Sandy, so I guess I could see what she's up to, but she's probably gone by now. No news from anyone else, either.

Saphnie: Maybe it's best to leave it be.

Me: Yeah.

Saphnie: I just realized I've spent 12 years in the education system if you count pre-kindergarten.

Me: And how does that make you feel?

Saphnie: Cheated and lied to.

Me: Uh-huh. Well, how was your last day?

Saphnie: Honestly? It was pretty tiring. I've been bombarded with yearbooks to sign all week. (Remember that I never asked for any of this before you say some snide remark on how lucky I am.) I didn't even know what to write in half of them, let alone the people to whom they belong! I was promised a new start when I moved here, but now I'm stuck with the reputation I've gained. What makes me so popular? Why are looks and clothes so important? Why do we value them above other things? It's all so superficial and materialistic and God, I need new friends. Believe me when I say I'd trade places with you any day.

Me: I might have to take you up on that offer! :-P

Saphnie: Why does popularity mean so much to you? You've been obsessed with it ever since we first texted. Care to explain?

Me: Well, before high school started, I had this girlfriend. Her name was Courtney. She'd moved to Arminster in eighth grade, but we'd only gotten intimate feelings for each other in April of that year. Anyway, toward the end of eighth grade, she sort of... changed.

Saphnie: How so?

Me: Things became different when she started voicing her opinions. To be fair, everything she said was true, but they weren't so much as kind or even necessary. The cool kids started hanging out with her after that.

Saphnie: Maybe it was the other way around.

Me: I know not everybody who's popular is generally mean and rude, and it may just be for their charisma. Kind of like you, I guess. So subconsciously, I've always wanted to be with the popular people to prove to her I could, y'know?

Saphnie: That's a dumb reason to want to show her up, but I suppose it's reasonable. After all, I am pretty charismatic (and modest)! So what happened to her?

Me: We went to different high schools, and I didn't hear from her after that, except for at a party I went to a couple of weeks ago. She's pretty much kept to the status quo.

Saphnie: Humans tend to have this solipsistic experience at around eight or nine years old when they realize they're not the center of the universe. I think your problem is you've latched onto that idea for too long. Your famous Ronald Reagan once said status quo is Latin for "the mess we're in."

Me: You just quoted Reagan. I think I'm in love!

Saphnie: Give yourself some time to get over Sandy first, why don't you? (^_~)

Me: Oh! And you'll never guess who Courtney's going out with: the same Jason you and Sandy both dated. :-P

Saphnie: That little prick. I hope he falls down a long and fiery hole with a bottomless pit. It's crazy how everything comes full circle with your ex dating mine and you having his old number. I know the world is enormous and it's simply a figure of speech, but it's a small world in terms of interconnected relationships.

Me: I guess we should be thanking him, since he's the reason we started texting in the first place, haha!

Saphnie: Yeah. I suppose you're right.

Me: Do you ever hear from your old friends in Oklahoma?

Saphnie: Not really. We didn't exactly end on the best of terms. Unlike Courtney, I didn't let popularity or whatever change me. People actually liked me for who I was! What a concept! They accepted me, but then I got sucked into everyone else's drama.

Me: What kind of drama?

Saphnie: What you have to understand is that therapists don't seek out their clients. The flies come to the web. I was sort of everyone's advice-giver who listened while they vented to me their honest feelings toward each other. Then they wanted to know the truth and weren't too happy about it (or me) in the end. I got this phone the summer I left and immediately got hate messages from every girl I thought was my friend.

Me: That's horrible. D-:

Saphnie: There's nothing scarier than having someone else's life in your hands, but it is (she sighs deeply) what it is. By the way, did you ever ask your one promised question?

Me: Not yet. I guess I'm waiting for the right time, or the right question.

Saphnie: Let me know when you do! I have to go help my dad pack for another one of his conferences. He'll be back in a week. Have a good night!

Me: You too, Saphnie!

Saphnie: Call me Saph. <3

Me: Hehe. Whatever you say!

fifteen days ago
SATURDAY
7:49 PM

Me: We had to leave the zoo today due to thunderstorms. I think I felt some hail, too.

Saphnie: You went to the zoo?

Me: Affirmative! It was just my folks and me.

Saphnie: How was that?

Me: The polar bears died, so their exhibit is being changed into something else. Same with the giraffes. It was kind of sad, to be honest. :-(

Saphnie: I don't like zoos or aquariums.

Me: Why not? You get to visit lots of animals you probably wouldn't get to see otherwise!

Saphnie: With good reason! Those polar bears probably died because it's so damn hot and unpredictable in Oklahoma. I bet the giraffes got their necks tangled together because their enclosures are too small to accommodate their stature. How would you like it if you were an animal trapped in a caged area so small you couldn't move around without stepping in your own crap? How would you like it if you were a fish having to swim around in the same foot by foot by foot tank while little children tapped on the glass all day? How could you possibly enjoy that?

Me: I've never really thought about it before.

Saphnie: Does anyone?

Me: Anyway, how's your day been?

Saphnie: Fine. I went to the beach. It's still too cold to swim, but it's nice walking along the waterfront.

Me: Still trying to hear the ocean sigh? :-D

Saphnie: That serendipity only happens once, it seems. Zeus and Poseidon have nothing on me.

Me: Is something wrong?

Saphnie: I guess my vision of the break isn't turning out how I had planned. There won't be any summer romances. I'll only be hanging out with the same people from school. I'm so sick and tired of it all. I miss Luke. I miss Val, too. I think I should take a nap.

Me: How are you and him?

Saphnie: Luke? I don't know. If he had asked me out again a few days ago I probably would have said yes, but not now. I think

I'm finally over him, but whenever I see him or I'm close to him or read his texts I get really anxious because I know anything between us will end badly and I'll get hurt again. I actually saw him at the beach today and hid behind a picnic table. All I wanted to do was run away, but I also wanted to push him off a cliff and run to the bottom to save him.

Me: I don't know how big of a place Windhaven is, but is it possible to avoid him?

Saphnie: I don't think I'll see a lot of him this summer, but some of the time. We associate with the same people and he lives close to a few of them. (What's the opposite of cabin fever?) I almost had to be with him last week when Jenny wanted us to go out with his friends while he was there.

Me: What do your parents think?

Saphnie: Please. What do you tell your parents? Mine know nothing about my social life. They trust me. I hate to say it, but Luke will probably have a new girlfriend in a month or so. I would honestly wait for him if he changed some of his ways. He has a lot of potential. He could go really far. Maybe I should stop trying to throw a car to the moon. Ground Control to Major Tom, right?

Me: Well, you'll for sure be seeing me next week! :-)

Saphnie: Does your sister live in Windhaven?

Me: Yep, so it shouldn't be too much trouble, haha.

Saphnie: We'll definitely have to plan something then! Not now, though. I'm too tired, but thanks for listening to me.

Me: Of course! Let me know how I can help. Anything you need!

Saphnie: A time machine, Jay. Sorry. Carpe diem!

Me: Nos vemos!

fourteen days ago
SUNDAY
9:59 PM

Me: Sorry to be texting you this late at night, but I think I came up with the perfect question to ask Mr. Metres!

Saphnie: I can't do it anymore.

Me: Do what, Saph?

Saphnie: This unrealistic and mind-boggling thought won't stop popping up in my head. "Everything will fall into place. Don't you worry, Saphnie. You will be happy and life will be okay." I have to do this. Aeternum vale.

I didn't know Latin as well as she did, but QuickSearch led me to find out "aeternum vale" means "farewell forever."

That's when I understood.

To hear the ocean sigh is to sense the calm before the storm, and Saphnie was describing herself that day. She was tired of slamming against the same rocks over and over again. She kept having to meet the same expectations. She felt caged.

She was suicidal.

I went through my contacts list and found her under "Saphnie." I had never added her last name, but that wasn't important at the moment, for this was a matter of life and death—a world with or without Saphnie Kane-Tachibana.

I selected her number. She picked up on the fourth ring.

"Saphnie?" I asked.

"I can't do it anymore," a scared voice answered. *"I'm so sorry."*

"Hey, what's the matter? Let me help you!"

"I have the gun. I have the gun, and I'm going to blow a fucking hole through my messed-up head. *Coup de grâce* or whatever."

"No—no, wait, I can help you! You're not alone in this—"

"BUT I AM ALONE! NO ONE CAN HELP ME! NOT MY DAD, NOT MY MOM, NOT MY FRIENDS, NOT VALERIE, AND DAMMIT, YOU CAN'T EITHER!"

"Saphnie! Saphnie..."

"What?! What more do you people want from me?!"

"Put the gun down!" I told her, and I could hear her crying. I took a deep breath. "Please, just tell me what happened!"

"My dad," she began. "He's been gone for one of his conferences. I was walking home early from the beach today and opened the front door. I thought no one was in the house, but I heard noises coming from my mom and dad's bedroom, and I saw—"

" ... "

" ... "

"Saphnie?"

"I saw my mom having sex with her former boss," she managed before she started sobbing. "SHE WAS FUCKING HIM!"

"I'm so... I didn't—"

"Mom's always saying she doesn't like how Dad sometimes gambles—BUT HE IS A GOOD MAN! HE WOULD NEVER CHEAT ON HER! So I ran outside and down the street and all the way back to the beach. I needed to hear it again. I needed to go back."

"What she did wasn't right, but you can't end your life—"

"I kept running even when it hurt."

"—because of something your mother did!"

"And it hurt so much."

She paused, her voice weak because of her sadness. I could hear her sniffle.

"You don't understand," she said. "My mom isn't happy with their marriage, and that much is obvious. Maybe my dad knows about it, too. If that's the case, then they're staying together for the kids… kid. I feel dead inside, and there is no afterlife for wilted flowers like me."

"You're not making—"

"Fifty percent of couples divorce in the year after the death of a child, whether it be due to problems in the household or the death itself."

"Let your parents deal with this, not you—"

"They won't handle this. It's up to me."

"They love you! Your friends—"

"They don't *love* me! They love an *idea* of me! The Saphnie in their heads!"

"You can't be blaming yourself for—"

"YOU DON'T UNDERSTAND WHAT IT'S LIKE BEING ME! I HEARD THE OCEAN SIGH BECAUSE I CAN'T MAKE PEOPLE HAPPY WITHOUT IT COSTING MY OWN HAPPINESS!"

"Please, please, *please* do not do this to yourself!" I shouted at the phone. We were both crying. "Wherever you found the gun, please, put it back!"

"Jay—"

"You can only do your part!" I paused, my voice quivering. "You can't do it all. You'll go crazy trying to change things beyond your control. Killing yourself isn't worth it. *It gets better!*"

"How can you fucking say that? How can you fucking know?!"

"I DON'T KNOW!" I screamed at her. "I… I *don't* know. I *don't know* the answers. But you shouldn't kill yourself. Not tonight. *Please.* There's always tomorrow to find that answer. There's always hope."

"And oceans."

"Hope and oceans."

We were quiet for a while after that, with only the sound of us breathing to indicate we were still there—both of us. I couldn't tell what she was doing, but I was shaking and sweating on my end.

"Okay," she said finally. "I won't do it. I don't know how I'm going to get through this, but I won't kill myself."

"Promise me."

"I promise. Thank you."

"I should really be thanking you," I said. She laughed, cute and comforting.

"Well, my phone's about to die—erm, running low on battery..."

"See you soon?" I asked, remembering my upcoming vacation.

"You'll see me soon enough," she assured. "But I am so tired. In the morning."

The silence returned, with only our sighs to keep us company. It was Saphnie who eventually hung up. When she did, I fell back onto my bed, feeling scared yet accomplished in a strange and endorphin-induced sense—that I had successfully prevented Saphnie's suicide. I knew in my heart I could have said and done more to help, but knowing she was going to be all right for at least another night was enough for me then. Even so, I felt the phone slip between my fingers and fall onto the floor beneath my bed as I slowly drifted into a deep, worried sleep.

I don't remember dreaming that night.

JUNE

thirteen days ago

I had almost forgotten my phone call with Saphnie when I woke up the next morning, but as I was taking my shower, the water reminded me of her suicide attempt. While it seemed so unreal to me, I knew I had been there, on the phone. It had happened.

I wanted to text her to see if she was OK, though I didn't want to bring it up just yet. If it had slipped my mind, maybe it had also slipped hers? So I didn't look for my phone.

It was the first of June, and my parents and I would be leaving for Windhaven in just two days to visit Elena. That meant packing clothes, making sure we had all our toiletries, and gathering enough electronics to keep us busy on the way there. I wasn't the type of person to pack last-minute, and this trip would be no different.

I devoted a part of the afternoon to getting started on the Spanish verb sheets Ms. Beckham had given my class for summer homework, which she had assigned in valid fear that her students would forget everything during the three-month break. I had finished a few by the time lunch was ready, and after some slices of pizza, I went up to my room and found my phone underneath the bed. No new texts. One missed call from Saphnie, twenty-one minutes after our conversation. No voicemail.

Me: Hello there! How are you doing?

Six simple, easy-going words. I waited for a response, and when I got none, I decided to wait by browsing the web: no new emails, no new information on the next Metres novel, and no new CoffeeFolder notifications. I was about to log off when I noticed the many posts on Saphnie's profile replacing the ones from her birthday. "You will be deeply missed," they said. "We lost a great one last night," and "I always saw you with a smile. God bless."

I was honest-to-God confused and had no idea what was going on. I scrolled through the incoming comments, reading every one of them, unable to comprehend how upset everyone was and how they were just as bewildered. I refreshed the page and saw that someone had posted a link to an online article from a North Carolina newspaper. I clicked it.

THE WINDHAVEN "PUBLIC" ONLINE
Death at Windhaven Beach
by Allan Gramen

Saphnie Kane-Tachibana, a 16-year-old student of Tallarico Bay High School, was found dead on the sands of Windhaven Beach.

The mother of Kane-Tachibana woke up to find her missing from her bed early in the morning. She filed a missing persons report and notified law enforcement.

According to police, who arrived on the scene around 8:00 a.m., the victim hit her head on a coastal rock and died after losing a large amount of blood. The victim was declared dead shortly thereafter. The medical examiner will determine the exact cause of death.

Police are ruling this case as an accidental death, and warn beach-goers to be cautious when swimming late at night.

The funeral is this Thursday at Memorial Gardens.

Saphnie was dead.

I re-read the article to be sure, then again, then again. I didn't know what to make of it, and the company's slogan—"Veritas vos liberabit"—seemed to ridicule my confusion. Saphnie was real, but this was fictional. There was no Allan Gramen, there was no missing persons report, and there wouldn't be a funeral at Memorial Gardens. She had made me a promise. She had told me that she would see me soon. My vacation to North Carolina was in *two days*. Saphnie wasn't dead, and I was going to see her on the beach. There was no way this was true.

I grabbed my phone and called her number, dreading every ring.

"Hi! It's Saphnie."

"Oh, my God, I'd heard—"

"Oops! You, uh, you got my voicemail." She giggled. "I'm not actually here right now. Sooo... leave me a message, and I'll call you back as soon as I can. Thanks. Um, buh-bye!"

I tried leaving a message, but I couldn't do it. I called again, and again, and again, but each time, she stuck to the script. *I'm not actually here right now.*

I couldn't deny it that time. I could sense it. But *why?* Why did I feel this much pain at the death of someone I had never met? Why all these emotions? I already knew the answer, although I didn't want to admit it: I'd gotten to know Saphnie in a way her parents and peers never had.

I went back to CoffeeFolder and read some of the newer messages. "An absolute beauty," one person wrote. "R.I.P. girl." Another: "i love you so much! u had such a pretty smile!" The most recent: "You will forever be in our hearts and will always be remembered." Did they mean forever loved in their memories? If that was true, what would happen when they died—how would she be remembered then? Would people pass down stories of her to countless generations to come and go? And even if so, what exactly would be remembered? Her "pretty smile," right? But she was so much more than that. *Saphnie was a living, breathing, complex human being.* She had worry. She had fear. She blamed herself for the death of her sister, as anyone else might have. And now she was dead. *Saphnie* was dead. And all that'll be remembered of her is a glorified image she never wanted to become?

I understood what Saphnie meant when she had heard the ocean sigh. These people weren't her friends, though I'm sure they had tried to be. She was tired of the same comments as meaningless as what she had written in their yearbooks. But Saphnie wanted a listening ear— she wanted someone to hear her own sighs for once.

And that someone was me.

I had failed her.

No voicemail.

Saphnie was dead.

twelve days ago

I was alone. The feeling was familiar, which made it all the more sorrowful.

I spent the day browsing CoffeeFolder, starting with Saphnie first— hoping that something had somehow changed, but nothing had. I next moved onto Lily, Ethan, and Ty, none of who had posted anything new. Megan had "liked" an unofficial tribute page in honor of Barrett Carpenter started by his father and the church. Sandy had changed her current location from Arminster to a town in Alabama. Both Darian and Nick had deactivated their accounts. Carl was sharing scripture and psalms, Sherman had led the robotics team to nationals, and Jason had changed his relationship status, as had Luke. Courtney's account appeared to be inactive. Ms. Beckham's son was having an extra tooth removed, to which she was asking for prayers and positive thoughts from friends and family members. Kukowski had only one status, posted from when he had most of his hair: "I'm going to start a farm where parents can send their kids so I can raise them properly." Someone had commented, "A pedophile in the making," to which he had replied, "I WAS REFERRING TO THE PUBLIC EDUCATION SYSTEM!"

There was nothing for me to post, so I logged off. This cycle would repeat several times throughout the day, but the end conclusion was always the same: I had nothing to contribute, so once again, I didn't.

Mom came into my room sometime after dinner. She was holding my blue-gray button-up in her right hand, and the left was placed firmly on her hip.

"I found this behind the dryer," she told me. "It must have fallen out while I was washing clothes last week, but I smelled it, and I hung out with enough of your father's friends in college to know that this is *marijuana!*" She held it out farther, as if I were going to sniff it, too. "I'm not stupid, Jakob! I pieced two and two together: You didn't go see a movie with your friends—you went to that Darian kid's party!"

"Mom," I said, "this isn't a good time."

"Not a good time?! Oh, I'm sorry, was last week a better time, or the week before when this actually happened?! You're just lucky my allergies had kicked in that day! When I talk to your father—!"

"And tell him what?! That I messed up?! I already know that—I don't need you reminding me!"

"Don't raise your voice!"

"STOP TREATING ME LIKE I'M A KID!"

"NIGEL! GET UP HERE!"

She threw my shirt on the ground and stomped off. I kicked it to the open door, sat on my bed, and ran my hands through my hair. I remembered Megan talking about how things had been so much easier before. Everything had changed in such a short amount of time, and she had been just as shocked as me, if not more.

Dad walked in. He briefly looked at the shirt, then knelt on one knee in front of me.

"Did you smoke any?" he asked.

"No," I answered.

"Did you drink?"

"A little."

"Were there consequences?"

"Yes."

"Did anyone get hurt?"

"Yes."

"Do you want to talk about it?"

"Not right now."

"Well, all right," he said, then stood up. "I personally think you've learned your lesson, though your mother might not see it that way. Still, when you're ready to talk, I'm here for you. But if not me, at least talk to someone. Someone you trust. Lord knows everyone needs one."

He put a hand on my shoulder, then left the room. I got up for the bathroom, but looked out the window in Elena's room, instead. As I watched the willow tree swaying in the faint breeze, I wondered what exactly constituted hearing the ocean sigh. An image? A sound? The definition of a breaking point was too vague, and perhaps that was the point.

eleven days ago

The car was packed and ready by dawn on Wednesday morning. Our drive to the airport was quiet, as Dad and I were too tired to hold a conversation. That didn't discourage my mother from trying, however, as she seemed to figure the proper method of responding to our argument the evening before was to simply forget about it.

"Anybody know a good joke?" she asked, first turning to my dad, who was driving, and then to me. "No? Oh! What do you call someone who keeps talking when no one's interested?"

"Karen, please," Dad pleaded with her.

"It's too early," I added.

"Fine, fine," Mom said. "I was going to say, 'a Democrat,' anyway." She hummed to herself. "Maybe some music will wake us up?" We groaned as she pressed a button on the dashboard and the beginning of a symphony started through the speakers—which one I couldn't have cared less about at a little after six o'clock in the morning.

Dad switched it to a local radio station. It played Shooter Jennings's soft and steady "Lonesome Blues" into the stillness of that morning's gentle air.

Arminster International Airport is a bit of a misnomer, as their planes don't fly outside the country. It's also tiny, which usually means it's crowded during the holidays. Somehow, despite it being two weeks into summer, there was no one other than transportation officers and airline employees there that morning.

After we went through security, we got breakfast via Taco Kick and carried it over to the empty terminal. Mom fell asleep after eating her chicken quesadilla, but Dad woke her up an hour later when we were ready to board. Because Arminster had so few planes going in and out, we couldn't go straight to Windhaven, instead having to settle with a connecting two-hour flight to Chicago, then a seven-hour wait until there was an available plane to Raleigh. From there, Elena would pick us up with her fiancé, proud surfer and radio host Kasey "the Boogeyman" Stafford.

***

The flight was long and uneventful to Chicago. In front of me sat two guys who looked a bit older than me: one had blond hair and carried a green, leather jacket; the other wore a beanie over his longer, red hair and a hoodie about three sizes too big for him.

"Good grades and community service just aren't enough for college résumés anymore," said the one on the left.

"Assuming you even want to go to some white-boy university," said the other.

"You have to stand out—be fucking different!"

"Or fuck someone who's different and put it online."

"Yeah. Not a handicapped, though."

A flight attendant asked if I wanted anything to drink, to which I reluctantly declined. By the time he came back to ask again, I was already asleep.

***

I woke up to my mom tapping my shoulder with news that we were landing. At first, I thought I was seeing the east coast out the window, but what I surmised to be the ocean turned out to be a pretty big lake. A while later, the pilot informed us that we could unbuckle and begin exiting her plane.

Inside the airport, which was significantly larger than Arminster's, we found where our connecting flight would be. Around one o'clock, we got hungry again, and Dad spotted a place called Horney Islander's with all sorts of hot dogs to try. I chose the San Francisco Dog and ended up enjoying the perfected bread more than the meat itself. We picked three stools to sit on as we ate our lunch and looked out to the busy crowd of tired people bustling to and fro—parents struggling for the attention of their many children, businesspeople rushing to catch their next flight—and I screamed when I turned to my right and saw Kukowski sitting crossed-legged on the stool next to me.

"WHAT THE HELL?!" I shouted at him. He looked at me, his head cocked to the side.

"It's a Chicago Dog," he said, wiping mustard off the corner of his lip with the sleeve of his patched jacket. "I thought, given the city, I should try—"

"Jakob, is something wrong?" Mom asked, worried.

"Do you know this man?" Dad asked, fist clenched.

"Yeah," I said, still baffled at Kukowski's presence there. "Yeah, he's my Chemistry teacher." I turned to him. "What are you doing here?"

"My mother passed away in January," he explained. "I took a plane the day after school let out so my sister and I could sort through her stuff. My sister kept some jewelry and clothes, I got the Christmas decorations, and we sold the rest without being too sentimental. Now I'm off to this fancy rehab facility for dipsomaniacs like me. Who knows? Maybe this one'll work out."

Kukowski looked at my concerned parents and laughed.

"Relax, Mr. and Mrs. Murchison!" he continued. "I applaud your capability to distinguish and interpret comedy in its natural habitat—and I mean that, really—but it's summertime, baby! Have some fun!"

He glanced at his watch. "Sweet mother of God's holy haberdashery!"

Kukowski crumpled up his napkin and tossed it in the trash. He secured his messenger bag, grabbed his worn briefcase, and said, "Have many good afternoons!" before leaving us with our hot dogs.

"Well, that was weird," Dad said, slightly perturbed.

"Definitely," Mom agreed, and we finished our meals.

I re-read bits and pieces of *Rudderless at Sea* while we waited in the terminal. I couldn't help wondering how long Saphnie had enjoyed the signed copy I'd had sent to her. I didn't regret writing her school's address instead of my own, but I did regret that *she was dead*, and it would probably be given away when her parents started going through her stuff—like Kukowski with his mother's belongings. I could imagine a *$tore Wars* cast member heading to Windhaven, finding the book in a run-down Verona Booksellers establishment, noticing the signature, and selling it for a quick hundred bucks. That idea alone angered me more than it probably should have.

I was thinking about this when a lively voice over the speaker system announced that our plane had arrived, and we could begin boarding. Next stop: Elena, then Windhaven. Not Saphnie.

We landed in Raleigh at seven o'clock Eastern Standard Time, losing an hour but gaining the next stretch of the journey. We rolled our luggage to the main doors and saw Elena waiting by her own luxury sedan with Kasey, whom my parents and I had already met when we had made a similar trip to visit them two years before. Back then, my dad wasn't too thrilled with the fact they were starting to move in together, but after hearing that Kasey's family was rich, he warmed up to the idea, so to speak—he was OK with it. My mother only wanted her happy.

"Mom! Dad!" Elena called out. She put her phone away and went to hug our parents and me. The four of us embraced, and I got caught in the middle of them.

"It's always good to see my baby girl," Dad said, then eagerly shaking Kasey's hand: "And you too, Kasey! That is a *really* nice car!"

"Tiny, too," Mom noted with a frown.

"Always a pleasure, Mr. and Mrs. Murchison," Kasey said. He was buff, tanned, and had blond hair that was long on top and shaved on the sides. I thought he was pretty cool. "This here is a quality Japanese-American."

"And the latest model year, too, I see," Dad affirmed.

"You know, Mom," Elena started, steering the conversation away from car-talk, "Benjamin Franklin once said something like, 'Fish and visitors stink in three days.' No offense, but don't you think two weeks are... oh, I don't know... a bit much?"

She considered this. "Yes, but I'm not a visitor. I'm your mother."

"Firm, but fair," Elena said, accepting defeat.

Kasey and I loaded up the crimson-colored car with help from Dad—who insisted on having Kasey call him Nigel—and then we were driving away from the airport and into the lonely night.

"We just have to take the interstate straight for about two hours to get to Windhaven," Kasey told us. "This road here is a beautiful thing."

Mom was the first to fall asleep, lodged in between Elena on the right-hand side and myself on the left. I started to write Saphnie a text about being in North Carolina, but then soon remembered I would never receive a reply. So I watched the scenery—earbuds in and Trent Dabbs's "Goes Without Saying" seeping into my subconscious space.

I awoke to the sound of wheels rolling over a gravel driveway. I looked up and saw Elena and Kasey's one story, ten minutes from the beach.

"We don't try to have grass because there's so much sand from the wind, even on the streets," I heard Kasey tell my father. "Some people have patches of it, but we don't bother. Some yards have cacti while others sprout trees. Some people buy boats, and the rest of us keep our cars. What can I say? That's Windhaven for you."

Even in the dark, I could see his point. The palm trees that mixed in with the sand were not long and slender like the ones featured so prominently in beach movies, but appeared short and swollen with uncomfortable-looking spikes on their sides. Some cacti with flowers were growing on the street corner, and the neighbors proudly showed off their motorboat (so truthfully named *Ship Happens*) in front of their garage. Save the warm weather, Windhaven, NC was drastically different than Arminster, OK. I liked it already in a pessimistic sort of way.

Elena unlocked the house door and showed my parents to their room while I dragged my suitcase to where I had stayed the last time. Kasey told me the AC tended to break down when the heat was brutal, so I ducked and turned on the ceiling fan to full-blast. The twin-sized bed wasn't as comfy as my own back in Greenland Hills, but here, I figured, what would be would be.

I was too tired to sleep, instead lying there in pools of sweat on my bed sheets. I walked around the house alone, admiring the stark contrast between the old-fashioned kitchen with white countertops to the more modern living room and the ninety-inch flat-screen TV plastered on the wall. I did this until my legs were tired, and then I went back to try and fall asleep. It didn't work, but it kept me busy until dawn, when I had finally given up.

ten days ago

Mom and Dad were the first to wake up, each making the other a cup of strong coffee. Next to awake was Elena, followed by Kasey, and lastly me around eleven, which was really ten back in Oklahoma.

Kasey had taken the day off to drive the five of us to Windhaven Beach for the first day of our vacation. We parked on the outskirts of the Ocean View Amusement Park, which I recognized from our last visit (POPCORN! CANDY APPLES! COLD DRINKS! FUNNEL CAKES! COTTON CANDY!). The sun-fun fair featured a carousel, a pirate ship, a single rollercoaster, and other rides and sideshows. I distinctly remembered walking the Hall of Mirrors with Elena when I was fourteen, laughing at how ridiculous we looked in a certain one (the joke was on us—that particular mirror wasn't warped), and riding the Ferris wheel with Mom and Dad, where a dozen or so seagulls soared above. I remembered feeling as free as those birds while looking down at North Carolina's jeweled coast and the little people consuming it. Only in going through these memories in my mind did it occur to me that not only had I been to Windhaven two years prior, but I had played on the very same beach where Saphnie was found dead. And yet, there I was.

Dad carried the cooler while I brought the towels. Elena ran toward the ocean as soon as she saw it, waving her hands and laughing all the way. She soon rejoined us, saying that for two people who lived so close to the shoreline, she and Kasey rarely found the chance to go.

"Now this is a real beach!" Dad exclaimed. "You've never been to Oklahoma, have you, Kasey?"

"No, sir."

"Consider yourself lucky. The lakes there consist of nothing more than dead catfish, annoying speedboats, and old men wearing one-strap overalls with a hand down their pants, yelling, 'Jo Anne! Get me another beer, will ya!'" He shook his head. "There are things in those waters the size of pickup trucks that will eat you alive, and you won't see them until it's too late."

"Out of all the places I've been," Mom said, "I had to end up living in the state where they had to *give* the land away. I can't even think of what someone would want to see in Oklahoma."

"The closest way out!" Elena deadpanned. They laughed while we applied our sunscreen before going out into the water. Kasey mentioned he wanted to take us all out surfing later in the week, and that seemed neat and everything, but as I looked at the people mingling on the beach, I doubted they were aware that *a teenage girl had died there* four nights before. If so, they acted completely natural as they went about their fun. Then again, they hadn't known her the way I had.

As I watched the children, teenagers, young and old people dancing and running in the shallow water where the tide met the wet sand, I wondered if Saphnie had been among the ones far below me when I had ridden that Ferris wheel. Had she been swimming in the waves that touched the shore and back again? Had we seen each other then, perhaps in passing, and I'd been unaware of it?

I turned and observed two bald men lying together on beach towels and all at once thought of how funny it would be if Kukowski and Carl ever met each other. The possibilities were endless—one's carefree attitude juxtaposed with the other's seriousness, although I could not honestly foresee such a meeting ending well enough for a second round of RH. (*Would Carl even drink alcohol?* I thought to myself. *Nah, coffee all the way.*)

"Family photo!" Mom declared, beckoning one of the bald men over to us. "Jakob, let him take the picture with your phone."

"How do you know I have it on me?" I asked.

"Because you never stop checking for texts!" Elena said, calling me out on my isolation. I nevertheless complied with my mother's wishes, giving the phone to the confused man and a forced smile for the picture.

After Mom's insisted "couple of more photographs," I got my phone back and returned it to the lone pocket on the side of my swim trunks, momentarily forgetting the disclaimers at the end of commercials and on the sides of packaging boxes: Water and electronics do not mix. It was like the time when I had gotten a paper cut during a Chemistry test, dismissed it, then washed my hands an hour later and remembered it again. So when Dad grabbed me by surprise and threw me into the surf, I stood up, mortified, and was as painfully aware as I had been when I'd applied the antiseptic, if not more.

"No... no, no, no, no..." I fished my Serenade out of the water as my mom splashed him. I showed it to them both.

"Aww crap," Dad said, understanding what had happened. "Does it turn on, at least?" It did, although the screen was so dark, I had to put it in direct sunlight to see anything.

"No worries," Mom said, putting a hand on me. "We'll get you a new one as soon as we get home, OK?"

I didn't respond, not knowing how. I had lost everything in such a short amount of time. There weren't any words to describe my heartache, and that was devastating on its own.

Everything was quiet.

———————————————

Once we were all beached-out, Kasey drove us back to the house and started flipping hamburgers out back (as opposed to bean or veggie burgers, since he was "only post-ironic during work hours"). He and Dad bonded while Elena, Mom, and I discussed how our dog had died from old age, Thunderbolt's latest *Annihilation!* adventure, how Elena was doing as a photographer for the *Public*, whether we were happy with the winner of *America's Next Top Foster Child*—stuff like that.

"Twelve children competing for the love of a rich couple on the coast?" Mom said, reciting the show's opening word-for-word. "That just doesn't seem right." She had kept up with the current season, despite this.

We all began to go our separate ways after our dinner of Kasey's burgers. I took Elena aside and brought her to my room, asking if we could talk. Elena had always been there for me when we were younger and before she had left home for college, and I still found myself needing my big sister every once and a while, especially then. With Lily, Ethan, Sandy, Megan, Ty—Saphnie—gone, I had never before felt so alone, even prior to having known all of them, when I had nothing to lose. Now that they were out of my life, I realized they were my *everything* to lose, and without them, I had nothing and no one to return to when the vacation was over.

"What's up, baby brother?" she asked, patting the edge of the bed, gesturing for me to sit next to her. I started with Saphnie, the first text, the help with the frozen pizza, *Rudderless at Sea*, and how I had met Lily and gotten closer to Ethan because of it. I told her about his birthday party, about meeting Nick and meeting Sandy. I shared how I had won the contest and sent the book to Saphnie, our different opinions on the story, her hearing the ocean sigh, the last few days, how I had called her, how she had promised me she wouldn't kill herself, and then reading about her death. And throughout my entire account for all that had happened the latter half of my sophomore year, Elena sat there and listened—didn't ask questions, didn't interrupt, didn't judge me. I had always admired her for that.

Elena wanted to know where the funeral would be held. I told her a place called Memorial Gardens, which according to her, was close by. I asked if we could go.

"Of course," she told me. "If I had known your friend had died on that beach, I obviously wouldn't have taken you. I'm so sorry."

I said it was OK. Saphnie wouldn't have wanted for her to be sorry, anyway.

nine days ago

It was the brightest day I had ever had both the pleasure and misfortune to live through. Kasey left early for work the morning of the fifth, leaving Mom and Dad to wake up and find Elena and me wearing all black. They were confused, at first, but gave their approval when Elena told them that she was taking me to a fancy theatre, which explained why I was wearing one of Kasey's suits (admittedly a bit too large for my size). I appreciated all she was doing for me.

We didn't know when the funeral was, as no one had posted it on CoffeeFolder, so we decided for noon and were in the car by a quarter 'til. She drove past the boardwalk and the amusement park, past the ocean and the pier, away from the gritty coastline and deeper into North Carolina. I rolled down the window to the smell of saltwater and a hint of seafood in the air. It was refreshing, to say the least.

We arrived at Windhaven Memorial Gardens a couple of minutes later. The cemetery was beautiful, with pink flowers and green trees wherever there weren't tombstones, and American flags swaying next to the graves of the veterans visited a week prior for a Memorial Day commemoration. In the middle of all this was a huge group of people dressed as dark as we were. Elena and I approached them and saw they were indeed here for Saphnie, circling around her casket being lowered in. We had arrived at the end of her burial, but we had still made it— that late good-bye was all that seemed to matter to me in the end.

Next to the open grave was a short man with thick, round glasses that kept slipping down onto his nose, partly from the sweat, but mostly from the tears he kept wiping off his face with the back of his hands. Beside him was a tall, Japanese woman in a black dress with sleeves. She kept clutching her pearl necklace while tears dripped down from her shaded eyes. Saphnie's parents were standing close to each other, but not close enough.

The woman began sobbing loudly when the dirt was thrown over the grave. I realized I wasn't the only teenager present, as it seemed the entirety of Tallarico Bay High School had shown up to pay their respects. One person I recognized was Luke Wilbourne, who had his arms around the waist of a girl with long, red hair. I wondered what they were thinking at that moment. I wondered how many of these people believed they were at one point close to Saphnie. "God, I need new friends," I remembered her telling me. I then recalled her commenting on Valerie's funeral and pondering who would show up to her own when the day eventually came. I wondered whether she would have been happy with the turnout. I wondered if she thought it would have come so soon.

People began to disperse after the funeral was over. Elena and I were heading toward the car until she bumped into a man she knew, and they began talking. He was a little taller than me and wore a suit similar to mine. He was cleanly shaven and had short, dark hair to match his sunglasses.

"Jay, this is my friend Allan Gramen," Elena said, introducing us. "He's a journalist for the *Public*."

"You wrote the article about her death," I noted. "That's how we knew to come to Memorial Gardens."

"That's right," he said, looking to where Saphnie was buried. "I didn't know the girl, but I always attend the funerals of those I report about. My brother was one of her teachers. He says she was a bright student."

"She was," I said. "Very articulate. Can I ask you a question?"

"Elena, can you give us a moment alone, please?" he asked her. She nodded, walked toward a tree, leaned on it, and pulled out her phone. He turned back to me when she was gone. "What would you like to know?"

"I was wondering," I started, then took a moment to collect my thoughts. "Well, you saw her body. Do you think it was really an accidental death, like you wrote, or, well... suicide? Your report said the medical examiner would determine the exact cause of death—"

"I've seen a lot of bodies in my line of work," he told me. "More than I'd like to admit, actually." He put a hand on my shoulder. "Her head was split open by a rock, kid. Why don't you let her rest in peace, all right?"

Gramen patted my back and went off to flirt with Elena. I wanted to scream at him. Adults were supposed to have the answers—where was mine? He acted as if a corpse is all she'd ever been, but that was only because he was just another person who hadn't heard the ocean sigh. He didn't know.

Elena and I went over to the grave spot when Gramen had left her and the cemetery was almost deserted. I noticed the bittersweet headstone next to Saphnie's plot belonged to her sister.

Valerie Anne Kane-Tachibana

Daughter, your faith has made you well. Go in peace. —Mark 5:34

Semper in Cordibus Nostris.

"That funeral sure needed some life, huh?" Elena asked me. I didn't respond. "Too soon?" I nodded.

We passed the 23rd Psalm engraved into a stone Bible as we left. I recited it from memory while resting my head against the car window, my eyes closed as Elena pulled out of the Gardens and turned on the radio.

"—to WHVB-FM, Windhaven. Can't get these songs just any-where." Kasey's voice was so smooth and persuasive that I was sure he could talk a bank teller into handing him the entire vault. "I'm all about getting you hooked on music you wouldn't have heard other-wise—and speaking of which! Today, I'm happy to play the latest single from Pulsar Skies, 'The Sun Sets on Me Now,' off their new album, *Lost at Sea*. Have at it!"

And so commenced the music. I couldn't help thinking of Saphnie while I listened, though I'm sure it came with the territory. The song started slow, kicked into full blast soon after, and came to a halt by the end with a reprise of the chorus:

I tried to chase you, dear.
I went to this world's edge for you!
And where have you taken me
Tonight? Tomorrow? Forever?
Don't leave me here for too long—
Without you I have nothing to live for.
Happiness has fragility, you know.
The sun sets on me now.
The sun has set on us.

"There it is, folks. You can get 'The Sun Sets On Me Now' via dig-ital download and any retailer that still sells good music, period. We're not hipsters. We're the contemporary youth composed of wasted ba-chelor's degrees and years of abandonment issues. Like I always say: If the jeans fit, wear them! And if they're too tight, who cares? We don't. And you? You're listening to WHVB-FM. *This is your Windhaven.*"

three days ago

My two weeks in North Carolina went by ever so slowly. Whether this was to give me time to remove myself from what had happened before the trip and to enjoy the vacation, I'll never know, just that neither happened. No matter what we did, all I could think about was Saphnie and her "accidental death."

Kasey had the weekends off, so on Saturday, we ran into ex-reality TV star Jake Palaver bumming cigarettes off compassionate tourists as we went to see the USS *Goodwin* battleship on the other side of Tallarico Bay. The top half was predictable, but once we went underneath the vessel, it turned out to be an enormous labyrinth of steel-plated rooms and corridors that would bring out the claustrophobia in anybody. It reminded me of how things can appear a certain way from the outside, and yet be completely different within—people like Nick, Sandy, Saphnie, everyone. They were so much more complex than I had originally imagined, which made me wonder what others thought of me. *The Suicide Kid*, I remembered. Was that what Saphnie had become? Was she the one in the statistic Ethan had shared with me?

I put those thoughts aside on Sunday and Monday at the Ocean View Amusement Park, where I rode every ride other than the carousel, as I figured I was too old for it. Kasey won Elena a plush seagull, which she loved, and that reminded me of how I was supposed to have made plans with Saphnie, and how we could have gone there, together. How I could have won *her* a stuffed gull.

Tuesday afternoon, Elena took our parents and me on a two-hour drive to South Carolina to go to the same Myrtle Beach that Saphnie was supposed to have gone with her alleged friends. The pattern was worrisome, but I wasn't in Oklahoma anymore, and might as well have been standing on foreign ground—*Saphnie's* domain, not mine. We searched for seashells along the shore, and when it got dark, we rented a cabin, which was made of the wood of the surrounding forest.

We returned to Elena and Kasey's home on Wednesday, only staying as long as it took to change before heading back out for Windhaven Beach. I spotted Mom and Dad that day sitting on a bench by the pier, watching the waves the ocean couldn't control. They were cuddling with their arms around each other, which was a pleasant sight for eyes as sore as mine.

I sort of felt as if Elena was taunting me by taking me there again, but I knew she wouldn't do that. Therefore, my only conclusion was that it was fate insulting me, not my forgetful sister. But for what? For not preventing Saphnie's death? Fate was acknowledging one fault of my many: that I could not stop the girl who trusted me with her life from dying to the late-night tides and a misplaced rock.

Thursday was another day at the beach, but first, we browsed the scenic boardwalk in downtown Windhaven—the USS *Goodwin* still in sight. I took notice of the flirty-eyed girls with their long hair and little shorts strutting in front of tanned guys in pastel tank tops that matched the houses. Their board shorts displayed their favorite brand of underwear each time the boys stretched their arms out too far, which was usually for the girls in front. I envied this group as I heard their laughter and the *flip-flop* of their sandals, walking around and soaking up the sun without a care in the world—*it's summertime, baby*. But I did not dare join them, as I was stuck in my own comfort zone, all while heavily wishing that Lily, Ethan, and Saphnie were there to join me.

We visited Jeremiah's for lunch, a seafood restaurant with grilled Yellowfin tuna as that day's special. I ordered it and ate some Kaiser rolls while waiting for the server. We soon finished our meal and continued on our way to Windhaven Beach. A Hispanic man with a large mustache stopped us before we could reach the car, which was coincidentally parked in front of what was Xavier's flower shop from *Together Forever*.

"*No te puedes morir por sobredosis de marijuana,*" he told Elena. Dad got between them. "*¡Te apuesto a que no sabias eso!*"

"What is he saying?" she asked me.

"He's probably another druggie wanting some proposition passed,"

236

Mom answered for me, then to the man, over-enunciating each syllable and shaking her head: "No. Thank. You. Do. Not. Want."

We walked away at a much faster pace to the car and arrived at the Atlantic soon after. I noticed a small boy darting his hands into the sandbar in hopes of finding that one, perfect shell. I saw two siblings building an impressive castle while a guy in a teal UNC Windhaven t-shirt ran straight into a crashing wave with his girlfriend squealing on his shoulders. I watched as a little girl cried each time the water nipped at her toes, and two bikini-clad teenagers wearing large sunglasses took pictures of themselves—their lips pursed and cleavage exposed.

I left my family and walked into the ocean. The backs of my feet got buried and released as the tide came up and returned out to sea in a matter of seconds, washing away any broken seashells with it. I could only imagine how she must have felt that night, alone on this beach where so many movies were filmed. I could only imagine. And that was the problem.

Standing on the beach where the water lapped was a girl my age and fairly petite. She had curly, copper-colored hair that formed neatly behind her head. I could not move my eyes from her, and she noticed. I tried my best not to look embarrassed when she flashed a smile and walked over to me. She positioned her pale body toward the water, and we stood in momentary silence.

"Did you know a girl died here not too long ago?" she asked me.

I glanced over at her, but her head was still turned, looking a sort of auburn in the afternoon light.

"Yes," I told her. "It's very tragic."

"The girl was my cousin. We came here for her funeral." She faced me. "I saw you there, Jay."

I stared at her. She laughed at my startled expression.

"Reagan Kane," she said, reintroducing herself. "Damn, it's a small world. I took your pencil at the beginning of last year, remember? And then I yelled at you for believing my namesake was that of... a certain president. Sorry about that. I voted for you, if it's any consolation."

"It's fine," I said, trying to sound reassuring.

She kicked at the wet sand before sitting down and crossing her legs. The saltwater sprayed her hair, which glistened in the Carolina sunshine.

"This fucking sucks," she told me.

"This fucking sucks," I allowed. It needed to be said. "I didn't know her or her sister that well, but it does."

"I didn't know her as well as I would've liked."

"It's shit they both drowned. And two months apart? I knew they were inseparable, but man, the irony in that. You never think death's a real thing until it comes out and gets you, huh?"

"Or worse, someone you know."

"Yeah."

"Yeah."

I think that was all we could have said at that point.

We parted toward our respective families. I had originally thought it was inappropriate for me to be on Windhaven Beach after Saphnie's death, but a whole group of grieving people vacationing there was even more unsettling. I didn't know whether to feel pity for them or merely contempt.

Elena nudged my shoulder when I returned. "Oooh, who was that?" she asked. "Did my baby brother find love a thousand miles away from home?"

"Her name is Reagan," I told her.

"Like the president?" Dad asked.

"Yeah, but do you *like* her?" Elena pressed.

"Come on now, Ellie," Dad said. "Leave your brother alone."

"What's going on?" Mom asked, frazzled. "Who's dating whom?"

We all laughed. Same ol', same ol' with the Murchisons. Family's family, as weird as they can be. That gave me hope.

After everyone had gone to bed, I took it upon myself to use what little I could of my phone to recreate my friendship with Saphnie—to find that same connection I'd had with her through another person. I ventured into online chatrooms, sifting through half-naked teenagers and suspicious links in an attempt to find her again and learn she was indeed alive, somewhere, anywhere.

Stranger: Hi.

Me: Hello! I'm a sixteen-year-old guy who just wants to talk with someone. No SextMe, no pics, nothing weird.

Stranger: Same.

Me: Oh, cool.

Stranger: No I mean I'm a guy I want to talk with a girly.

Stranger: heyy 16 ukraine girl

Me: Hi there. I'm a sixteen-year-old guy who just wants to talk with someone. No SextMe, no pics, nothing weird.

Stranger: nice =) Super powers you wish you had?

Me: The power to rewind time, probably. Yourself?

Stranger: wanna cam with me? brunetteteen16 on Hairy Gurlz

Stranger: HEY

Me: Hey. I'm a sixteen-year-old guy who just wants to talk with someone. No SextMe, no pics, nothing weird.

Stranger: IM TO YOUNG BUT FEEL THE SAME WAY

Me: Haha, all right. What's up?

Stranger: THE SKY

Me: I suppose. How old are you?

Stranger: 12 WATS YO NAME

Me: Jay. Yourself?

Stranger: NICKI

Me: Nice to meet you, Nicki. Have you heard of Pulsar Skies?

Stranger: BRB JAY DONT LEAVE ME

Me: OK, I'll wait!

Nicki never wrote me back, and two hours later, Nicki disconnected from the chat. I eventually found a girl from North Carolina, but talking with her then just wasn't the same as it had been with Saphnie, who I truly did not want to replace. So I, too, disconnected, and I, too, was left wondering what I'd said to permanently end our conversation.

two days ago

On our last day—a Friday—in Windhaven, Elena and I returned to Memorial Gardens with our parents. Elena told them we were going to sightsee, but she and I were a little more meaningful than that.

We parked near the area of tiny grave markers belonging to babies and toddlers. Everything about this final resting place seemed so dismal to me—almost too final. Farther within the cemetery and among the "Beloved Mother," "Our Sweet Sister," and "In God's Loving Care" inscriptions, we came across Valerie's grave and Saphnie's brand new headstone.

Saphnie Maydelle Kane-Tachibana

You are beautiful, my darling.
There is no flaw in you. —Song of Solomon 4:7

If tears could build a stairway, and memories a lane,
I'd walk right up to Heaven and bring you home again.

It was my only physical proof of her existence, and yet the epitaph seemed to go against everything Saphnie believed in and much, much more. "No flaw," huh? And what memories would be building a lane? Why did they believe she would even want to come home if this is what she would be returning to? She had hoped to be finally resting in peace, undisturbed. Why bring her back from that? I couldn't comprehend that her own parents didn't know her well enough to see how inaccurate it all was. I wondered what my own parents knew of me and what I truly knew of Saphnie. One thing was clear: Death was never meant to be romanticized. There's nothing romantic about it.

"God, I'm such an idiot," Dad said, bending his knees to first touch Saphnie's grave, then Valerie's.

"What's wrong?" Elena asked, putting a hand on his back.

"I know a Mr. Kane-Tachibana," he explained. "He worked for Adveston in Arminster until he transferred to the North Carolina division. He was a small man, but boy, did he have a big heart. I saw him last at a business meeting in Chicago a couple of months ago. The guys and I made fun of how noticeably exhausted he looked, but I had no idea."

Dad couldn't bring himself to finish the confession.

"Sixteen and eighteen," Mom observed, checking the dates. "That's just too soon." She turned to me. "If I ever lost you..."

I looked down and realized I was standing right above Saphnie, or whatever was left of her, anyway—the fresh dirt and insects between us to serve as a grim divider. That unsettled me, and when we got back to the house, I went to the guest bathroom, looked at my reflection in the mirror, and puked into the toilet. I flushed it down with what I hoped were all my worries.

Making use of my childlike stupidity, I briefly thought not of her death, but of Ronald Reagan's. His daughter observed that when he opened his eyes for the last time, the so-called Great Communicator looked directly at his wife with tenderness and affection. "If a death can be lovely," Patti said, "his was." But I couldn't fool myself, and I knew this was not the case with Saphnie.

I took out my phone, positioned it underneath the light, and tapped "Create Message."

Me: Saphnie, I cannot describe to you all these emotions I'm feeling. It's silly. Absurd, even. Why am I missing you when I barely knew you? I don't understand. Why did you have to go and get yourself killed?! YOU PROMISED ME, SAPHNIE! YOU PROMISED ME THAT WE WOULD GET TO SEE EACH OTHER AND HAVE A GOOD TIME AND HAVE FUN AND NOW YOU'RE DEAD AND I DON'T KNOW WHAT TO THINK BECAUSE IT WAS "ACCIDENTAL" AND IT WASN'T YOUR FAULT AND NOW YOU'RE DEAD AND IT'S *MY* FAULT AND YOU PROMISED YOU WOULDN'T KILL YOURSELF AND NOW YOU'RE DEAD AND ALLAN GRAMEN IS AN ASSHOLE AND NOW YOU'RE DEAD AND YOUR PARENTS ARE UPSET, I'M UPSET, MANY PEOPLE ARE UPSET, BUT THEY DON'T KNOW WHAT TO BE UP-SET ABOUT BESIDES KNOWING ONLY THAT YOU'RE DEAD YOU'RE DEAD YOU'RE DEAD AND NOW YOU ARE DEAD.

Tears fell onto my Serenade's screen—it wasn't just the deceased who needed peace, it seemed. I closed my eyes and opened them again, but I still couldn't see past this overwhelming feeling of guilt.

I never sent that text, just as she hadn't left a voicemail. In one week, it would've been six whole months—half a year since my birthday and her original text message.

I dreamed I went back to Windhaven Memorial Gardens. It was raining softly, and I was alone, so I fell to my knees and dug with my hands to reach her. I clawed at the dirt with my nails until they cracked and bled and became one with the groundwater.

But the casket was empty. There was no one to meet. And then I was in the casket, looking up at me—past me, wondering. And I was looking at myself in the grave, but I was still inside, staring at me, who turned into Nick, then Sandy, then Megan, then Ty, then Ethan, then Lily, then Saphnie. I was all of them, and they were me. I was nothing, and so were they.

I buried myself in that box, and I floated out to sea.

one day ago

We awoke at three in the morning for the long drive to Raleigh. Elena had to get up early for work, so we had all said our good-byes before—with many more tears to accompany it. ("No, I'm... I'm not crying!" Dad had insisted. "Those were just some... really good burgers!" He then proceeded to cry some more.)

Dad decided to drive that night after he had recomposed himself, as ninety percent of the odyssey was on the same, single stretch of interstate. A multitude of sleepless nights had finally caught up with Kasey, so he accepted Dad's offer without a second thought.

"OK," Kasey began, yawning. "To get onto I-40, you just turn right and drive to the—Nigel, are you listening?"

"Nope."

"Huh?"

"What?"

" "
"..."

"..."

"Just take a left at the light."

"You got it, chief."

We arrived at the airport at around six in the morning. It looked as if everybody on the eastern seaboard wanted to get out of North Carolina at the same time as we did—the line to security seemed to loop around the inside and back again. We somehow got to our awaiting terminal before takeoff, and from there, we were then permitted to board with the final passengers. My parents and I got separated on the plane's seating arrangement, though I didn't mind. I wasn't there to talk.

Our plane landed in Chicago at nine o'clock Central Standard Time. Because we were so hungry and tired, we didn't bother with the hot dogs or the chance to bump into Kukowski, instead heading straight for the coffee and fruit smoothies. A brain freeze and almost two hours later, we were sitting in a crowded, stuffy terminal for people waiting to go to Arminster and a couple of other south-central cities. But as soon as the plane before ours arrived, everyone but us got up to leave. It looked as if we were the only ones going to Oklahoma. Figured.

A few other weary travelers wandered over as time passed, and when a tiny plane showed up, and we began boarding, the seating arrangement didn't apply because of how empty the flight was. I chose a window seat and watched Lake Michigan as the plane took off. I admired the way it blended into the sky, rendering it almost impossible to tell where one ended and the other began.

One noticeably nervous man sat in the same aisle I was in, by the opposite window. I asked him if he was OK. He said he was fine, but a little worried. I asked what he meant by that. He told me there was a job interview for him as a pastor in Arminster, but he was afraid the Native Americans might come out from their reserves and lead an attack during his stay. I smiled for his ignorance and assured him there was nothing other than prejudices to fear. He seemed relieved to hear that.

"We're having a, uh… slight malfunction with the landing gear, but it shouldn't be much of a problem," a flight attendant announced a little over an hour and a half later. Her hair was dyed yellow and buzzed in the back. "Wait a minute… The captain has just informed me that we are now indeed landing. The weather is ninety-six degrees Fahrenheit, and the local time is 12:14 in the afternoon. Thank you for flying with us! If this is your first visit to Oklahoma, we hope you enjoy your stay. And if you're a resident here in Arminster, *welcome home*."

I believed the woman, as the outside was so hot that I could feel the heat on my face when the hard sunlight hit against the window. I looked out to see us descending toward the trees, which appeared small enough to be used for a diorama display. The rivers and creeks were a murky brown, which was despairing after leaving the North Atlantic Ocean and Tallarico Bay beside it. But as we got closer to the ground, I saw a long, slightly-curved highway that looked like an erect penis. I, the only teenager on the plane, couldn't help laughing.

We departed the aircraft after abruptly striking against the runway—"Nice job with the landing," Dad remarked to the captain as we walked by, luggage in tow—and set foot once again into the city's all-too-familiar airport. I winced once we got outside and the sun made contact with my skin. The temperature in Windhaven had been in the eighties while we were there, but here, it was in the upper nineties *in the shade*. I imagined this would take some getting re-used to.

My parents found the car with relative ease, then loaded up the trunk, and we hit the road. North Carolina was such a different experience that it felt sort of wrong coming back. But as we drove into Greenland Hills, and I saw our peaceful house—so loyal and inviting—I felt glad to be back, without question.

I got out, grabbed my only suitcase, went to my room, and collapsed onto my bed. To sleep in the comfort of one's own home is a good feeling, which I verified with a long, overdue, and much-needed nap.

The rush of the air conditioning was soothing, like wind rustling through palm leaves.

today

We sat in the living room. My parents drank their early morning coffee while I was on the couch.

"Can one of you drive me to church?" I asked, breaking the silence.

"We aren't exactly dressed for the occasion," Mom said, still in her robe and pajamas.

"I wouldn't need you guys to go in," I added, "only a ride there and back."

"You can't drive yet?" Dad asked.

"Mom won't let me," I said, staring directly at her, but she looked away.

He shrugged. "Who am I but a simple man to deny my son access to the Lord? Be ready in ten."

I went upstairs and threw on some jeans and a button-up, rolling up the sleeves. I brushed my teeth, straightened my eyebrows with my forefingers, and was at the front door with a minute to spare.

"Nice," Dad said as we got into the car. He turned the radio dial and stopped on a classic rock station playing "Champagne Supernova" by Oasis. It seemed strangely appropriate. Almost morbid. Yet finally, I understood.

––––––––––––––––

"The bells seem happy today," Dad noted as we drew nearer.

"They do that every Sunday," I pointed out.

"Still," he said, "it's better than never at all." I couldn't argue with that, instead thanking him for the ride and shutting the car door before watching him drive off and honk his horn twice.

I walked inside, up the stairs, and into the room where the youth group met. Megan and Ty were watching the TV, and Carl was at the podium.

"Jay!" he exclaimed, running over to hug me against him. I tried to hug back, but one of my arms was caught in his embrace, so it was a bit awkward. "How have you been?! I'm so sorry about what happened last time—"

"It's good," I said, laughing. "Honestly. I'm just happy to see you." He smiled at this, and I went over to Megan and Ty.

"Hey, Jay!" Megan said, standing to hug me as well, which was odd, as she had never done so before. I hugged her, anyway. It was a welcome change.

"I thought the Second Coming of Christ would arrive before you did!" Ty joked. We fist-bumped, apologized, and laughed with each other. Megan asked for my phone number, and because Ty felt left out, I exchanged my information with him, too. The Serenade might have been useless—it didn't always want to turn on when I needed it—but I felt it was a necessary step in getting my friends back.

"You both have the same last name?" I asked, squinting at my broken contacts list.

"Well, duh," Megan said. "We *are* brother and sister."

"Oh!" I said, embarrassed. "I thought... Uh, nevermind."

"What's the matter?" Ty asked, a wide grin on his face. "You look redder than when we turned eleven, and I walked in on Megan trying on a training bra. Besides, I'm—"

"For Christ's sake!" Megan exclaimed, whacking him on the top of his head with a couch cushion, then whispered: *"Not before Mom!"*

"Hey now!" Carl piped in from the other side of the room. "Third commandment: 'Thou shalt not take the name of the Lord thy God in vain!' That's somewhere in Exodus. Look it up!"

It was then when Lily and Ethan walked in, hand in hand. Upon seeing me, Lily ran over and wrapped her arms around me. Her hair was much longer than when I had first met her in January, and I noticed Ethan's complexion had cleared up significantly as well. He came over and hugged me, too. And in that moment, I felt truly loved and cared about. These were my core group of friends, and whether I was popular didn't matter to them.

"Let's just… forget it all ever happened," Ethan suggested. "Bridge under the water!"

"Ethan and I talked it over," Lily explained. "Right, babe?"

"Yes, ma'am," he said to her, then smiled at me. "We can't lose you, man. We like you too much!"

"Plus we've already invested too much of our time into you," Lily joked. "You were quite the fixer-upper."

"Thanks," I said, smiling. "You both are great, you know that?"

"Well…" Ethan started.

"Don't sell yourself so short!" Lily said to him, laughing.

He paused, then put his hands on his hips. "A short joke? Really?"

She smiled as she rolled her eyes and turned to me. "We certainly try," she said, then to Carl: "And sorry we're late!"

"Yeah," Ethan added. "Lily over here only takes *right* turns." She playfully shoved his upper arm.

"Not a problem!" he told them. "Better late than in the counsel of the ungodly." He then cupped his hands around his mouth for dramatic effect as he shouted, "Good morning, fellow disciples of Christ!"

"Good morning, Carl," we all said. "We're ready to learn about God's grace and demonstrate His abundance of love toward our fellow people."

"Amen!" He was still loving this. "Taking attendance now. Let me see… Twins Megan and Tyler are here—"

"You're *twins*, too?" I asked them, shocked.

"And I'm the older one!" Ty said, pleased with himself.

"But you don't, like, look alike?"

"We're fraternal twins," Megan answered. She was enjoying this.

"—Trisha? Anybody seen Trisha?" Carl continued. "Dag nabbit, where is that girl? OK… Phillip's on a mission trip, I know that… Lily and Ethan are here… Jay's back in good business… Will? No Will? Megan, where's your boyfriend?"

"He's home sick with a cold," she told him. Ty looked over at me and nodded.

"OK, so Will's absent." He paused to think. "Am I missing someone?"

We were already in a circle around the podium by the time he had finished. Carl smiled.

"As some of you know," he started, "I won't be here next week due to a youth ministry conference I'll be attending in Chicago—which I actually have to go downstairs in half an hour to prepare for—so this sermon will be shorter than usual." He paused. "What's today's date?"

"Probably June," Ty noted.

Carl shook his head. "Well, next Sunday is also Father's Day, and I've always loved my dad. He was my role model, he baptized me when we lived in Arkansas, and he taught me everything I know about Christ. He was a man of strong faith. My dad also worked as a cop for forty years, gaining a lot of respect from not only his colleagues, but even the inmates and people he arrested. But one day, he was caught in a riot and was almost stabbed to death. I want to say he was lucky, but he had to be hospitalized after that. I had to watch him turn into a vegetable before he got his wings this past April." I noticed a tear fall from his cheek and onto the big Bible on the podium. "He was a very kind man, in and outside the church. I don't know why God let him die like that.

"If you're like me," he continued, balm in every word he spoke, "and have had something truly awful happen to someone you care about, you've probably asked yourself why in the world God would permit something so horrible to happen to them. You all know the universal question: Why do bad things happen to good people?

"My dad and I were close. I know a lot of friends who did not have a good relationship with their fathers. In my deepest hurt, I asked God—yelled at God—why He took my dad and not one of those who weren't around for their children. Even after all these years of knowing the Lord and walking with Him... I let Him know I did not think it was fair.

"I'm unsure of how to explain what began to put the pieces of my heart back together, but God met me right there and then, and I felt His love in the darkest moment of my life. God let me know He understood my brokenness, as He had also unjustly lost someone He loved deeply. His only Son was crucified—a man who knew no sins, the Bible says. Jesus most certainly did not deserve to die the way He did and most definitely did not deserve to die for me. But God had a plan, and Jesus did it out of obedience to the Father. So it is true that life is not fair. Yet the Bible says that God exalted Jesus after his crucifixion, and that same power God used to raise Him from the dead will be with you through all the storms of life when you learn you can depend on Him—when you learn that you don't have to have all the answers.

"I still miss my dad terribly. I don't believe time heals all wounds, as they say. Will the circle be unbroken?" He smiled faintly toward Lily. "Sure, it's easier today than it was the week he died, but some days are as if there's still a hole in my heart. Father's Day without him will hurt like I just lost him. But now I stop to thank God for the wonderful man He blessed me with to call Dad. I thank Him that one day, I'll be reunited with my father, and I'll never have to say good-bye again. For now, that's enough.

"Kids, God wants you to place your trust in Him and to know that He will always be faithful to His people. While the loss of my dad was truly sad to bear, I knew that God was in control of everything, and He would not leave me in my time of need. 'The Lord has comforted His people and will have compassion on His afflicted.' Book of Isaiah, verse 49:13."

I glanced around the circle to see everyone was looking away—Lily was crying, and Ethan had his arm around her. Carl knew this was a touchy subject, and perhaps that was his reasoning.

"Let us pray," he said, and we all stood up to hold hands. "Dear Lord and Heavenly Father, we thank You for all the blessings You have allowed into our lives. You created us with a yearning to connect, share, laugh, and love—the greatest gifts of all. We pray that You put Your angels all around Mr. Carswell as he serves overseas, ease Megan and Tyler's mother of her Huntington's, and please tell Dad I wish him an early Happy Father's Day."

I thought of Mr. Kane-Tachibana and what he must have been going through. How would he spend his Father's Day? Would anyone be there with him? Would he celebrate at all?

"From injustice, we pray for hope. From hatred, we pray for love. From grief, we pray for understanding. 'Wash me thoroughly from my iniquity. Cleanse me from my sin.' We ask this in the name of our Lord and Savior, who is Jesus Christ. Amen."

"Amen," we all agreed, and although Carl allowed us to talk to each other for the remainder of the hour, I went up to him, instead. Arminster is a small enough city—an urban island in a rural sea—so I thought it would be worth a try.

"Hey, Carl," I began, and he looked at me.

"Yes, Jay? How can I help you?"

"Did you... ever know a Saphnie?"

He sat down on one of the plastic chairs and thought about this.

"I did," he told me. "I served as a crossing guard maybe ten years ago for an elementary school. This little girl named Saphnie would come up to me each day for help getting across the busy intersection. I'd do that whole *got-your-nose!* bit on her, every time, and she would stand there and let me take it without any intention of getting it back." He smiled. "Why do you ask, may I ask?"

I trusted Carl as I trusted Elena, so I told him, sparing most of the details for time's sake, but allowing the gist of it without sugarcoating.

"Saphnie was a sweet girl," he said after a while, sadness in his eyes. "I was told she was very generous—always a giver, even when she had none. Maybe that's why she let me take it? No, that's silly. My nose is fine." He sighed. "There aren't nearly enough worldly mansions for the kind folks who deserve them. I'm so sorry, Jay."

"I am, too," I allowed, "though she probably wouldn't have wanted me to say that. Saph wasn't a big believer in apologies for things beyond our control."

"I'm not so sure," he said. "I believe sympathy is a needed under-standing."

I considered this.

"Yeah, you're right," I told him. "I'm sorry about your dad, so that makes sense." I looked down. "Do you think... did she follow through with her suicide attempt? I mean, was it my fault? I know that's selfish of me, but I... I don't know."

"From what you've told me," Carl began, "Saphnie was a lonely girl surrounded by a lot of people. She needed someone to talk to about her issues with school, her parents, and then the loss of her sister. She sought you, Jay, and what an honor that is! Yet you are under the im-pression that when she couldn't contain her emotions and took death as a last resort, you failed to keep her from dying at Windhaven Beach.

"The truth of the matter is neither of you are at fault. She was seek-ing something better—something we will never be able to truly com-prehend, as the pain of others is not for us to judge. But know that you did all you could to calm the tide, and Saphnie did all she could, too. There's no use thinking otherwise." He gave me a slight, hopeful smile. "This sermon was unfortunately appropriate, huh?"

"Unfortunate or not, it's what I needed," I said, then sighed. "I wish I had been there. I should have texted her more often. I shouldn't have been so—"

"Hey." He pointed to Lily, Ethan, Megan, and Ty. "All's forgiven to those who are remorseful. Don't you ever forget that."

"Thank you," I told him. I felt a tear in my eye, and I let it sit there and build up before wiping it away.

I heard a familiar voice from the entrance.

"Sorry I'm late! I got stuck behind this person who refused to take a left, so I had to go the long way—"

I turned around and gawked at Courtney, who wore a flowery sun-dress and pristine, white shoes. She looked just as shocked to see me.

"I knew I was forgetting someone!" Carl said, walking to her and urging me to follow. "This is Courtney. She's been here with us these past two weeks." Then to her: "It's good to see you again this Sunday!"

"Thank you," she said to him, unsure of how to address me.
"Jay Murchison," I said, extending my hand. She smiled.

I went out of my way to hug my dad when we pulled up to our house and got out of the car. He was confused, at first, but then understood and embraced me. Once inside, we saw Mom already had paninis ready for lunch, so we washed up, gathered next to her, and ate our food—barbeque sauce dripping down our cheeks as we talked with each other.

I was about to go up to my room after finishing when Mom reached up to lead me toward the backyard. There, she sat on the porch steps and gestured at the spot next to her. I followed.

"Elena..." She paused, and I watched her look toward the willow tree. "Elena told me what happened, and I owe you an apology."

We sat in silence. I could hear her sniffle before she continued.

"I know I'm not the perfect mother. Your whole life, I've sheltered you because you've always been my baby. Things were so much simpler when you were six years old and just about anything was an adventure in your eyes. But as we moved, you grew up, and Elena went off to college... that was rough. I pushed my feelings away and held on to you even tighter, which was a disservice on my behalf. I mean, for crying out loud, you didn't even know how to bake a frozen pizza!"

I laughed, and she joined me. My mom was a lot of things, but she wasn't self-centered, and if she had time to reflect, she would.

"I'm getting older," I told her, "and in two years, I'll be leaving, too. But I'll always be your little boy—no matter how freakishly tall I am."

"You get that from your father's side," she said, smiling. "But know that you can trust me, as I trust you."

We hugged tightly for several long, peaceful moments. Any other time, and I would have felt embarrassed to be held by my mother, but not then. Ignoring my phone vibrating in my pocket, ignoring the chirping of the birds and the buzz of the insects, ignoring the world for a passing of seconds, I felt at home.

"If it makes you happy," she said, dropping her voice almost to a whisper, "you have my permission to get your driver's license."

"Thanks, Mom," I said. "That means a lot."

"Although I don't think your father will want you driving either of our cars for a while," she added, and we laughed again.

I looked up at the sky momentarily before going inside with her—the both of us for once in mutual agreement—and checked my phone halfway up the stairs. ONE MISSED CALL: LILY CARSWELL, it read. I returned it in my room.

Lily: "Hey."

Me: "Hey. Sorry about your dad. I didn't know—"

Lily: "It's OK. I worry sometimes, but Carl was right in that I need to have a little more faith. But anyway, I called to say I'm sorry about what happened at the park and our phone call afterward. I'm also sorry about your friend Saphnie. I overheard you talking with him about her, and it sounded so awful—"

Me: "Yeah, it was."

Lily: "Yeah. But other than that, was your vacation a good one?"

Me: "It was hard to forget about, but that's OK. Not all beaches are fun and sunscreen."

Lily: "And you're going to be all right?"

Me: "I'll be fine. Don't worry about me."

Lily: "But I do."

Me: "Thank you." (Pause.) "How about you, Ethan, and Ty?"

Lily: "We're stopping with the pot, if that's what you mean. Megan told her and Ty's parents, who spread it to mine and Ethan's. We'll find better ways to manage. And as for Ethan and I..." (Pause.) "We've worked some things out."

Me: "That's good. It's none of my business, but I'm happy for you both."

Lily: "Thanks. How are you and Sandy?"

Me: "I don't know. I haven't talked to her since school ended."

Lily: "She was sobbing after we left Darian's party. Granted, I was, too, but for different reasons. Anyway, she kept going on about how she had cussed and how she felt terrible about it. We had a good-bye party for her the Sunday before she left. It was nice, but I don't think she'll miss Oklahoma."

Me: "With this heat, I know I didn't."

Lily: (Laughing.) "Oh, hey, did you hear Carl's getting a divorce?"

Me: "I did not. Is that a good thing?"

Lily: "For him, yeah. He deserves better. It took them long enough!"

Me: "Well, good for Carl, I guess."

Lily: "Pretty much."

Me: "…"

Lily: "Darian stopped by my house yesterday and apologized to me for some personal things. She was upset and crying. A lot of people think of her as this bubbly party animal, but she's really sweet once you get to know her. She hates the notoriety she's gained, which is understandable. She's had her CoffeeFolder, Chipper, Photofixer, and SextMe all taken down. She says she's done with them, and I don't blame her. I didn't know how to comfort her, though, so we sat around and ate ice-cream while watching reruns of *House of Love*. I don't know why I'm telling you this. Ethan would find it dumb."

Me: "I think I've got Darian's number. Tell her to call or text me sometime. I want to tell her something."

Lily: "Huh? OK, I can do that." (Pause.) "You could've asked Megan out, you know. Today at church, I mean."

Me: "Doesn't she have a boyfriend?"

Lily: "I'm not sure she's really into Will."

Me: "I want to be single for a while, I think."

Lily: "What? How come?"

Me: "I need to sort out my thoughts—time to reflect."

Lily: "About Saphnie?"

Me: "Yeah."

Lily: "That's fine. Do what you need to do." (Pause.) "Did you ever end up asking your one question? From the contest you won?"

Me: "Not yet, but I do have an idea, so thanks for reminding me."

Lily: "Absolutely! That's what friends are for, right?"

Me: "Right."

Lily: "Well, I guess I'll let you get on with your Sunday then. Mention me in your letter?"

Me: (Smiling.) "Sounds like a plan, Stan."

Lily: "Oh, stop it, you!"

I shut the door and opened the blinds for natural light before signing into CoffeeFolder to look for the address I needed. I found it and noticed that people had stopped posting on Saphnie's profile. The last was Luke Wilbourne, a week after the funeral: "I'm so sorry, Saphnie. I'm so sorry."

I was about to log out when a voice in another tab spoke through the speakers and announced, all happy and cheery: "Third-class mail!"

From: TSC — TEMPORARY SIMULATIONS CORP.

Dear valued customer,

Unfortunately, it has come to our attention that the TSC Serenade 7-Plus Ultra Pro cell-phone models contain a glitch which prevents a small percentage of text messages from being received by the user. We have looked into the issue and have found the undelivered messages in storage, which are being forwarded to your phone, free of any charges. I apologize for the inconvenience this may have caused to you and your recipients.

Regretfully,
Niall Phuket, CEO

Saphnie: What I said yesterday wasn't entirely true. I'm afraid of death. I'm afraid of the pain it will inflict and the chances and experiences I will miss. Maybe my opinions will change. Who knows? I sure don't.

Saphnie: HAPPY NEW YEAR! *\(^_^)/*

Saphnie: CoffeeFolder's advertisements are so weird. Sometimes they're accurate and display ads for things I might be into, but that SextMe app? Not so much. ("Personalized Porn!") I RE-PEATETH UNTO THEE: NO NUDES!

Ethan: Dude I just pissed in a national forest

Sandy: Thanks for putting up with my weird family today. I didn't ask them to go with us!! Anyway, I had fun. Great movie! Want to come over sometime?

Saphnie: Humans are too complex to be defined by a single word. It bothers me how some people can't seem to understand that. It's like how people can listen to you, but don't truly hear a word you say. That's what I mean by hearing the ocean sigh.

Sandy: You texting me first would be fantastic...

Sandy: I know you would never cheat on me. I can just get so paranoid sometimes. I'm sorry. It won't happen again. Forgive me? Please?

Sandy: There's laughing with and laughing at. I'm not sure I want to know which you're doing.

Ethan: Hey man. Wanna hang next Sat with me and Ty? Going to the lake and stuff

Lily: I know I don't normally text you, but Ethan and I apolo-gized. He says you are forgiven. I'm sorry this all happened. I'm sorry for what I've done to you. Please give either of us a call.

Saphnie: I hate this, Jay. I really hate this. How come you're the only one who gets me?

Darian: Happy early half-birthday. It'll be mine, too. I'm text-ing you to say I was wrong. I've made mistakes. I care too much and take the little things too personally. I believe we're a lot alike, you and I, though I understand if you take that as an in-sult. Even so, have a good summer. – Nick

It was a sad, necessary realization: My perspective had been skewed much more than I'd imagined. Apologies were due, but like Luke's, it was already too late. The damage had been done.

I went through my contacts list and read the names aloud: Bradford, Ethan; Burroughs, Darian; Carswell, Lily; Goldsmith, Sandy; Hawley, Megan; Hawley, Ty; Murchison, Dad; Murchison, Elena; Murchison, Mom; and Saphnie. I changed her information to "Kane-Tachibana, Saphnie," and Darian's to "Behr, Nick," before setting the phone—damaged to begin with—beside its charger.

I closed the Internet, opened up a blank document, looked across the hall, and then began this letter to you.

"The best way to write to a writer is to write the way a writer would write."

Here we are, a week later, twenty-one days since she passed. There might be some spelling mistakes and grammar issues, but please bear with me, as I'm only sixteen. I'm certainly not asking to get a reply this long, but I felt that for you to answer my question—which I'll get to in a moment—you needed to view the entire picture, and I didn't want to forget anything.

I know you might not read this. Aunt Nancy was an editor for a literary magazine before she died, and she couldn't read stuff like this for fear of being sued. So I understand if you don't get around to read-ing all of this, as long as you know this is for me, too. And Saphnie. They say that absence makes the heart grow fonder, and while I hope to God that's not the case, I realize now there is truth to the statement.

I want to remember Saphnie for the girl she was.

While writing this to you, I have come to the conclusion that supposedly great people aren't always great. They're only as magnificent and wondrous as we make them out to be. We live in a society that lives off the whims and wills of the rich and famous: Hollywood actors, rappers, pop stars, and rock bands—they each influence our conception of what we believe is popular, what we view as the norm, and those who fall into neither category.

Saphnie wasn't great, despite what her headstone may suggest. She had flaws beneath the surface and was ultimately misunderstood. Her friends thought of her as this amazing girl, when in reality, she was like any of us. Does that deprive her of the right to be remembered? I sure hope not, as there was so much more to her than that.

Though as much as I complain about them not knowing Saphnie, neither did I. Her favorite colors, her passions, her inspirations—all I do not know and fear I never will. I was so caught up in my own life and my own problems that I rarely, truly bothered to talk with Saphnie about her own. I was ignorant and reckless with no excuse. I have my many regrets.

Of all euphemisms for death—which doesn't sound like a real word anymore, although it certainly is a real thing—I like "to buy the farm" best. Back during World War II, the idea for most soldiers would be that if they died in combat, their death benefit would serve to pay off their family's mortgage. So if that happened, the soldier would lead a peaceful lifestyle on a farm in heaven or a place of supreme happiness and bliss. Maybe Saphnie is strolling through that nice, quiet pasture, or perhaps she's buried at Windhaven Memorial Gardens like she had hoped to be. Resting in peace, right?

My aunt once said that life begins with a single push—her words, not mine. I didn't know what she meant back then, and I still don't to this day, but I take it she was reminding my family that a new beginning is sometimes necessary for us to continue our journey. It's possible that's what Saphnie needed. Truth be told, I see her sitting on an island in the middle of the ocean. Sounds like paradise.

Mr. Metres, when it said that I had won an answer to any one question, it never specified to which story. While I do have a few regarding Edward's, his isn't the one I'm interested in right now.

Who was Saphnie Kane-Tachibana, and what will be remembered of her? I have written to you all I could gather from our five-and-a-half months together in a vain attempt that I won't forget her. But in the end, time knows no personality and who we were on this earth. It only keeps the solid things—the only impressions we truly leave behind. That bothers me, as I should have paid her closer attention, and I should have seen the signs. I understand that writing this won't make her immortal and won't bring her back. If this were *Rudderless at Sea*, she would not want there to be a single, valid answer, and I would not deserve it. Yet I am undeniably selfish—a habit that has led to this final request: I have told you of my account, I have my question, and I need to know.

Did Saphnie kill herself?

I now understand what it feels like to hear the ocean sigh. There is much to be done, but I am so tired. In the morning.

Jakobson "Jay" Wayde Murchison

ACKNOWLEDGMENTS

Thank you to my mother Grettel, who has always believed in my ideas, and to my little sister Gracie, who puts up with me far more often than any older brother deserves.

Thank you to my mentors over the years: Dr. Kathy Goff, Nancy Christy, Sarah Walker, Tara Waugh, and Bea Hoxie, for teaching me everything I know and for fully supporting me in everything I do and dream of doing.

Special thanks to Mary Faith Flores, Duncan Carson, Giselle Fuselier, Essence Collins, Audrey Still, and the lovely Bryna Frohock.

Blessings to my uncle and aunt, Steven and Cielo Valverde, respectively, and thank you for providing the setting that sparked my inspiration.

Last, I must express my gratitude to the Cochrans, Valverdes, and the Frohock family. Thanks for understanding.

. . .